FIREBIRD SERIES – BOOK ONE

THE GIRL WITH STARS IN HER EYES

DAWN FORD

Scrivenings PRESS
Quench your thirst for story.
www.ScriveningsPress.com

Published by Expanse Books,
an imprint of Scrivenings Press LLC
15 Lucky Lane
Morrilton, Arkansas 72110
https://ScriveningsPress.com

Printed in the United States of America

Paperback ISBN 978-1-64917-195-5

eBook ISBN 978-1-64917-196-2

Editors: Erin R. Howard and K. Banks

Cover by Linda Fulkerson, bookmarketinggraphics.com

Map illustration by Andrew Torres.

To my husband who has patiently waited for my dreams to become a reality and who gave me as much room as I needed to make them come true, I love you beyond words.

ACKNOWLEDGMENTS

For my readers, I hope *The Girl With Stars In Her Eyes* has taken you on a journey along with Tambrynn and Lucas into a brand new world full of magic and curious creatures, both good and evil. If I have managed to pull you in for the ride, my job as an author is successful.

As a writer, I must thank God first and foremost for gifting me with this story. It was He who made my fingers fly across the keyboard that first day when three chapters flew into creation on my computer screen. I was immersed into this fairy-tale land then and each time after as I worked with Tambrynn on bringing her story to life.

For my husband and family who have supported me and let me dig into their brains for ideas and schemes, I'm eternally grateful for your love. You are the stars to my night's sky. I love you more.

To my critique groups, the Fictionistas and the Engravers, you held me to the greatest standard and took a diamond in the rough and created a gleaming story that I couldn't have done without you. I am in your debt. I have been blessed to find some amazing editors and cheerleaders who have also guided me into making this book the best it could be. I want to especially thank Ben Wolf and Janeen Ippolito who dug into the guts and pulled out the best parts. It's dirty work, but so worth it!

Thanks, also, to Andrew Torres, who created the map at the beginning of this book.

And to Linda Fulkerson and all of the staff of Expanse Books and Scrivenings Press, I am humbled by your belief in me and this story. It is a part of my heart and soul, something I trust to very few. You all are incredible and amazing, and I'm so glad to be on this journey with you.

PART ONE

1

A brisk autumn wind pushes against the heavy manor door when I step outside for midday chores. The sky is stony and overcast, promising a coming storm.

Face to the sky, I smile slightly. I take a deep, crisp breath of the chilled air. I'd been here less than a week, but with one month left until my birthdate, I can almost taste the freedom it brings. No more winters shackled to a wooden pole awaiting my next assignment or grueling hours of thankless servitude. The end of my indentureship is near. At last, I'll be free and able to search for my father.

Wind whips my face and my hood slips. I hurriedly clutch it to hide my hair that I'd pulled in a tight bun. I didn't have a chance to rub more coal dust in it this morn to darken the silver tresses.

Little Nellie, the newest maid, steps through after me, glancing at the forest that lies beyond the boundary of the Broodmoor Estate. "Tambrynn, is it true the forest is haunted?" Her eyes widen like brown saucers as she runs to stay beside me as we head to the barnyard.

My joy disappears like dried leaves darting about in the wind, and I press my lips together. "Who told you that nonsense?" I couldn't tell her the truth. The forest isn't haunted. I am. Haunted from my past and my curse. One only needs a glance at my eyes or hair to know I'm different. However, I've been careful to keep the hood over my head and not be noticed by most of the staff since arriving the past week. For once, I'm thankful that scullery maids secure little attention. Only Cook and Mrs. Calvin have seen me without my covering.

Cows bawl in the barn next to the chicken coop as we walk up to it. The wooden latch on the door always sticks, and a humming sensation that starts in my gut answers my unspoken *call*. The bolt releases as if well-fitted instead of wedged too tight. It's just a little nudge, not enough pull that Nellie would notice and not enough to sap my strength.

Recently I'd learned how to *call* objects with more control, so the wood flips loose easily, though there's a spark of blue static that travels between my hand and the door handle. I shake my fingers to get rid of the sting, confused. Though I haven't always been able to restrain it, *calling* has never bitten me back before.

Hens squawk and dart about, kicking up dirt as we enter, tossing dusty clouds in the air. Nellie's clasped hands are red and chapped from scrubbing the hearth earlier this morn. Knowing she's a recent orphan, my heart twinges at her fate. I was the tender age of eight, Nellie's age now, when Mother died and I first became indentured. It had taken me the ten years since, moving from place to place, to become tough enough to survive. I consider what to tell Nellie.

Glancing at the trees, I shiver, but not from the cold. "Nellie, there's nothing haunting that forest. Whoever told you that wants to scare you so you don't try running away."

She looks up at me, her face alight with the trust only seen in the young and naive. I'm heartened when she doesn't flinch as she looks into my eyes, something even adults cannot manage. Mother lovingly said I have stars in my eyes, as if my star-shaped pupils were magical. But then she'd been brutally murdered by wolves, and I realized Mother was the only one who thought my eyes and hair were acceptable. If only everyone could be as innocent and nonjudgmental as Nellie.

I touch her shoulder, longing to protect her as I had not been. "You'll learn soon enough the tricks they use to keep us obedient." I leave her to gather eggs so I can get the grain and water.

A high-pitched wolf howl from the forest startles me. A flock of birds in the trees along the forest's edge explodes into the sky.

Tambrynn, danger! A voice inside my mind calls out. I haven't heard that voice in a long time, and it's as shocking as the howl. It's familiar to me as my own voice and snippets of visions flit through my mind of a young, handsome man with dark eyes and dark hair. Could it be my father? I have no real recollections of him, but who else would I recall but him? He's definitely not any of my previous employers. Yet I hear this voice, always warning me, and see the cloudy picture of him in my mind.

My heart pounds painfully in my chest. I pray silently to the Kinsman that *they* aren't coming again, but even as I say amen, I fear my words are all in vain. The beasts are never far away from me, even if they're only memories that plague my dreams at night.

And once again, I am unable to stop the images of Mother's broken body from returning to me. The beasts are blurry in my memory, but I recall the evil that rolled like waves of fog off of them. I'm shaking as I press the memories back inside the darkest recesses of my mind.

I clasp the hooded shawl tighter as I walk beyond the barn to the well house. There's no movement, no menacing shadows. No monsters hunting me. I struggle to calm my breathing. I can't let fear affect me as it always leads to my undoing. And here there are too many eyes watching at every turn, especially Cook's favorite snoop Adelia. I shake my head, trying to dispel the emotions churning inside of me.

The rope scratches my calloused hands as I send the bucket down the stone well and wait for it to sink and gather a full load of water. It's heavy as I unlatch it from the rope, but luckily, I only have one to carry instead of the three like my last employer's home, which had required more than one trip.

Another barking howl rings through the trees. *'Danger is coming!'* The masculine voice is closer this time, desperate, and sounds almost as if he stands over my shoulder. I stagger. Water sloshes over the bucket, soaking through my thin stockings. It pools inside my worn leather shoes. Cows' muted bawls filter through the barn as they hear and sense the predators.

My chest tightens with an old, familiar fear. I can't let it cripple me again, not when I'm so close to being free. "Stop it!" I whisper over and over, hands and eyes clenched tight until I regain my bearings. Finally, the voice recedes and is gone. I hasten to another shed to gather the cracked corn and millet. My gaze darts about to keep watch for any threat and I end up spilling the grain in the dirt. Not wanting to be chastised for waste, I quickly scoop up the feed and dirt with my hands into the bucket, wiping my gritty, damp hands down my stained apron. I've eaten worse, and the chickens won't notice.

When I return, I find Nellie on the coop floor, sobbing. Her egg basket lies askew against the wire fence, with several eggs broken and oozing on the dusty ground.

"Good heavens, Nellie. What happened?"

"A magpie scared the ch-ch-chickens, and one flew at me." Nellie hiccups. "I couldn't open the door, and I dropped the basket trying to."

I glance at the shadows that seem to move along the forest line. Hair on my arms prickles against the wool sleeves of my dress, and I fight the dread that creeps into my soul. Fear or anger causes me to lose control of my cursed ability to call things. And when that happens, someone always gets hurt.

I count to twenty slowly, silently, then assess the damage.

"We've got almost two dozen. Maybe there are more in the pantry than I remember." Another glance at the forest shows no hint of immediate danger, so I hand her the grain, dump the water in the wooden trough, and give her a weak smile. "You finish tending the chickens, and I'll take the eggs to Cook."

Turning toward the manor, I press a hand against my churning stomach and resituate the hood that had dropped away from my hair. The wolves outside or the maids inside? Neither is desirable.

The heat from the kitchen stove warms my chilled body as I step into the pantry. Odors of malt vinegar, red onions, and salted bream sting my nose. I find more than a dozen eggs preserved in salt. I place the extras into my basket to take to Cook and set it aside to re-cover the crock.

Adelia breezes past me into the pantry. "I thought I saw you sneak in here. I need to start on Mistress's custard, or it won't be cooled in time. Where are those eggs?" She grabs for the basket. Her crisp white apron over her blue smock is startling against my stained hand-me-downs.

She steps on my foot with a smart-looking heeled boot, and I jerk sideways, bumping the basket. Eggs fly up and out. I juggle four eggs, *calling* the others to keep them from dropping. However, they break in their rush to reach my waiting hands. Yolks drip through my fingers and down the front of my worn dress. More eggs lay broken on the floor.

Even worse, my hood has fallen to the ground as well, leaving my hair and face exposed.

Adelia's eyes are wide and she gasps. "What they said about you is true!" Her laugh is condescending. She stares at me as I glance away to try to hide my eyes, knowing there's nothing I can do about my hair. It seems like forever before she turns from me and steps over the mess on the floor.

She counts the remaining eggs out loud, and I concentrate on her white cap atop her dark hair to still my anxiety. Her small, upturned nose wrinkles in distaste, and I wonder how she can breathe so easily through those narrow slits. "Twenty-six. Not nearly enough for what we need. You've ruined the tea." Adelia's tone is as sharp as her tongue. "We'll see what Cook has to say about this."

Though smaller than I, Adelia's grip bites into my wrist. I try to bend down to grab the hood, but she yanks me through the pantry door before I can grasp it. I hurry to keep up with her, wishing I could disappear into the floor as my damp shoes squeak. The sick feeling I'd get ever since my first employer, Farmer Tucker's wife, declared me an evil spawn spreads through my veins.

The other maids stop and stare, curiosity overruling their current duties. Adelia and I stumble between the women and the wall, making our way down to Cook. I clench my jaw and fists as the weight of their inquisitiveness turns to judgment. There's nowhere to hide. I can't lose control in front of everyone.

With a whoosh, the kitchen door opens and Nellie blows in

with the wind. She halts at the sight of Adelia dragging me behind her. Tears well in her big, brown eyes.

"What is it now?" Cook's sweaty brow wrinkles as we approach. Her wiry black hair, having come loose from its bun, flutters wildly about her chubby head. Short and stout, she stirs a bubbling stew.

Adelia flings my arm down as if I'd just burned her. "Tambrynn has ruined the tea, mum. She dropped the eggs. We've less than two dozen left." A triumphant glow spreads around her freckled face.

My fingers itch and tingle. It isn't the first time I've wanted to poke each spot on her face, jabbing my dirty fingernails into her flesh. I shake the cruel thought off and tamp down my instinct to strike out.

"Twenty-six," I retort. "You counted them yourself." The rest of the maids gawk, motionless. No help, no empathy offered. I don't know why it always surprises me—their reactions. My scalp stings from the effort to keep my distress under control. Again, I inhale a deep breath and exhale slowly, trying to work through the anger and shame spinning circles in my stomach.

Cook pounds her fist against the butcher table, and the girls plucking peacocks scatter. Downy feathers scurry through the air. "Twenty-six or not, it *won't* do!"

She wipes her hands on the stained apron tied across her rotund waist and flinches when she looks me square in the eyes. "I told Mistress Broodmoor not to take you on, cheap though you come. Don't think I didn't hear the talk. Strange things happen around you. Just look at you." Cook waves a chubby hand at me. "I knew it wouldn't be long before your wickedness reflected upon me, and I refuse to be the one punished for it. If it were up to me, you'd be in a workhouse where you belong."

Icy fingers of anxiety steal the heat from my face. "I am neither criminal nor infirm." Nor am I evil, but I don't say that for fear of being struck. I twist my dress with my fingers. My wrist aches and bears marks from where Adelia grabbed me.

My gut buzzes. Once again, I'm thankful no one else can feel the power that rests inside me. However, pots hanging from the rafters clank together and utensils on the table rattle. The maids' voices around the room rise in alarm. I'm losing control.

Saying a silent prayer to the Kinsman, I dig my fingernails into my palms to remain focused. "Your pardon, but they were only eggs."

Cook scowls. "You insolent, stupid girl." She spins and throws me back against the sturdy block table. Her reddened cheeks puff out with every heaving breath she takes. To focus, I stare at the mole on the side of her face. A dark hair sticks out of the center like a cat's whisker.

"*This* is what impertinent maids get." She flips the metal arm holding the kettle over the flames outward. The stew splashes and sizzles down the side of the black pot. Cook yanks me away from the table and thrusts my hand over the bubbling contents. I clench my fingers together, but the steam still blanches my skin.

In a flash, I *call* out with my mind. It's instinct. I can't stop it. My eyes burn and I blink. White light explodes behind my eyelids. A butcher knife from the table sails through the steaming air. Cook's eyes bulge as the knife flies past and thuds deep in the wall behind her. Blood drips down the side of her face where the hairy mole once was.

As soon as the power inside me is released, I sag back against the table for support and to catch my breath. My hands glow with a bluish light. I shove them behind my body. I don't have time to wonder about the radiance, though, as the kitchen breaks out into riotous chaos.

Cook's screams join with the other maids'. She points a shaking finger at me. "H-h-her eyes! They lit up like fire! She's a witch!"

The door to the kitchen opens and slams against the wall. The head housekeeper, Mrs. Calvin, enters the room. She's imposing and her face is flush with anger at having been interrupted by the noise. "What's going on in here?"

Cook continues to sputter and point. "Her. There. Tambrynn. Her eyes flashed and—and—" she stutters but then takes a deep breath. "Look at what she did to me. I *told you* she was dangerous. Do you believe me now?"

I brace myself and struggle to stand at attention while my hands land on a warm peacock carcass. The knots inside my stomach tighten. "I didn't, Mrs. Calvin. She was going to stick my hand in the pot, and—"

Adelia's grin turns from wicked to innocent in the blink of an eye. She rushes to Cook's side. "I saw it. She threw that knife at poor Cook."

Mrs. Calvin picks up a cloth and, with smooth strides, is beside Cook in a moment. She presses the cloth to the wound with a steady hand before directing an eager Adelia to hold it in place. She glances at the knife stuck in the wall and then glares down her thin nose at me, her small lips puckering.

"You were warned when you came here about your behavior, Tambrynn. You're dismissed. Go to your room and pack. Since we're all busy with guests until this eve, you will wait to be collected and sent to the stocks as soon as someone's available to take you. Do not leave your room."

"The stocks? But I've committed no crime!" Tears blur my sight as my stomach does furious flip-flops. "Please, Mistress."

"No crime? You attacked Cook." Mrs. Calvin points toward the stairs leading up to the servants' quarters, her head turned away from me. "Go. Now. And don't even think about running. If I find you missing, we'll send the hounds."

I stiffen at the threat. Hell hounds, as they're dubbed, are trained to kill by scent and are used for hunting as well as tracking down anyone who tries to escape from their indentureship. The animals are known to be vicious and often bring back the escapee in pieces.

The maids' faces are filled with a mixture of horror and mirth, but no one dares move. I run past them all, catching the stricken look on Nellie's face. I try to smile at her in encouragement but fear it comes out as a grimace. Her pain and fear only add to mine.

I glance at the forest through a tall window as I hasten up the stairway, already feeling the cold shackles against my skin again. A magpie sits on the ledge, watching me. Its eyes are familiar, and I'm overwhelmed by fear.

The bird's presence is a harbinger of the beasts. Neither is a good omen.

2

Particles dance upon the chilled air, moving at my command. They flicker and twirl in the light of a small candle that has melted into shiny globs over a tarnished metal holder. A thin film of snow accumulates on the windowpane, fulfilling the promise the sky made yesterday.

Nellie pokes her flushed face in my open door. "Tambrynn! Good, I caught you before you left." She steps into the open doorway, her hands behind her back. "Gads, it's freezing in here!"

I stretch my stiff limbs and stand. I reach for the shawl that isn't there and self-consciously rake a hand across my silver, braided bun. The shawl hasn't been returned to me, and I miss its protection. "Adelia sent word that I was not to have any coal or wood last eve. As if being dismissed isn't punishment enough." I nod toward wooden planks balanced on crates that serve as my bed. "Sit?"

"I can't. If I get caught ..." She holds out an old brown cloak with shaking hands. It's long, several sizes too big for Nellie. "I found this in my room when I arrived. Must've been the last maid's? Anyway, it's far too big for me." A noise echoes from the stairway. Nellie glances behind her, sighing in relief a moment later when nothing materializes. "I'm sorry you were dismissed. It's all my fault."

I'm touched by her generosity and take the cloak from her. I curl my chilled fingers in the fabric. "It's not your fault. If Adelia weren't so vindictive, there would've been plenty of eggs. She's the one to blame."

Nellie glances up. Tears well in her eyes. "Still, I wish it hadn't happened."

I ignore the bees buzzing in my stomach and force a smile. "Me, too. Don't believe everything they tell you, okay?" I wrap the cloak around myself, thankful for the added warmth. I flick the hood up to cover my hair. "Thank you, Nellie. This is the kindest thing anyone's done for me in a long time."

Before I can button the cloak, Nellie is gone. I whisper a quick prayer for her and myself and tuck my arms inside the sleeves. Though it was much too large for Nellie, the cloak is still a bit small for me, falling short of my dress that I'd had to lengthen with other disposed dresses, but I'm thankful for it.

Mrs. Calvin's heavy footsteps sound in the hallway. "It's time, Tambrynn. The attendant will get your things. You need to get moving. 'Twill be dark before you get to Pauper's Square in Grousefield." She levels a harsh glance toward me, though not directly into my eyes, as if waiting for me to answer a question.

I bite my lip to keep my expression neutral, but I can't help the glare I give her, daring her to look at me. I wait a moment before I respond. "No need for an attendant, Mistress. This is all I own." My possessions are few. The leather case I clutch was given to me by an old dairymaid years before, and all I own fits easily inside its small confines.

Cherished among my belongings, though, is an ornate

silver ring. Larger than a signet ring, it has an elaborate tree carved into the metal. Etched inside are words in a strange language I can't read. In the moments before she died, Mother told me it was my inheritance, my salvation, and that I should watch for a man who wore the same ring. He'd bring me safely home.

It had to be my father, though she never spoke of him. I desired to search for him. As a child, I had dreams that he was a king and I was his lost daughter. Like the fairy tales Mother told, there'd be dragons and a handsome prince to put the ring on my finger and return me home to my castle.

The disapproval on Mrs. Calvin's face is a douse of cold wash water.

I sigh, knowing no one would believe the ring, or anything so pricey, would be mine. So it remains tucked inside the scraps of cloth and feathers that make up my pillow.

"Need I inspect your case before you leave?" Mrs. Calvin's narrow nose cuts a sharp line between two charcoal-colored eyes.

I match Mrs. Calvin's glare, looking down into her pinched face. Let her get her fill of my strangeness. By the end of the day, the stories about me will have spun out of control, and I can only imagine the false atrocities I will have committed. "You may look through whatever you wish. I hide nothing." A half-truth, but my conscience is clear.

The cloak is frayed and has a couple of holes, but she flings one side and then the other open to see if I have anything stashed inside. The movement makes the hood fall, and, at that moment, she glances up into my eyes. I have the satisfaction of seeing her momentarily cringe.

She opens the case and rustles through it as if on a mission, finding only a stained dress, worn shift, undergarments, and stockings. She leaves them in a messy pile. My pillow and blanket she picks up with the tips of her fingers. Her face pinches as if smelling something rotten. She drops them, then turns and walks out to the hallway without another word. Her black skirt swishes as she moves, and the heels of her boots echo through the hall and down the stairs.

I start to replace the hood but stop. A hot flash of defiance rises inside me, and I decide I want to observe their discomfort. I tidy my clothes before stuffing the pillow and blanket inside and hurry after Mrs. Calvin.

I wind my way down the servants' stairs, my suitcase in hand. I spy Cook standing in the shadows of the kitchen with a grin on her face while she waits for me to pass. Had Adelia not lied, and had Cook not been such a bitter, hateful woman, I never would've lost control. Cook won't miss the mole anyway. Maybe she'll thank me when it heals, and she no longer resembles a fat cat.

I remember what I told Nellie about the forest and running away. I'd finally have the freedom I so desire.

No. Surely Mrs. Calvin will send notice to the commonwealth office. If I were ever to be found, I'd be recognized too easily. Even if I could conceal my hair, my eyes would give me away—they're too unique. I'm indentured with no rights, not even to defend myself against anyone's accusations. I'd be sent to the noose. It's a common enough fate for disobedient servants in Tenebris. I fight to hold back the bitterness rising in my throat.

The noise in the kitchen mutes. Hushed words are muttered behind servants' hands. Sweet scents of baked goods fill the air, making my empty stomach pinch with hunger. They'd obviously recouped from the egg devastation of yesterday.

Mrs. Calvin and I march in a procession, reminding me of

the formality of a public hanging in the market square. There's no escape, no use running away.

I hold my head high. My hair, which I'd rebraided and pinned in a bun last night, pulls tight against my scalp as we move through the kitchen, past curious workers at the wooden tables, and toward the back hallway to the pantry. All eyes are upon us, except for Nellie's. She has the grace to turn her head as Mrs. Calvin proudly escorts me in full view of everyone who witnessed yesterday's events.

My chest burns as I swallow my humiliation even as I relish their disbelief and flinches. I refuse to leave without a final act of retribution, though. I swing my hand up to feign pulling at a loose hair behind my ear.

Responding to my unspoken command, the rug bunches up under Mrs. Calvin's feet, and she topples to the floor with a squeal. My lips quiver as I restrain a laugh. Without looking back, I march past her and out the heavy door to the waiting carriage that will take me to my new prison.

Flocks of birds fly overhead. Unlike me, they're headed for a better place.

The driver, a slight man, nods me to the carriage quarters instead of the upper bench without even a glance at me, thank the Kinsman. It is a rare indulgence, to be sure, one I will take advantage of. To my dismay, the magpie perches on the open door. A cold gust of wind ruffles the bird's inky feathers, and though it stares at me, I refuse to look into its dark eyes. It twists its head back and forth as if sizing me up. *Flee*, screams the voice in my head. I swivel around, wishing it were my father, but there's no one here besides the driver and me. I avoid the magpie and grasp the handle to heave myself into the cab.

I take in the dark, forbidding forest. There's no place to run. I swing the carriage door shut, and the bird flutters away. Its repetitive chatters sound like it's saying, *come, follow me*, over and over. I quench a sudden urge to do what the bird asks. It's ridiculous. Birds don't talk, let alone try to save the likes of a scullery maid.

The carriage creaks under the weight of the driver. With a crack of the whip, the horses jerk into action. We're on our way.

Finally alone, I loosen my posture and unclench my hands. The bruise on my wrist burns from where Adelia gripped it yesterday, so I cradle it to my chest. My bravado extinguishes, and tears dampen my cheeks. I had tried this time, really tried to control myself. Freedom had been so close. A knot of defeat and anguish settles in the pit of my stomach.

The driver heads west onto the narrow road that coils through the dark woods, the quickest path to Grousefield. As Nellie said, all the maids think the forest is haunted. But I've found that people fear that which they can't explain.

And I've learned much of life defies explanation. Like me.

I pray silently to the Kinsman for a miracle to end my servitude forever. An appeal for him to end my cursed gift. It never seems to get answered, but I continue to ask nonetheless.

No one believes in the Kinsman here, at least no one I'd met. But Mother had, and she'd passed that reverence on to me. Even if the almighty Kinsman didn't listen to the petitions of someone as insignificant as me, it doesn't hurt to try.

I pull the quilted pillow and blanket from the case, put the pillow behind my head, wrap the cloak tight, and curl into a ball. For added warmth, I tuck my hands under the fabric. Since I'd worried about when Mrs. Calvin would come to collect me, and it had been so cold, I'd had little rest last eve. I'm grateful to be the only passenger. Otherwise, I'd have had to sit outside with the driver. I don't envy him this trip, having to face the icy wind and the snow starting to fall.

The wind rocks the coach, the motion lulling me to sleep. I dream of Mother planting herbs in her garden, of picking flowers and playing with a dark-haired boy whose voice speaks to me in my mind. I'm jolted, and the dreams scatter like seeds on a stone floor.

It takes me a moment to gather my wits. The carriage shifts and lurches to the side. The motion throws me from my seat across the interior of the compartment. I fight to sit back up, but we are moving too fast, and the road is too bumpy.

What is happening?

"Whoa! Whoa!"

The driver's alarmed calls set my heart pounding so hard I can hear the beats in my ears. I catch the door handle and pull hard to regain my balance, but the handle moves, and the door opens. The hinge bends and detaches. Mounds of snow and tops of brush weed assault me in a blur of brown and white as I dangle from the hanging door frame.

Frozen flakes pelt my face sharp as needles. My head spins, and I pull myself back inside the carrier as the door moans and cracks. Though the interior was by no means warm, the air and snow steal what meager protection the cab held.

My eyes dart to and fro as I try to make sense of where we are. Nothing looks the same as a week ago when I traveled through the forest the first time on my way to the Broodmoor Estate. The carriage's curtain lies crumpled on the floor, tripping me as I scramble to get to my feet. Through the falling snow, I view our precarious position. We're headed directly for several trees, all larger around than Cook's waist.

We're going to crash.

3

The carriage's wheels slide at dangerous angles along the snow-thickened landscape. The front of the vehicle creaks and groans as we shift sideways. I peer around the door and witness the shaft keeping the horses attached to the buggy busting in half, and we're tossed the other way. Another creak, and the shaft snaps to pieces, straps flying in every direction. Freed, the horses thunder off together.

The motion and slick snow keep the carriage sliding around, and fear spreads like spilled oil through my being as the driver curses his luck. I spy the driver's white-knuckled hand on the bar above the carriage used to hold luggage. The vehicle slips sidelong, and the trees are now coming at me directly. I have no choice. I have to jump. Clutching my belongings, I take a deep breath and throw myself out into a mountainous snowdrift. Like jumping into a river, I'm engulfed in a pool of cold whiteness.

A holler pierces the air as the side of the coach crunches into a massive fir tree, throwing the driver off. He lands with a grunt against the next trunk, not far from where I lay. Snow swirls in the wind above his crumpled body.

Snowflakes gather against my eyelashes, blurring the sight of the rumbling transport as the remaining intact portion splits open against a thick bank of oaks.

Silence.

Has the driver survived? How will we get out of here?

My feet slip as I stand, and I sink back into the bitter cold cushion of snow up to my waist. I've lost my pillow and blanket, but I use the suitcase to help me stand, and I fight my way through the snowdrifts to make my way over to the wheels' path and then beyond to the driver. He's sprawled and twisted—dead amidst the jagged remains of his seat. His mouth is wide open in a silent scream.

I cover my eyes, remembering Mother's torn and twisted body. I bite my lip against the tears which threaten to come and raise a shaking hand. No one deserves to be left like this, so I *call* the snow to bury him under a blanket of white. "May you meet your Kinsman this day, and may it be a blessing."

I wade to where the carriage wheels shuffled the deep snow aside, so I can stand. I mentally check each part of my body. A few bruises, to be sure, but nothing seems broken or sprained. The cold wind creeps through my wet clothes, and I shiver uncontrollably. I've never seen it snow like this before. Ever.

I wonder how far from the estate I have traveled. The sky above me is a haze of white, giving no indication of time. I massage the skin at my collar to lessen the hot barbs of fear that sprout up my neck.

Brushing the snow from my cloak, I stamp my feet to remove the clumps under my skirt that cling to my stocking-clad legs. If only I owned a pair of boots instead of my shoes, worn through in several places. My toes are already soaked and frozen, despite my wool stockings.

"You've been in worse situations. Keep your wits." I imagine Mother, who was never one to back down without a fight, saying the words I speak aloud to myself.

The stark white landscape blinds me. Closing my eyes, I reach out instead with my abilities to feel for signs of a cottage or barn. I *call* for something. Anything. A log. A rope. Boots.

A soft object touches my hand. I open my eyes and see ... the quilted pillow and the blanket? Not at all what I'd expected, but I'm grateful to have them, along with my ring, back. Another try brings me a soggy envelope. I turn it over. The ink is blotchy from wetness, but it is a letter addressed to the Magistrate.

Well, maybe the Kinsman does answer prayers after all. Should I leave it in the snow? Perhaps I can figure out a way to gain my freedom with it. I fold the paper, tuck it safely inside my chemise strap, and say a quick prayer to the Kinsman for safety.

The spark of joy I had when I called the letter dies as I turn in a circle trying to gauge where I am. I remember overhearing about hunting cabins in the woods not far from the mansion. I refuse to return to the estate and perish in the stocks. If I'm going to die, I will do so trying to get free.

A biting wind blows, and I struggle to breathe as I move through the drifts. Thankful once again for the cloak Nellie gave me, I tuck my pillow inside and button the cloak tight over it. I drape the blanket over the hood to hold as a shield for my face against the biting flurries. Standing as I am, my sleeves barely cover my hands. Without gloves, I can feel the cold down to my bones. It won't be long before they turn numb, which will lead to frostbite. I consider leaving the case behind, but I will need a change of clothes wherever I end up.

Around me, the wind whirls the flakes in waves as they fall, the patterns moving as if chasing me. A bird cries above me, and I look up into the dark undersides of the tree branches, a stark contrast to the whiteness. Somehow the bird's squawks sound like my name. I stumble but manage to catch myself, though I drop the blanket.

Another gust of wind jars me with its force, and crystals pelt my face. A dark shadow moves out of the corner of my eye. I sense it hovering over me. I shake the blanket free of the powder and thrust it back over my head to ward off whatever otherworldly beings might attack. Maybe the forest *is* haunted. *Nonsense, keep your head!*

I place a trembling hand on the hard bark of a nearby tree. The solid sturdiness of the trunk grounds me, slowing my churning thoughts to a more sensible pace. I gather the brown cloak closer and slog back to my case. Only the handle shows above the solid blanket of white. I can still see the broken pieces of the carriage, but they're quickly becoming covered. It won't be long before I lose any sense of direction. With my jaw set, I trudge through the white fluff with my head down to ignore the lurking shadows.

My body soon numbs to the cold. On and on, I plow through a thick ocean of cold, silently praying I'm not moving in circles.

At last, the wind dies down, and the snow eases up. Sunlight struggles to pierce through the dying storm. The trees thin out and I dare a glance up from the ground. Ahead, dark against the waning light, stands a cottage. Without smoke or lamplight, it appears to be unoccupied.

My hands and feet are frozen, so instead of knocking, I bang the case against the door. There's no answer. Could it be one of the hunting cabins I'd overheard the maids talk about?

Chitter. Chatter. Rustling feathers dart beside me.

A magpie. Surely not the same one from the estate. It can't be, can it?

My heart pounds in my ears. "Shoo, you beast!"

As I thought—it had been a bad omen.

Mustering up all my strength, I shove my shoulder into the heavy door. It gives and I tumble inside, bumping my head on the doorframe as I do so. I kick the door shut before the bird can follow and plunge into stale darkness.

A few moments and several blinks later, my eyesight adjusts. Slivers of light frame the window shutters. I open one. There's no glass to keep the draft out, or as I realize belatedly, creatures.

Outside on the windowsill, the magpie perches, staring at me. It pecks at the weathered frame, stretches his long black wings, and hurls his body at me, claws first.

I scream and slam the shutters.

A wintry stillness rests upon the inside of the house. Any noise, save the bird, is shielded by the thick mounds of snow beyond the log walls. I can make out the shape of a table and chairs, the fireplace, and a ladder that leads into a loft. Picking up my belongings, I dust off the table as best as I can and set them on top.

My hand brushes against cold glass in the middle of the table. A lantern! I spy a darkened room behind the table and the light cast from another shuttered window. Gritting my teeth, I slowly unlock and open these wooden shutters. No birds. Nothing shrieking at me. Though the light is dim, it helps me see well enough to inspect the cottage.

First is the kitchen, and I find several containers and bags of supplies with small amounts of flour, salt, and oil. Garlic and some root vegetables hang on a nail on the wall. They're dried up but surely still edible. I smile. My luck has changed. This little house has everything I need. More than I've had for years. And more dust than I'd seen in years as well. Possibly it had been abandoned in haste and forgotten—or the owner died, leaving no one to claim his property. I search every corner, pleased to discover a pile of dry wood and the flint and steel needed to start a fire, and so I do.

Within no time, the warmth of the crackling fire loosens my stiff hands, and I get to work. As I gather snow in a large kettle, I catch sight of a scrubby pine limb to scour away the wet footprints from the now-muddy dust that's thick everywhere. The lantern is full, so I have plenty of light to check out every dark corner while leaving the loft for when the cottage warms up a bit more. Though it's chilly in the cottage, I'm energized and work up a sweat. I strip down to just my chemise and underwear while searching and scrubbing.

I melt snow and add it to the flour, salt, garlic, and oil for a simple flatbread to ease my empty stomach and decide to rehydrate the vegetables later for a soup. The last time I'd eaten was the eve before the escapade with the eggs. That had been only a few scraps taken when Adelia hadn't been looking to supplement Cook's favorite meal for the indentured servants: cold cabbage and turnip green hash. While the dough cooks beside the hearth, I gather snow to heat in the kettle to wash my clothes.

I could stay here until my birthdate. It makes perfect sense. I clutch the drying missive from Mrs. Calvin. The script is mostly blurred except for my name and her signature. If I played it right, I could convince them I'd served the end of my indentureship without incident, and then I could be free.

I had days until my birthdate, so I just needed to wait it out and not starve to death while doing so. I've lived on less than what is here.

Luckily, this cabin looks to have been abandoned for a while, so I don't believe I'll have any interruption now with the storm burying the woods. Not even the heartiest of hunters would dare go out in this mountain of snow until a good thaw.

Soon I'm exhausted from hauling snow to boil to wash my clothes. I decide to bathe. It has been months since I'd last bathed and longer since I last washed my long hair. Though still silver, my scalp is coated with coal grime, and the tresses are greasy. I scrub hard, ruining my stockings doing so, but it's worth it to feel tingly and clean once again.

I study the silver strands of hair from one side of my head in the glowing firelight as it dries. It's almost as if it reflects light itself and my lips twist painfully down. Mother had brown hair and brown eyes, and I'd always teased her I was a changeling left by a fairy. She'd counter that I'd been born of the stars and that the moon had left me at her door on the eve of the brightest night. I was her starlight princess. A tear glides down my cheek at the bittersweet reflection.

The scent of bread browning against the warm hearthstones breaks my reverie and, shaking off the memories, I flip it over so it doesn't burn.

Satisfied with the fruits of my labor, I change into my extra shift, now-dried dress, and stockings, and am toasty warm at long last. I lay down on my freshly washed and dried blanket and pillow, and I'm lulled into a doze.

Bang. Thud. Something knocks against the front door.

I jolt, my heart beating hard and fast. I search the room for the makeshift broom made from the evergreen branch. The magpie, after making a ruckus for a time, has long since disappeared. Could this be the owner or another soul wandering the forest?

The door handle moves. There is no board for the latch. Why had I been so naïve to believe I was safe?

My breath hitches as the door opens. Wind whistles

through and snow spirals in, becoming slush on the warmed wooden floor.

The magpie flies in, slipping through a hand-width opening. *Scream! Squawk!*

"Oh, no. Not you again." I chase the bird. It must be ill because it doesn't fly. It runs from me, leaving wet footprints to pool on the wooden floor. "Shoo! Be gone, you monster!"

Wings flapping and beak wide, the magpie hurtles at me. Feathers graze my face in a soft, yet determined attack as it screeches. I flail and jerk away from the crazed assault, only to trip over the makeshift broom. I fall and land on my bottom, my long hair flying crazily over my face. I hastily brush it away so I can see. Anger burns in my chest as I grab the branch and swing. I land a square hit.

The bird skitters across the floor and over the threshold into the snow. I stand and quickly run for the door to jam it shut.

I lodge the thick evergreen limb into the bar brackets on each side of the frame. I *call* a heavy, wooden bench from across the room and prop it against the door. I barely notice my strength weakening from using so much of my ability as the blood pumps furiously through my veins.

The scratching against the front door stops, and my breathing eases. Moments later, however, something hits against the back door, and my fear rekindles. I *send* the iron kettle across the room to block the door. It lands on the floor with a thunk and dirty water sloshes over the side of the heavy pot. Sweat beads on my forehead from the effort.

The noise stops. After a lengthy silence, I open the window not far from the door and glance outside at the doorway. No bird. Maybe the vile creature finally flew away.

I turn to gather the kettle to dispose of the dirty wash water outside and slip in a puddle. My feet fly out, and I land with a gasp on the hard floor. I can already imagine the bruises I've undoubtedly gained. The bird flies in the open door, cawing at me as if laughing.

Instead of diving at me, it swoops up, clasps the handle on the door with its claws, and shuts it with a bang. Its dark outline expands into something much bigger.

Terror crawls up my spine.

Oh, Nellie, I was wrong. So very wrong.

There are ghosts in this forest.

4

The forest must be haunted, because before me stands a ghost. A most handsome one, but a specter nonetheless. He's also as tall as I am, which is quite disconcerting. I choke back a scream and stumble backward.

He steps toward me and I notice he has sleek black hair that sweeps down to his collar, a strong nose and jaw, and strangely shaped, dark eyes. His pale white skin stands out against his black tunic and breeches.

He smiles before speaking. "Are you going to sit there all day with your mouth hanging open, or are you going to scream?"

I shriek and scramble to my knees to dart behind the kettle. "Don't you touch me, you devil."

"Look, you obviously don't remember who I am. But, I am neither the devil nor the ghost you surely believe me to be. I'm here because you're in danger. That's what I've been trying to tell you for the past half-day." His smooth baritone voice flows with a mocking tone. His voice is familiar, somehow. But I can't place it.

I squint, trying to gauge his motives. "I'm only in danger from you, someone I don't know and have never met before. Leave now, or I'll cook you for supper, you foul creature."

"Oh, will you now?" Laughter drips from his words. He folds his arms against his chest.

My hands ache as I grasp the pot tighter. "I'll chop you up into small pieces and use your bones to stir the stew." I wish I possessed strength enough to toss him back outdoors, but my arms quiver slightly from fatigue.

But surely, I've become infirm. A bird does not become human. Yet I remember a darkly dressed man, who I thought was my father, quite similar to the man before me. I shake my head. This is obviously not my father. He's not old enough to be.

He leans forward, and again I'm struck by his height. "Tell me, do you intend for me what you did to Cook? I do hope you'll be careful. I've no moles that need removal."

I grasp the rim of the kettle. "You should be afraid. Look at me. Everyone who sees me knows I'm a witch, cursed. Don't you know I can hex you as well?"

Firelight makes his face glow as he takes another step toward me. "I know many things. In fact, I know you are not dangerous. A bit clumsy, perhaps."

"I've powers you can't imagine." I never mention my abilities, but I'll use it to get him to leave if it comes to that. Better he thinks me a witch than assault me. As the thoughts rush through my mind, I realize my hair is untied, loose around my head. Surely, he can see how strange it is.

The blue-black of his shirt glows in the light. But his gaze imparts a seriousness that doesn't match the mirth of his grin. "I'm more than aware of what you are capable of, my lady. Shall I give you an example?"

I back up toward the fireplace. "I'm no lady, and you'll not live through the night if you take another step." Behind me, I motion with my fingers and *call* a sharp piece of broken stone to my hand. It lands silently in my palm. It's sharp enough to cut if necessary.

"Oh, but you are a lady to me." He continues as if I haven't just threatened him. "Now, for instance, I know you thought fairies switched you at birth because you looked nothing like your mother." He stretches his hand out toward me, and I'm fascinated at the pale, slim fingers that spread out much like the feathers I surely must've imagined moments before.

I'm speechless for a moment and then gain my wits. "That's preposterous. Everyone knows there's no such thing as fairies." I had believed so many years ago.

"No? I know your mother's full name was Cadence, though she went by Cady here, and you wore your favorite purple dress until it was in tatters when you were in your eighth year. I loved when you wore it. It went so well with your stunning hair."

My mouth hangs open, and I snap it shut. I run a hand through my hair and twist it self-consciously with shaking fingers. No one ever complimented my hair. And how did he know what I looked like? I blink before changing the subject. "Anyone could find out my mother's name. It's on public record at the Pauper's Cemetery." At least I believe it was. There was no way for me to find out for sure since I'd been indentured and not allowed to visit her grave.

As for my dress, it had been the color of my favorite purple flower, which Mother grew in our garden. We never knew the flower's name, but the dress was the softest fabric I ever owned. Tears sting my eyes. I was wearing it when Mother died, but it had been thrown away since her blood had soaked it.

How can he know? Has he spied on me?

"Would you like me to recite the bedtime story about how the moon took a piece of the brightest star and created you, leaving you at your mother's doorstep?" A fond smile graces his face.

I frown at him and pain tugs at my heart. I'd never told anyone about those stories. They'd been my secret since Mother died. She'd been the only one who saw anything good in me. I'd been doomed since the day she died.

His brows furrow in what seems like disappointment. "What about the ring? Didn't she tell you it was the key to your salvation? I have one as well." He holds out his hand. On his third finger is the same signet ring as the one hidden in my pillow.

This can't be right! I always believed the man with the ring to be my father. It was definitely not some annoying bird-ghost-man.

"No." Saliva fills my mouth, and I swallow it back. I study him harder. His narrowed, dark eyes *are* familiar. And his skin, almost as pale as my hair. I've seen him in my childhood dreams. The boy who could change right in front of my eyes. He played with me. But it can't be! It was my father, not a boy. I twist my neck, rolling my shoulders.

My feet burn from stepping too close to the fire. Panic wells up inside me, and the crocks in the kitchen clank. I clutch the sharp stone tight. "You're wrong."

He raises a hand to his ear. "Am I? Do you hear the call on the wind? You know that sound. It has followed us—you in particular, these past ten years."

I move the edge of the stone so it faces outward. One good swipe and this bird, this ghost, this man, will regret attacking me. "I hear nothing, save you."

A mournful howl silences me.

The beasts are back.

My feet stick to the floor. I fight back the memories as snarls sound from outside the cottage. Fear runs wild through my veins, and I dash toward the ghost and chop at him with the sharp edge of the stone.

The ghost ducks away and I smack against the wall. I let out my own snarl in frustration.

He crosses his arms over his chest. "I'm not your enemy. Use your abilities, Tambrynn. Think. What is it you do best?"

"Sweep the floors. Polish the silver. Clean the fireplace." I spit the details of my résumé as I had on the pauper's block several times. Belatedly I comprehend he used my name. "How do you know my name?"

His eyes, the shade of sparkling coal, level at me. Something in them kindles a memory, but as quick as it comes, it vanishes.

"I—I've always known," he says absently, rubbing a hand through his sleek hair. He whistles. "So, you're nothing more than a domestic, equal to a scullery maid."

I bristle at the regret and pity in his voice. I dislike being pitied worse than being controlled. My attention turns to the front door as the snarling is accompanied by scraping. In haste, I fling my arms wide and hurtle the kettle toward the door, not calling, but *pushing*. It's instinct from fear. It clatters against the threshold, denting the wood and leaving a wet trail behind it. It's heavier than anything I'm used to calling, but instead of weakening, I'm emboldened.

"Astonishing job, my lady!" He speaks with a note of pride.

I spin toward him. He's supposed to be intimidated, actually scared by my ability, not enthused by it. Who is he? "What kind of worthless man stands by as a helpless girl does the heavy work?"

A louder wail from the front of the cottage silences my angry tirade.

The ghost continues as if he hears nothing to be concerned about. "If you recall, you think me a devil. Do devils labor? I think not."

"Devil or not, you're a man. *Do* something!" How can he remain so calm, just leaning against one of the chairs when danger surrounds us? So, he thinks he can stand around and do nothing? I sneer at him. "Maybe a good dousing is required." I lift my hand toward him.

"What are you doing?" His voice edges a bit higher than before.

"Me? I'm just doing what I do best." I swing my fist and *push*. Hard.

He jerks and shoots across the cottage, arms waving, and flies into the pot with a big splash.

He's stunned at first, then manages to get out of the kettle without falling, though his clothes are now soaked and dripping on my cleaned floor. "I believe that's the first time that's happened. And your eyes lit up. It's incredible. You're growing stronger. I came back just in time." He wrings his shirt out, the puddle beneath him growing.

I ignore the beasts. "What do you mean?"

He rubs droplets from his face and runs his fingers through his dark, damp curls. "You pushed the kettle and then you pushed me. Have you done this before? I've only seen you draw objects to you, and I've never seen your eyes glow."

I frown at him, confused. "How do you know what I can do?"

His face contorts and he sneezes. More of the soapy water drips from his hair. He resembles a wet kitten that doesn't enjoy baths, and I can't help the giggle that escapes.

"You always did love to play games." He slicks back his hair.

Snuffling noises sound by the door. Panicked, I send one object after another flying against the front and then the back entrances. Hidden objects I hadn't seen cascade out of the recesses of the loft until piles stand guard at both sides.

"Well done, my lady. If I may ask, next time could you at least try to miss the innocent?"

I whirl around and spy the man eagerly devouring the bread I baked. A fork dangles in his damp hair and a red spot swells on his cheek. Though I'm starting to tire, anger spurs me on.

"Innocent? You're not innocent. You're a thief!" I lunge at him, but in a blur, he changes into a bird and I grasp empty air.

A dark feather flutters down and lands at my feet. Crumbs fall in a pile where he no longer stands.

Whootle. Cheep. The magpie flies up, disappearing into the shadows of the loft.

A scrape rattles the back door, and it almost breaks. *The beasts. They're going to get in!*

My heart hammers in my ears. If only I could recall how I saved myself the day Mother died. We were just entering our cottage when they attacked.

As tall as men, their wolf heads were grotesque and twisted. Their teeth were sharp, as were their clawed hands. They attacked without provocation and I'd screamed, pulling every bit of my power within me to stop them. Mother pushed me behind her, yelling something in a language I didn't understand, and a warm wind rushed over us. My eyes were closed the whole time and when I looked up, the beasts were gone. I'd survived with a single scratch, yet Mother lay in front of me, shredded by the beasts. It happened so quickly, like what I did to Cook, I scarcely remember it.

Boom!

The door quakes against the hinges and the floor trembles beneath my feet. Dust scatters everywhere. Sweat trickles down my temple.

I seize a smaller branch from the edge of the fireplace and prepare for battle. Like Mother, I'll fight until the end if need be. I concentrate on the center of my being, where I gather what's left of my strength.

I tense, facing the door at the front of the cottage, waiting for the onslaught, stick balanced in my hands.

Silence.

Moments turn to minutes. I stand up from my crouched position and listen. No noise. No sound. Nothing. Are they waiting for me to let down my guard before they pounce?

"Ahem." The ghost stands where he stood before, but this time behind me, his arms crossed over his chest. Not even a ghost could move so swiftly and so quietly!

I turn toward him, clutching my own chest and breathing hard. "You're insufferable. I should like to skin you and feed you to those beasts."

"Brave words for one so small. At least I would be deposed on a full stomach. I did thank you for the food, didn't I? It was quite good for one who doesn't usually cook." A crooked grin slides up one side of his face.

I study him, curious. "How do you know me so well, and why are you dry? You were sopping wet when you flew off and left me to defend myself against those vile creatures." The flames sputter like my words when I toss the stick back into the fire as I turn over the impossible words I just uttered. A man flying. It simply isn't done.

"There's much I need to tell you, my lady. But, not now. I believe we're safe for the moment, so I bid you good night." He tips his head, and I notice his arms moving in an arc—like before when he'd changed into a bird.

Now he decides to be a gentleman and bid me goodnight? Fury darkens my vision. "Stop, magpie." I *push*. He halts. I raise my fist and he is suspended in midair, surprise flashing across his smug face.

5

"How do you know me? Are we truly safe, and where are you off to?" My senses sharpen as I hold the magpie-man in the air. My hands are steady but tingle in an invigorating way, unlike anything I've experienced before.

He thrashes to no avail. I hold him, and his feet dangle knee-high from the floor. My focused anger allows me to direct my will with steady control. The thought of it makes me giddy. It's the first time I've maintained such discipline over any object, much less one alive and moving.

"Do you hear the beasts?" he asks, his hands fisted by his sides. "No? I took care of them as you requested with my extraordinary talents." His voice holds the slightest tremble, almost as if he fears me. He blinks and sighs. "It's been a long day. If you'll please release me, I'll leave you with the fire to keep you warm."

"If you haven't already noticed, you're not in control right now. And you're not leaving until you answer some questions." I pinch my fists tighter.

He winces, and then his face slackens in resignation. "All

right. Please let me go, and I'll tell you what you want to know."

Fatigue cramps my body, and I fight to stand. I won't be able to hold on much longer, but I'm determined not to show my weakness. "You promise not to fly away?" It's unbelievable to ask such a question, but in these circumstances, necessary.

"You have my word."

I study the solemn expression on his face. He seems sincere, but even if he's not, I need some strength left just in case.

He drops harder than I intend, but I don't apologize. My knees shake from the effort, and I am unable to keep it from showing.

"My lady, if you are tired—"

I silence him with a glare. "Who are you, and why do you know me so well? *What* exactly are you? Why did you follow me?"

He bows gracefully. "My name is Lucas, my lady. I have been with you since you were a babe. Well, except for a short time, I'm afraid. But, I am, and forever will be, your faithful friend and Watcher."

I cross my arms in disbelief. "You're mad. Completely, intolerably mad."

"I assure you I am as sane as you, Caller."

How did he name my ability? Mother was the only one who ever knew. She's the one who told me I was a Caller, and I'd used that title for it ever since. "Have you been spying on me?"

"I am charged with keeping you safe." His chest expands, much like a preening bird.

"Safe? You call this safe? And who, pray tell, are you keeping me safe from? Pauper's blocks? Or my master's whip? Cook's ire? When did you keep me safe?" I think back to the ten years since Mother died. Not even the Kinsman had found it in his mercy to keep me from being sold over and over again. I certainly wasn't safe with masters who thought me cursed and then treated me as such. He's obviously lying, but why?

He glances down to the floor and shifts his stance. When he glances back up, his eyebrows are scrunched, his pale face is flushed. "You must've noticed that you and I don't look like anyone here." He waves a hand up and down his body with a dramatic flair. "Are we not taller than anyone you know? Our faces don't resemble those who live here. We're not the same." His dark eyes are unwavering as he stares at me.

Bitterness floods my tongue, and I study him. There is something familiar—like I've known him before. Still, it's too far-fetched to consider. "This is unbelievable. Perhaps I'm a real fairy and we're from the moon?"

"Nothing quite as romantic as that, I'm afraid. This kingdom, Tenebris, is not your home kingdom. We—you, your mother, and I—are from Anavrin, where there are different races. This is why you look nothing like the Tenebrisians. Surely you didn't truly think you were some sort of devil's spawn because of how different you look?"

His words sting because I'd considered it too many times to count. "You've no idea what it's like being told you're evil day in and day out for ten years. There's nothing else that would explain this." I grab some of my hair and point to my eyes. "Silver spun hair and star-shaped pupils. Not to mention how much taller I am. If I'm not evil, why do I look like this? What am I?" I think back to Mother's stories about the moon leaving me on her doorstep.

He frowns. "Unlike Tenebris, Anavrin has different kinds of people. You and I are a mixture of races, allowing us to use some of the abilities of whichever race we're descended from. You're half-mage, a magic-user, and half-eldrin, a special race of holy people. Your mother was an eldrin gifted with healing and protection. I am half-djinn, a shape-changer, and half-voyant, meaning I can connect to others with my mind."

I hold my hand up to stop him. "Wait, so you're saying there are other people out there who are like me? I'm not the only one?" Tears sting my eyes. How many times had I been treated like an outcast, someone who is cursed?

"You are unique, but you're not the only one."

"But I don't believe in magic." I wipe the moisture from my eyes.

He hesitates as if considering his next words. "How else can you explain your ability to call objects?"

"I don't know. Just not magic." It is too impossible to believe. Calling objects is one thing.

Magic spells are quite another.

He takes a deep breath and lets it out. "You are exceptional. Before you were born, your mother survived a dark magic attack. Though she was unmatched when it came to healing and protection, you somehow absorbed some of that dark magic." He stops, possibly awaiting my reaction.

I have no idea how to react to such nonsense. Dark magic, indeed! His tale surpasses some of the old maid's myths I've heard.

When I say nothing, he continues. "The moment you arrived, you were special, distinct in not only your looks but your abilities as well. No one is born able to use their gifts, yet you were. You're not like anyone, but you are not wicked. Evil is a choice, not something you are created to become."

"If Mother was unmatched in her skills, why was she murdered by beasts? Shouldn't she have been able to fight them off? And if I'm as great as you say, why couldn't I fight them off? This makes no sense."

He shifts as if wanting to touch me but withdraws. "You did fight them off, which is why you lived and your mother didn't. She died trying to protect you and was unable to recover herself. It seems that this kingdom isn't favorable to magic, as you may have noticed. It's the only reason I can think of why, as strong as Cadence was, she didn't survive the attack."

"Why did Mother have to die? Why were we attacked at all?" My throat constricts, and I'm unable to ask any other questions.

"Your ability to call shouldn't be an actual ability. Even the most powerful dark mage can't do what you do without first accumulating an incredible amount of power. With you, it's innate, a natural gift that you've always been able to access. When that mage who attacked your mother found out about your budding calling ability, he came after you. He will kill you to get it. That's why Cadence brought us here to Tenebris."

I scoff at that. It's all so fantastic. I've never heard a more fanciful story. I cross my arms. "How would he get my ability if he kills me? Who is this mage?"

He takes a deep breath, and his eyes pierce into mine. "Your—"

Pounding halts our conversation. Can wolves knock on doors? If I am half mage and magpies can turn into men, then wolves can sprout hands and manners and knock before entering. I must be delirious. Possibly, I've frozen out in the forest and am imagining this whole thing. I take a deep breath.

"Don't answer the door, my lady." Lucas changes to a bird and flies into the loft area, leaving me alone again.

Where is he going now? "Watcher, my bucket." Spit flies from my lips, and I swipe them angrily with my sleeve. "Keep me safe, ha! Can't even stay in one place long enough to hold a conversation." I grab the limb back from the hearth. It glows orange at the end. I'm ready for another fight.

"Let me in." The muted voice is deeply masculine and quite

demanding. The air around me thickens, and I'm drawn to open the door. I step forward, and then a warm sensation bubbles in my gut and spreads outward. Tingles, different than my calling ability, sweep across my body. As soon as the prickles reach my head and toes, I take a deep breath. What is going on?

The pounding starts again, this time with more fervor.

Could it be the previous owner? Surely not, since the cabin looked to be vacant for quite some time, and an owner would simply walk in without knocking. My skin glows again with that strange bluish tint, which is disconcerting. I shake my hands, but it doesn't leave or dim. Who would be out in this snow? Something isn't right. I take on the brusque manner I'd heard my mistresses use often. "I should think not. Be on your way."

Shivers spread across my scalp like someone's massaging it.

The sensation intensifies to a pull as if a tether is attached to my mind. "Tambrynn, it's your father, Thoron. Let me in."

6

My father? I lower the branch as shock steals the heat from my body and the bluish radiance around my skin disappears. I shiver as the coldness descends over me.

More of the pull tugs at me. I step back, blink, and the sensation is gone. Lucas had mentioned mages who could perform magic. Is this my father, or is it someone trying to get to me like he'd said, wanting to steal my ability? I slap my free hand to my head. This can't be happening.

However, doubt creeps in my heart. I've always longed to find my father, more so since Mother died. Could this really be him?

"Do not open the door. That man outside may be your father, but he is as dangerous as the beasts that killed Cadence." The magpie—Lucas—speaks up behind me.

I turn and glare at him, a hand clutching my chest. "My father? Here? Why shouldn't I open the door to him?"

"The dark mage I was telling you about is Thoron, your father. He's why we left Anavrin. The reason you look different than anyone else. His magic somehow affected you, making your hair silver, causing your pupils to be star-shaped, and giving you the ability to call."

I'm stunned. "My father?" Surely Lucas is wrong. Why would my father want to harm me?

Lucas's eyes narrow to slits as if he can read my thoughts. "Mages are not good, Tambrynn. He's evil. The beasts that killed your mother were his. He controls them, and I assure you they will do the same to you. You cannot trust him." His gaze holds mine with a passion that quickens my pulse.

I fling my arms out, and embers from the limb I still grasp fall to the floor. "And I should trust you? After you tell me I'm half-mage and then say they are bad. I don't know you any more than whoever that may be." I point to the door, and the pounding continues.

"You do, but you've forgotten. This kingdom twists magic in ways I don't fully understand. It's dimmed your memory of me just like it did for me of you." He places one hand on his heart and reaches the other out to me. "Please, I beg of you to believe me."

"I—"

The door rattles against the objects still blocking it. "Daughter, I've searched for you for years. Please let me in." His voice is smooth, almost caressing my ears. But, something in the lilted tone reminds me of Adelia when she'd tattle. The words hold no emotion, a hubris of sorts that rings untrue.

I fist my fingers in my still-damp hair, pulling the tresses tight. Too many sensations and emotions collide inside me. Longing for my father. The familiarity that beckons me to Lucas as a friend I wish to trust. The memories of my mother's broken body. Who do I believe?

"Have I injured you?" Lucas's teasing nature turns somber, almost serious. His alabaster skin glows in the light of the fire. "Have I done anything untoward? I admit I did partake in your supper, but I haven't had a decent meal in several days. I've been busy throwing the beasts off our tracks. Now I recognize it wasn't just the beasts, but their master as well. I won't be able to keep you safe if you let him in. He's too strong for me. And I've vowed never to let you come to harm."

This is truly a waking nightmare. "What kind of harm?"

The door glows as if on fire, but there's no smoke. I squint.

Lucas glances to and fro nervously. He gestures to the door. "He's using dark magic. Tambrynn, we must hurry." He reaches out a hand to me.

"Tambrynn, let me in." The air around me grows heavy, and there's an invisible yank on my mind again, stronger this time. My neck strains against the pull.

More strange tingles sweep over me. I'm panting by the time I shake it off. I rub my aching nape.

"Please trust me. I can tell you sense it. Thoron is evil. He doesn't want a reunion with his long-lost daughter. He wants to steal your ability. Come, we can escape if you'll just put your faith in me." Lucas's open hand, the delicate fingers resembling feathers, stretch out to me. His eyes beg me to believe him and take his hand.

The feeling of familiarity nags at my consciousness. I see in my mind a younger boy in much the same stance, beckoning me to play with him. I can hear myself squeal his name and laugh while he chases me playfully.

"How can you save me if he is evil and controls the beasts? No one is that strong. I can't fight that."

Lucas's gaze sharpens. "You did once. And I am more useful than you might imagine, Tambrynn. I think both of us are strong enough now, and I'll be able to change you. We can fly away, and then I'll explain everything when we're safe." He moves toward me, hand still outstretched, close enough I can smell him. My heart pinches. He smells of grass and wind, just as in my dreams. Another pang of knowing flits through my mind and I peer at him, trying to connect this man to the boy from my dreams. They look alike. They smell the same. Why have I forgotten him?

The man outside begins speaking in a loud voice in words I can't decipher. They're similar to the words mother spoke when we were attacked all those years ago. The doorway brightens as if the sun radiates off it. I gaze at it, conflicted. For so long, all I wanted to do was be free to find my father. Now he's here. My hand twitches, wanting to open the door, but I restrain myself. What if Lucas is right?

Lucas steps closer, his hand shaking now. "Please, my lady, we have no time."

The door explodes. Wood shards pierce the air. I throw out my arms to keep the wood from hitting me. *Stop!* Warmth floods over me from the center of my being, radiating blue in a sphere around me. I fist my hands and the fragments stop mid-air. I stare at the circle surrounding me and the scattered particles of wood suspended in the air in front of me. Has time stopped? I've never done anything like this before. Then I glimpse beyond the bluish glow toward the man, my father, moving through the shattered door.

He's much younger than I would've imagined, closer to my age than someone who should be my father. And he's tall. Taller than Lucas.

He steps inside the cottage and swipes his hand across the dangling debris in front of his face without surprise. They drop to the ground when he touches them, plinking against the floor. The rest is still in the air. He's slim with dark hair parted down the middle. There's a gray streak on one side of his head. Though he just destroyed the door as easily as I call objects, he doesn't look evil. In fact, he's quite handsome, but his eyes are cruel, and his smirk is condescending.

"We meet at last, daughter." He bows his head slightly, but he never takes his eyes off me. "The rumors are true." He studies my face, and I can almost feel his look trailing across my hair. His stare holds a cold calculation. It's the same gaze I have suffered many times on the pauper's block—judging me, evaluating how valuable I could be to him.

I don't know what to say, so I'm silent. I continue to study him back until I see two beasts step toward the threshold behind him. They're just as I remember, with warped features, dark skin, sharp teeth, and claws. Fear shoots through my body and then anger on top of it. My mother is dead because of them. And *he* is their master.

Appalled, I step back and unclench my fists. The wood pieces that I've held in the air fall to the floor in a chorus of wooden clinks. This is not the father I wished for. He is just as Lucas described—vile and depraved.

My father smiles as he turns and waves a hand toward the beast on his left. I see the ring on his finger, a replica of the ring Lucas wears and the one hidden inside my pillow. "Do you like my pets? They've been trying to find you for so long."

I grind my teeth. "They killed my mother."

"That was unfortunate." He shrugs as if it is a trivial matter. His smile returns, but is not reflected in his eyes. "Won't you introduce me to your friend?" His glance at Lucas is disdainful. He steps forward and I notice the shadows near him are more like a layer of smoke hovering around him.

My skin tingles and my hands glow blue again. Though concerned about the faint light, I concentrate on my father. "I would if he were indeed my friend." Lucas stiffens at my words, but I know how dangerous people work. Show partiality to anything, and they use it against you. My first instinct is to protect him, as I had with Nellie. It's as inborn as my calling ability. Besides, I now believe him.

My father laughs. The sound is cold and derisive. "Did your mother never teach you any manners?"

It's my turn to stiffen, but I try not to let him see. "She might've, if she hadn't been murdered by your filthy beasts." I nod toward the animals behind him.

The beast's nose and mouth are elongated into a wolf-like snout. Black nostrils flare, and a yellowish drool glitters on its taut, cracked lips. Instead of whiskers, the leathery snout is covered with what looks like a mustache stretched too far across the malformed muzzle, reminding me of the quills of a porcupine. Ivory, jagged barbs form teeth sharp enough to easily tear flesh. The misshapen nose gives way to a more normal-sized head, though the ears are exaggerated—wider and more elongated than a normal wolf. The grotesque skull rests upon a hunched masculine body. Now I recognize they're more person than beast, though the glittering eyes say no such thing.

"It's a shame about your mother." Thoron tsks and shakes his head. "Come, let me make it up to you." The hand he waves toward the open doorway is smooth like a gentleman's hand, with no calluses. There are black symbols scrawled across his wrists and neck up to his cheeks, much like the tattoos I'd seen on sailors in the seaports. But these are somehow different. They move, wavering in place like a ripple on the water.

I bide my time as I gather all of the energy I can to the center of my gut. I wish I weren't so tired from lifting Lucas and throwing items at the doors.

"I think not." I reach behind me and call my pillow closer so I can make a quick escape if possible, and it edges across the floor soundlessly. I pray that I am strong enough to get past Thoron and the beasts. However, the pillow catches his attention and his fake smile disappears.

"You're not thinking of leaving, dear daughter, are you?" A

red glow surrounds his hands. They snap with light, popping like a wet log on a fire.

I give Lucas a side glance. Of the two, I trust Lucas. Though he claimed I am part-mage, I don't have actual magic like the man in front of me. Or if I do, I don't know how to use it. However, I do have some abilities, and I'm willing to use them to get out of this cabin.

Before I can call the pillow to me, a light flies from Thoron's hands and I brace my arms in front of my face. It's hot, I can feel the heat, but as quickly as it hits, it bounces back toward Thoron. He swipes a hand, and the glowing light glimmers and dies.

Thoron's face screws up in a grimace, his eyes flash with a reddish glint, and I have to wonder what I believed was so handsome about him. He's incensed and roaring.

"Tambrynn, your hand!" Lucas whispers behind me, but Thoron sends a crackling ball at us. It darts faster than the first one, and I am unable to put my hands up in time to push it back. It hits me and I am lifted into the air. Needle-like pain digs into my skin. Then I feel the tugging, like a seam ripper on thread. The pull is stronger than before when Thoron was behind the door.

I land on the floor, hunched and shaking, a sheen of sweat coating my body. I should be bleeding with a thousand cuts, but my arms are lit up with a bright, blue glow. I *push* harder than I've ever pushed and send Thoron back through the door and into his pet beast.

"My lady, now!" Lucas yells and grabs my hand while clutching my pillow under his other arm.

Tickling tingles spread across my body. A whirlwind of air washes over me. My stomach flip-flops and my sight spins. Looking around, I realize we are no longer in the lower part of the cottage. We're perched in the rafters of the house, looking down upon where we stood moments before.

An odd lightness forces me to throw my arms out in an effort to still the wave of dizziness that rolls over me. Feathers instead of fingers splay before me, but they aren't inky black like Lucas's. They're gleaming silver. I hadn't believed Lucas when he said he'd change me. I open my mouth to yell, but only a garbled *cackle* comes out.

Thoron disentangles himself from the beast. He glances up in the rafters. Light flashes and he flings crackling magic our way.

"Follow me." I hear the words in my head. It's Lucas's voice. He darts down and around the flash and Thoron in a blur of blackish blue, flying out of the broken doorway.

I wobble on the rafter, my wings spread wide to keep me balanced. Thoron's magic grazes my feathers, but luckily there's no pain this time. I tuck my wings on my back and glare down at the man who is my father. For so long, I'd longed to find him. My dream breaks to pieces in my heart. In its place, I now wanted—no, I needed—to destroy him. Avenge my mother's death. But I have to survive first.

I pace and lean over the ledge. I want to follow Lucas, but I'm unsure of exactly how. I stretch my wings as another flash of light smacks me directly in the chest. I wobble, shivering as the magic moves across my bird body. A glow explodes from me, forming a halo a hands-width from my body in all directions. My father's magic dances across it like soap on a bubble. Light glimmers in a circle around me.

Thoron screams in fury and his beast dodges past him, jumping up toward me, but I'm too far up. I stretch my wings again, and with a silent prayer to the Kinsman, I teeter awkwardly, dropping between the beast and Thoron, my wings open wide. I barely manage not to hit the wall on my way out of the cottage. I can't see straight ahead and have to keep turning my head from side to side to get a good look at where I am headed. I skim the branches on one evergreen tree and dodge snow that's piled high on another.

The sky is growing darker and it's getting harder to see. I slam into tree branch after tree branch while I continue to adapt to my new sight. I can't find Lucas anywhere. I miss a couple of branches when I hear several snarls and high-pitched howls from the direction of the cottage. It's not just one but several different voices, barking and snarling. In my struggle to see, I hadn't noticed how many beasts there were.

More snaps erupt from behind me. They're too close.

Hot shivers slither down my spine as my legs dangle off a low-hanging branch. I never imagined dying like this.

7

"*Tambrynn. Follow the sound of my voice.*" Lucas's words fill my mind.

I make it onto the limb and turn my head side to side to search for him. My avian heart beats erratically. I can't tell where he is.

"*Over here,*" he calls out. To my ears, it's a *chitter*, while I hear the words in my mind.

I follow the sound of his bird's chatter and spot his dark form perched on a large evergreen branch. I shriek. Instead of a harsh sound, it's melodious, which frustrates me as it doesn't reflect my irritation. Off once again, I push my wings harder and totter sideways, right in the path of a tree limb. I arch my back to stop, but the forward motion continues to move me as I collide with it. I'm sent in a spiral and drop deep into the snow below. It's cold, and I cannot get a grip with my hands, and then remember it's because they are wings. Flapping in a circle, I make it out of the snow and back into the air. Finally, I locate Lucas.

The beasts snarl and howl and I can hear Thoron cursing as he trudges through the drifts of snow.

"They have trouble tracking us through the air, and the snow makes it difficult for them to travel as well. Though we're safe for the moment, focus on your wings. They'll help you to balance."

Focus on my wings? Balance? I've never felt so out of my element as I do at this moment. I yell out again to tell him so, but my words are a quivering song. I dart directly toward where he is, intent on landing, but I almost slam into him. He stretches his wings out, side-stepping me in a graceful dance. Pain explodes as I strike the hard bark and land, my body twisted on the branch. It feels as if I've broken a wing feather or two. Needles and snow rain down. Indignation fills me.

The magpie sends me a sideways look as I lay sprawled across the massive evergreen branch. *"There are several things to get used to when becoming a bird. Especially the eyesight. Your eyes see out sideways. It'll take a while to overcome, though that wasn't bad for a first-time flyer. I knew you'd take right to it."*

"Take right to it? You call this taking right to it? You must be mad!" The words shoot out of my mind and I attack. He ducks my attempt and I dart past him inelegantly on my new bird legs. How do birds move on such small appendages? Panicked, I grab at a small nearby branch with my beak and use the force to swing around before soaring out of the tree altogether. I land in a heap on a nearby tree branch across from him.

Lucas is trembling as if from laughter, and I glare at him, first with one eye and then the other. *"Are you amused by me?"*

"Not at all, my lady. Nice stop, by the way. You may want to cease trying to attack me and the tree and allow me to lead you out of here before they find us. When we're safe again, you may drop me into another kettle, if you so wish."

"I do wish." I fluff my feathers, ridding them of the snow clumps.

"Follow me, my lady." Lucas darts off the branch, making it look much easier than I know it is. Reluctantly, I patter to the edge of the branch and try to stay airborne.

The howls and snuffling of the beasts disappear as we fly away from my father. The sun has fully set now and the trees thin out as we soar over flat meadowlands.

My wings strain and burn from fighting the wind currents as I follow after Lucas. Although I weigh less than a small loaf of bread, I tire soon after we leave the evergreen tree. We fly for what feels like hours, and my energy is spent. My body bobs and my wings falter as I struggle to keep up with my leader. *"Lucas, please. I can't continue."*

"We need to go a bit farther, my lady. The beasts will track us if we don't put enough space between us quickly."

High above, the moon lights up the sky. *"We have to go back and get my things. I have no clothing. Nothing to change into."*

"Whatever we have in our possession goes with us when we change, especially our clothing. All you need is the ring, and I grabbed the pillow before we changed. I promise it will be fine." His confident voice irks me until a wind catches my wings and they cramp.

"Where are we going? I cannot travel much longer." My voice is breathless, weak.

"I will explain things to you when I locate a safe place and can land. It's hard to recognize where we are with all of the snow, so please let me concentrate."

I fume in silence as we fly for what seems like another hour. Soon, the snow grows less and less until the land below us is no longer white. The autumn trees are thin, their leaves rustling to catch up with our shadows. It's a sight to behold.

As a child, I always wondered what it would be like to soar through the sky like a bird. A memory blooms in my mind, sending shivers across my body from head to toe. It was of

Lucas, changing into a bird in front of me years before. It's why I was curious to fly. Now I know what it's like—tiring!

A sideways gust hits me. Pain tears through my right wing and it spasms. Like a stone falling from a hilltop, my body drops. I tense, waiting for impact.

A wheat field stretches out beneath me. Golden shafts cut and waiting to be baled soften my landing. The scent of the field mixed with dew is comforting. I right myself, but my wing continues to ache. Perhaps if I rest for a small moment, I can take flight again. Only for a moment ...

The magpie swoops down, startling me. *"My lady. You cannot stop here. We don't have much farther to go. We will be safe away from here."*

"I don't hear them. They haven't pursued us this far." I labor to catch my breath, knowing my mouth is wide open and panting, yet I can't pull together enough dignity to restrain myself. *"We are protected here and I am quite unable to continue. Please, let me break for a short spell."*

"Protected like a light on a hill," Lucas murmurs, but I barely hear it. A tug on my wing breaks through my consciousness. His infernal voice is in my ear. *"You cannot rest now, my lady. Danger is upon us."*

"I cannot ..." The ground disappears beneath me. A cool rush of air and then warmth as I'm carried. I will my eyes to open, but my lids grow heavy. Sweet darkness encloses me.

————

A bawling cow shocks me awake. My right arm burns as does my throat. Flashes of memories slog through the thickness that encompasses my mind. Where am I?

"Good eve, my lady." The pleasant baritone voice is familiar. "I'm glad you're finally awake."

In a burst, it all floods back to me. That man—Lucas! He changed me into a bird. I jerk up to complain, but it comes out as a melodic shriek. I have no lips, no hands. The magpie-turned-man stares at me with a bemused smirk on his very human face. Behind him lies the dim interior of a barn's loft. The scent of dust and hay tickle my senses.

Unlike the girls I've cared for, I have never been subject to fits or spells of vanity. However, glancing at the silver feathers bedecking my body affects something deep inside me. Screaming, I dart back and forth, flapping my winged arms. "Trill—*good for nothing*—chirp—*unscrupulous*—chir-chir-chirrup—*unbelievable gall* ..." Once again, lovely notes escape my beak when I'd prefer the sound to reflect my annoyance. It only serves to irritate me more.

"Whoa, whoa! My lady. I saved your life by changing you, so you're quite welcome. And I bring you a peace offering." He drops my pillow and flourishes a cloth sack onto the planks of the loft before me. "Food and water." He pulls a flask from his pocket and places it beside the cloth.

"Wouldn't it be nice if I could use my hands?" My anger sounds like a beautiful song.

It's all his fault. I attack, clawing at his hair. I jerk upwards, ignoring the pain in my wing, and the silky strands spring taut before slipping away. I tumble through the air and land against a hay bale.

"Ow! That hurts." He rubs the spot on his scalp. His pale cheeks flush.

Hay pokes my feathered body from across the side of the barn from Lucas. Dust and bits of fodder cloud the air. I fluff my feathers before I recognize what I'm doing but am relieved when several poking pieces are dislodged.

"I didn't realize you'd be so surly, might I add ungrateful, when hungry. Maybe I should just leave you to your distemper." He picks up the sack and moves toward the ladder that leads down from the loft.

My heart thuds. *"Don't you dare leave me like this!"* My trilling song is shrill, but not very threatening.

"If you ask nicely, I might be inclined to remedy your situation." He smiles at me from a crouched position. His teeth are a surprising white against his pearly skin.

I've used up what little energy I had on my outburst, and my heart beats so fast I fear I might faint. My body aches. My eyes can't tear. And no matter how I try, the bag doesn't move at my call.

"Sorry about that." He chews on a piece of hay. "When you're new to changing, or you're too tired, it's nearly impossible to change back until your body is capable of the shift. Though you're stronger than before, changing is new to you. I, however, have been at it for years and am capable of changing back and forth at will. It'll take you a while to build up your endurance. Now, the sooner you calm down, the sooner I can change you back. Any more noise and we may alert the farmer, and you won't get a chance to eat this delicious meal."

He unrolls a portion of freshly baked bread from a cloth. Its warm smell envelopes me before I see it. Next, he reaches down to the ladder and produces a spoon, twirling it in his fingers dramatically. Then he lifts a wooden bowl filled with a dark rich stew which he must've set on the ladder while climbing up.

Bending over the soup, he draws in a deep breath. "Ah. Ready to eat?"

My stomach twists painfully, so I bob my head in meek assent. I hop over to where he sits next to the ladder.

His finger strokes my beak where my chin should be. "Return."

Tingles spread through my veins. I close my eyes against the disorder in my brain. Heaviness expands from the center of my being, working its way to my toes and fingertips. Even my hair weighs me down, and I collapse on the floor, panting. Although dressed, without feathers covering my entire body, I feel exposed. But I am relieved to be human again.

My relief is short-lived when I remember how I came to this place. I swing my fist.

8

Lucas ducks. It's as if he knows what I'm about to do before I do it. I let out a growl of resentment.

"I understand your frustration, which is why I'll forgive you this time. You need to eat if we are to continue." Though his words are light, his expression is serious. He holds the bowl out to me again.

My stomach cramps. I pinch my lips together and grab the food but fumble with the spoon, having lost the ability to use my fingers for a few moments. Uncaring of manners, I gulp it down.

"Easy. You'll give yourself a stomachache." He covers the bowl with his hand.

I swat it away. "Don't ever change me into a bird again."

"I must remind you that we had no better alternative. I don't go around changing just anyone into animals. I've never changed anyone else before. Good thing it worked, yes?"

I stop eating. "You didn't know?" My hands clench as I tamp down the desire to swing at him again.

"Well, there was an optimistic chance since you are

susceptible to magic. Cadence used to say as much when you were little, and when I saw your hands light up and you put up a magical barrier, I figured our abilities combined would be strong enough to change you." His smile is smug. "I am surprised that your feathers are as long and beautiful as your trilling song. I fear you will not blend in with the birds here on Tenebris, however." He runs a hand through his silky black hair.

Frustration digs inside me. "Why is it that I can never go anywhere without it being a spectacle? How is it that my father shows up just as I'm lost in the woods? And where exactly are we headed?"

Dust floats in the waning sunlight and the scent of hay fills the enclosed space. I notice the area near the wide window is from newer wood as if added on to the barn years after it was built. Bales of hay line the other side of the barn where a hole in the floor is open to drop down the bales. My heart pricks with longing to find some place to settle—to call home. I pick the spoon back up to hide my thoughts.

Lucas's smile is sad. "There is much I need to explain, and I fear there are some things I don't completely understand myself. But if you have patience, I'll explain what I can. It may seem a bit far-fetched, like the fairy tales your mother once told you."

I swallow wrong and choke and sputter. "Fairy tales, indeed. Spoken by a thief magpie who turns into a ghost and then changes me into a bird with a mere touch? All we need is a dragon to be slain."

His chuckle is sardonic. "Would an evil mage do?"

Crumbs stick to my dress, and I brush them off, trying to act indifferent though my hands still shake with the distress of the past several hours. I take the flask of water sitting next to the bag and drink enough to clear my throat as I consider the events since Lucas flew into the cottage. I wipe my mouth on my sleeve.

I scowl, remembering my father. "Am I dreaming? It can't be real. Thoron doesn't even look like he's old enough to be my father. And why didn't I remember you at first?"

Noises of animals shuffling make me nervous, but Lucas doesn't seem to notice as he's deep in thought. "Thoron must be using his magic to keep from aging. Many dark mages are compelled to use their power and live forever, though I don't know one who actually has. Those beasts are people whom Thoron ritually murdered and used their life force to strengthen his dark magic."

I choke on a drink of water and sputter quite unbecomingly. "But, if they're murdered, how—" I gasp. Luckily, I've eaten all of the food, or I wouldn't be able to eat another bite. Unluckily, it churns in my gut.

Lucas nods as if sensing what I can't put into words. "From what I understand, it's a form of necromancy, forbidden magic that turns dead beings into animated ones—not alive, but able to function as if they were. They do his will, follow his orders, and can only be stopped when the mage is killed or dismembered or burned." He shivers. "But as you've noticed, it's very hard to get that close with his beasts as his constant shadow."

My eyes unfocus, remembering my father's despicable nature. I tuck the pillow to my stomach, knowing I wouldn't have believed it had I not seen it myself. "It's unfathomable. No wonder Mother never mentioned him. She'd never say anything, even when I'd try to get her to talk about him. I regret ever wanting to find him. But why have I forgotten about you?"

His face pinches in thought, and his eyes narrow to mere slits. "Tenebris is a kingdom without magic. It reacts strangely to it. It's like the atmosphere itself negates abilities or absorbs them somehow and wipes out memories linked to magic. I've experienced it firsthand. For too long, I remained in bird form, staying close to you but not knowing why. I'd watch you do your chores or travel to a different area, sometimes boarding one of the carriages to accompany you. I never left your side." His words end on a wistful note.

"What happened to make you remember?" I ask, curious.

Lucas leans back against the loft entryway, dangling a leg on the ladder. "When Thoron and the beasts entered this kingdom, I felt it. It was like bees stinging the inside of my bones, leaving me breathless at times. The next day after having dreamt of you, I awoke in my natural form, a boy, wearing this ring." He holds his hand up. The ring glimmers slightly in the sunset coming in from the wide hay door left open.

The loft looks familiar, like Lucas had before, and the memory of the first place I stayed after Mother died comes to me. I'd been banished to the barn after the farmer's wife had caught my favorite milk cow in my bedroom one morn. I'd called the poor animal to my room in my sleep. I'd been whipped for the first time there. Surely this isn't that farm. I shake the difficult memories off.

Lucas drops his hand to his lap, a wistful, almost tearful look on his face, though it's hard to tell with his narrow, slanted eyes. "It took me a couple of days to remember, but when I saw you after I changed back, it all came back to me. I recalled your smile and laughter as we played together as children." Color fills his pale cheeks, and his lips move slightly upward. He sighs. "The memories returned. I promise I'll never forget again."

I let out a deep breath. There's much I sense he isn't saying, but there's already so much to take in. "Where do we go now?

What do we do? How do we escape from Thoron and his beasts if he has magic?"

Horses whinny and stamp their hooves in a stall below, breaking the stillness around us. I view tackle and tools nailed to the walls beneath Lucas's perch by the ladder. "Cadence had always planned on returning to Anavrin. As an eldrin, your abilities don't normally manifest until you mature in your eighteenth year. She believed you both could return to the eldrin's mountain fortress where you could be taught the ancient ways and hone your abilities." His eyes shift, not meeting mine.

"If that's true, why did we leave Anavrin in the first place?"

He hesitates, and his shoulders hunch. "Eldrin are a noble people. They believe only the pure should have access to treasures such as the holy writings. Anyone of half-blood is impure, unworthy. Your grandfather, Bennett, was furious when he found out Cadence was pregnant by a dark mage. But your grandmother, Madrigal, was not like the other eldrin. She fought for the rights of the mixed races, founding villages to keep the homeless and orphans safe. She set up schools and healing centers to help those in need."

He hesitates but continues. "That's where I met your grandmother. I had been abandoned as a young child. Like you, I had to fight for food to eat and a place to sleep. I was lucky, though, because at an early age I could change into small animals—mice, mainly."

Tears sting my eyes and I reach out a hand. "I didn't know. I'm so sorry, Lucas." His hand is cool in mine. The wind picks up outside the building, whispering through cracks in the walls as moonlight replaces the sunset in the loft door.

His smile is endearing, and I can see the younger Lucas from my memories with that smile. It's so unlike how anyone looks at me that my breath catches for a moment in my chest.

He darts a look past me. "Madrigal found me on the streets, starving and beaten for having tried to steal some bread. She brought me to a small village she'd built at the foot of the mountain. For the first time, I was taught to read and write, how to shift into different animals and even people. I learned how to control my mind-reading abilities. That's where I met Cadence and you."

I pull my hand from his. "Did you say mind-reading?"

His grin is sideways as he gathers the bowl, spoon, and flask. "Yes. As I told you before, I'm part voyant. It's what allows us to mind speak when we're changed. But it's mainly a sense of emotions. It's not that I know what you're thinking exactly. It's just that your intentions are easy to read in the glimmer in your eyes."

That explains so many things. "So, when I attacked you after you changed me—"

He rubs his chin. "I knew that you'd be upset. And you were." He chuckles. "I mostly just watched your eyes and the tilt of your head. You were very intent on coming straight for me, so I ducked." His shrug is slightly dismissive.

I don't quite believe him, so I change the subject. "If the eldrin think someone like me unworthy, why would Mother want to return since I wouldn't be accepted?" My laugh is bitter. "I'm not accepted here because I look different. I have strange abilities no one understands. And the kingdom I'm from would be the same, wouldn't it? You said it yourself. I shouldn't have this ability to call things."

His pale cheeks flush again, from his neck up to the top of his high cheeks. "Maybe. I don't know. But I don't think it's safe to stay here any longer. It was too easy to get lost in my bird form, and it shouldn't have been so difficult for you to remember me. I was with you until you were in your eighth year. If we return, both of us will have a chance to get stronger." He purses his lips. "We'll find your grandmother, Madrigal, or others like us, and we can learn everything there is to know about our gifts."

I've yearned for somewhere to belong for so long, eager to search for the father I thought I remembered. How silly it was to believe Lucas to be my father. My heart plummets again with the knowledge my father is evil.

But Mother never mentioned my grandmother, either, which makes me wonder why. Would I truly be accepted, or would I be an outcast there as well due to my mixed blood and my appearance? A tear slips from one eye and I swipe it away. "And you think my grandmother, this Madrigal, will accept me, even with how I look? She won't reject me because I'm ugly." I run a hand through my hair and look away from Lucas.

He is silent for a long moment. I glance up to see him staring at me with his mouth wide open. "I've never seen anyone as beautiful as you, Tambrynn. Not in either kingdom. You are blessed and a blessing. Just because the Tenebrisians are superstitious and ignorant does not mean they're correct in how they judge you. Do you think any of them could've fought off Thoron in that cottage? They would've wet themselves and ran for the hills."

I can't help my laugh, but tears still sting my eyes. "Why was I born this way? I don't look anything like my mother and nothing like my father." I lift a strand of my hair. "How did I end up being so different?"

He leans back again. "Cadence only implied it had something to do with Thoron's magic. She never got into the details, if she knew them."

"So, I'm just some oddity." I run my fingers through my long hair, twisting it tight against my scalp.

"Only in the best possible way." He stands, picking up the bowl, spoon, and bag.

"I remember thinking you were older. But you've barely aged. How can that be? And where were you when Mother died?" I ask the last questions quickly, heat sweeping across my cheeks.

His narrow eyes widen and he sits down abruptly, disturbing a cow that moos loudly in response. "Cadence had sent me to find the clerics. She'd hoped since she was an eldrin and they often traveled to different kingdoms, she could request their help. It took longer than we anticipated for me to find their sanctuary. There was no sign of any living cleric, and then when I found their scripts stating they were starting to forget, I knew we were in trouble."

"By the time I found you, the Commonwealth had sealed your fate as an indentured servant. I tried to change you once while you slept, but I wasn't strong enough. So, I stayed with you, and it wasn't long after that when I began forgetting, staying changed as a bird longer and longer until just recently."

I study his face, his slim but muscular body. Though I remember him as being younger, it isn't much younger than he appears now. His pale face is still unlined, fresh-looking. He's only a few inches taller than I am now, and I recall barely coming up to his shoulders when I was in my eighth year. "That doesn't explain why you don't look much older than you did before."

His face turns thoughtful. "I was told that djinn don't age when they stay changed in animal forms. I'm unsure why. They don't often do so for long periods, however, because animals tend to live shorter lives. Since I've spent much of my time the last ten years as a bird, we are probably the same age right now." His crooked smile returns briefly.

I relax against the hay bale behind me. For the first time in a long time, I'm fed, I have a soft place to stay, and a friend.

Comfort unlike any I've had for too long sweeps over me. "What if we stay here, changed as birds and living our lives free as if my father doesn't exist?"

He's quiet as he considers my words. "We'd forget who we are. You'd stick out as much as a bird as you do a girl, and who knows how long we'd live? One year? Two?"

Though there's sense in what he says, my meager hopes are dashed. "You're probably right."

The floor begins to vibrate beneath us.

"What is that?" I can't help the alarm in my voice.

Lucas glances around. "Magic."

Instinctively I call out to my abilities and my hands glow slightly. I shake them. "What's happening?"

"Your powers. They've been more unstable since I first noticed Thoron's presence."

Chills race across my skin. "Does that mean he's near? Has he found us so soon?"

"You slept for a day, my lady. Plenty of time for his beasts to find us."

A day? I faintly hear the beast's howl. It's not near, but close enough. Out of fear, I *call* out, again by pure instinct. A pitchfork sails toward us from across the expanse of the barn, aimed right for Lucas. I scream out to him, but it's too late. The sharp edge of the metal winks as the light reflects off the tine before it sinks deep into the ladder's wooden frame.

Feathers explode into the air. The animals break out in cries and loud brays.

"Lucas!" I cover my face. What have I done?

9

I poke my head over the ladder and glance past the pitchfork stuck in the wooden planks to the floor. I don't see a bird or a body, but it is getting dark, and it's hard to tell. Is he lying on the floor injured where I can't see him? Guilt and shame make my hands shake. Through the dim interior, I spy several horses, a mule, and a donkey. The horses and mule settle down, but the donkey keeps braying.

Where did Lucas go? Should I go down and try to find him?

"I'm sorry. I didn't mean to. I couldn't help it." My whispered words are drowned out by shouts. I curse myself for drawing the attention of the farmer. Heart racing, I ease into a shadowy corner of the loft.

Footsteps pound into the building and a yellow glow of lamplight accompanies them. "Ho there. Settle down, now. Boys, you look by the horses, I'll check on the cows in the corral. We'll corner that wolf this time." A masculine voice barks out orders, and several footsteps scuff on the hard flooring below. Something about the voice is familiar, but I can't quite place it.

Wolf? They think I'm a wolf? A mournful howl drifts on the night air. It doesn't sound close, but I slink back into the dark corner more. Is that a real wolf or one of my father's beasts?

Sweat trickles along my brow and I hold my breath. If Lucas is injured, will he be able to get away? How will I escape without him? If it's my father, how will anyone escape his beasts? My stomach twinges as my food threatens to come back up.

Thunks and clatters assault my ears. The animals' bawling restarts. I can't blame the poor creatures. Metal clanks of shovels being grabbed gives me chills. They'd mentioned wolves, but would they threaten an intruder with such tools? I need to get out of the loft, but how, without being seen?

I utter silent prayers to the Kinsman for Lucas's safety. For our safety. For the howls to be from real wolves, not Thoron's beasts. My heart hammers hard in my chest.

"That's no wolf wot done that," a younger man hollers. The noise in the barn stills.

"Wot coulda done it?" Footsteps echo closer.

Sheer panic grips my chest. Caught again. The pitchfork's handle is like an arrow pointing straight at me.

"Hey! Over there! Get him!" More chaos breaks out, feet and hooves shuffling, loud grunting, and the thumping of falling objects. The movement sends dust into the air.

I pinch my nose to keep from sneezing. If only I could see what was happening. Yet, I am relieved the attention is drawn away from the loft.

"That way! Outta the barn. Don't lose him!"

Silence. Even the animals seem to hold their breath. I pick my way to the edge with care in case someone is left behind, waiting. A black feather is pierced with one of the tines and sticks out at an angle, indeed looking like an arrow. I gulp down the guilt, but tears sting my eyes.

A sickle lays askew on the stone floor beneath the ladder, and oats are scattered beneath a saddle lying on its side in the dirt.

If I hurry, I can find an escape. However, the pitchfork blocks a clear and easy path to the bottom. I rub my sweating palms down my woolen dress and grab for my pillow. A shadow passes over me, and I freeze in place.

Scree. The magpie lands and paces the edge of the loft before turning back into a man.

"You—you're alive!" Relief is a sweet welcome. I resist the urge to hug him.

"Yes, no thanks to you." Though his words are accusing, his tone is teasing. He rubs a a tear in the arm of his black shirt. I see a strip of red on the pale skin beneath.

It's my turn to blush at seeing his muscular arm. "Please accept my apologies." My voice cracks as my guilt returns.

"At least you sound remorseful. We cannot stay here now. I led them off on a hunt for a wolf, but they will return when they cannot find me. The only way I see of getting out of here safely is to fly."

"Oh no. No, no, no. I don't care how many animals you can become. I'm not changing back into a bird." I back away from him.

"My lady. As your Watcher, I am charged with your safety. I promise I will turn you back as quickly as it is safely possible."

Baying hounds join the men's shouts. Voices grow closer.

"Will this never end?" I frown at him.

Sadness gleams in his eyes. "Not that I've found yet. But we must hurry."

Clutching the pillow, I place my hand in his and brace for the change. My stomach whirls as I am transformed again into a bird. Jerking upward, we are once more air-bound. In a flash, I catch the wind just outside of the barn doorway and follow behind Lucas. The conversion is easier this time, if only a little, and flying not as awkward.

"Look at tha' lovely birdie. Supper's on me tonight ge'lemen." The man who speaks hurls a stone in our direction and I feel the air as the stone narrowly misses hitting my head.

It's like being back on the auction block where it was commonplace to toss rotted food or rocks at the bound servants who didn't find a placement. My blood heats up. I turn my head sideways to get a good look at the brute.

Another stone narrowly misses my right wing, and one of my silver feathers floats on the wind. I fly in a wide arc to inspect our attacker. My heart beats quicker as I recognize the face of one. Although it has been years since seeing him, the eyes are the same beady ones that plague my dreams. I knew the loft was familiar! It's Farmer Tucker's, my first employer after Mother died. I hadn't recognized it because the loft had been enlarged to hold hay. It had only previously been big enough for one person to crawl into and sleep.

Farmer Tucker's younger son is now a man, taller and broader shouldered than his father. The scar on his cheek and cowlick remains the same, though. Along with his incessant insinuations about my mother's death, he was the joker who came up with the idea to hide the cattle and then blame me. I'd been sent to the paupers block the first time because of him.

Hatred, hot and fluid, surges through my tiny veins. I turn back and, with a loud trill, dart for the man's head. His hair is thin at the front, bare on top, but long in the back. I grasp a stringy mass at his nape with my claws. Arching my long wings, I yank hard.

He screams in pain and swings at me. I fly above him and back down for another stab. I pull again. This time I succeed in yanking a chunk away.

None of the men move to help him. They roar with laughter and point at him.

Empowered by their amusement and the man's distress, I move in for another onslaught. This time it will be his ugly, condescending face. I fly upwards, turn, and tuck my wings back a bit to make a swift assault—

"Tambrynn, stop!" Lucas flies toward me, knocking me sideways and out of flight.

I teeter as my flailing wings catch me. *"He's nothing more than a vile coward. Do you know what I've suffered because of him?"*

Lucas crooks his head toward me. *"I understand your anger with this man. I recall his misbehavior at your expense. But if you continue your attack, you are no better than he."*

His words sting. Although I don't want to be held in the same regard as the farmer's son, resentment from having been mistreated for so long digs like claws in my heart. I want revenge for all of it. *"But—"*

"We need to keep going, my lady. He's not worth the time we're wasting. Did you not hear Thoron's beasts?" His voice is full of impatience as it explodes in my mind. *"This man's fate will be the best revenge. We do not go through life without bearing the fruit of consequences. He will reap his own rewards, if not now, then when he meets his Kinsman."*

Begrudgingly I follow behind him. The sun is completely gone now and I can no longer hear Farmer Tucker's dogs braying at this animal or that. From above, I recognize the old oak and small copse of trees where Mother and I would gather mushrooms and roots. Her knowledge of the plants that we used for tinctures or treacles had been our only source of income.

We travel in silence until the skeletal remains of a house come into view. The moon shines brightly upon what I remember as the front room of my childhood home. I know beyond that lies a small kitchen. A large bedroom should complete the home, only it is no longer there. Tears blur my vision as we descend.

Lucas flutters to the ground. His body unfolds as it changes back to his human form. Tears glitter in his eyes as he opens his palm to me. I drop down into it, heavy like the emotions still churning in my gut.

"You know where we are, Tambrynn? I know the bitterness you've held inside for so long. I was full of it once myself. But the only thing that comes from embracing anger is destruction. Do you want to be like your father who murdered your mother and wouldn't hesitate at taking your life to gain more power, or would you take after your mother who would never condone the revenge you so desire?"

His lips are gentle upon my head, but my soul is weighed down with his words. Tingles spread across my body as I change back, but I am barely aware of them. I drop my pillow and swipe wisps of hair away from my face as I step toward the door frame.

A memory of Mother pops into my mind and I see her as vividly as if she were truly standing in front of me. Her dark hair and shining brown eyes. The heart-shaped face that was quick to smile. I know Lucas is right. She would've scolded me for my actions. I turn from thoughts of her to inspect the house. My home once. Too long ago.

The charred wood is rough beneath my hand. I can almost feel the heat as I picture what happened here. A cry wedges in my chest, sharp as a knife and hot as a poker.

I step away from the door to the shattered front window. Its blackened glass teeth open in a wide scowl. Snarling at me. Trying to devour me.

My body quivers. "Who would do this?"

Lucas moves toward me. "It was the hottest day of

summer. You were awaiting hire in Havershire when I felt it, the biting inside my bones. I searched, led by my voyant ability, and found them here, the beasts. They used torches, uncaring that there was a family who had moved in after—"

"After they'd killed my mother," I finish his sentence. Pain crushes my heart. I recall that summer. It had brought a drought, and after many moved away to find food and jobs, I'd been lucky enough to have constant hire for quite some time. Until an incident with a handsy stable boy left the boy with a cracked skull and me back on the block once again.

"After the beasts, yes." Leaves and glass crunch under Lucas's feet as he moves beside me. "I wasn't going to bring you here, but you must know the danger you're in. Many are coming. I sense them, Tenebris senses them. When you, Cadence, and I first came here, there were strange storms, almost as if this kingdom were rejecting us. I didn't recognize the connection until the beasts came after you and your mother. If only I'd known storms are a sign that Thoron and his beasts entered Tenebris."

He pauses. "That storm two eves ago wasn't normal. I fear the strength of that storm and what it might mean about Thoron. How powerful he's become."

I can't think about that for now as I step closer to the cottage I'd shared with Mother. My shoes leave indentations in a layer of ashen dirt on the ground as I walk. I breathe deep and can almost smell the smoke. I long to touch the walls, to bring the cottage back from my memories, but I can't. "It has been a lifetime since I last walked across this threshold."

"I know, my lady. Almost ten years." The moon shines bright on his pale skin, making him look more like a ghost than before.

My feet are weighed down as though walking through water, and my steps falter. "It feels like a hundred."

"Yes."

Only crumbling rock and long-cold cinder remain beside the stone walls and fireplace. I was happy here before the beasts came and destroyed my life. I clutch my hands into fists on my lap.

A mixture of emotions flows through me. It is almost too painful to bear. Memories of Mother. Dreams of finding my father and having a real family. Images of me playing with Lucas. I stand and step toward him. My breath hitches in my chest. "I remember you." I recall Lucas's face, his laugh. My insides dance as I recall my girlish infatuation with him. He'd been kind, as he is now.

Warmth flows over me as I remember I was safe and loved, but sadness quickly follows. "Is there another reason you brought me here?"

Lucas walks over to the doorway and stares across to the crumbling stone fireplace, still intact, but scarred from a fire too big for it to hold. "Once I was like you. I wanted to strike out at anyone who'd hurt me. I began to treat others as brutally as I'd been treated." He stops and I turn to see him studying the dark sky. "Your grandmother Madrigal changed all of that. She understood when I acted out. She never made me feel like a half-breed. And I changed."

His footsteps toward me puff up ash and dirt. "When Cadence asked me to come with you, at first I did it because I wanted to repay her and Madrigal. And I thought it would be a great adventure." His laugh is low. "They both thought you'd be safer here, away from Thoron. Untrackable. We three would come here, live for a few years and go back after Thoron forgot about you. But he didn't. He came back for you. And I wasn't there to stop it."

I put my hand on his arm. "How could you know?"

Tears glisten in his dark eyes as he shrugs. "We're not safe here. I figured it out too late. Your gifts, my gifts, are stunted in this bleak kingdom. You'll never become strong enough to defend yourself here. You'll have a chance to learn and grow if we return to Anavrin."

"*This* is my home." My voice cracks, and I sink to my knees in the dying grass where I once played.

"Part of why I brought you here is for you to say a proper goodbye. This was only meant to be your home for a short time. Tambrynn, you have to believe me when I say this. You were born unique in looks and ability. You know how hard it is to hide what's different about you. Especially here."

"Why now?" I wipe my damp eyes with my sleeve.

"You're maturing into your eldrin abilities. Each day you get stronger, which is why I was finally able to change you when I did. Thoron knows how old you are, and that could be why he's come here. Or he could be planning something more evil, I don't know. Even though you're only half eldrin, you're stronger than any half-blood I've known. I fear his true motivations." The warmth of his body reaches out to me, our shadows stretching and blending into the rubble of where I'd danced barefoot with Mother.

"All mages are drawn to power in a most ruthless way, which is why it's forbidden magic. And murder, the kind your father has done, perverts the soul. Killing is the least he'll do. He may not give up until he's stolen your soul or worse."

"Worse?" A cold shiver runs down my spine. I stand to get off the chilled ground and dust the dirt and dead grass from my dress. Although I don't want to believe it, I have vague memories that don't make sense. Fear and running and crying. Visions explode in my mind, and I sift through them like pieces of a dream you can't remember the next morn. "I remember Thoron had ahold of me. He was hurting me, and I did something."

"I can't believe you remember that. Thoron found where Cadence had hidden you in my village. Madrigal saw through his disguise. I believe you did as well. You ran from him when he approached you. But you were only three. He caught you easily and he—" Lucas stops and clears his throat. "He tried to steal your abilities."

My eyes widen as I stare into Lucas's glistening, narrow depths. His lips are twisted and he looks paler than before. "What stopped him?"

"You did." His voice is deeper, his words full of meaning.

"I did? How?"

He steps closer to me. "Nobody knows. Before anyone could act, there was a blinding blue light. The next thing we knew, Thoron was thrown back away from you. His beasts were gone. The stronger villagers attacked him. I picked you up and ran to Cadence. That's when Madrigal stole the rings. She and Cadence hastily made plans to travel to Tenebris. But you were lethargic, so they needed someone to go with them. I volunteered."

Tears drop onto my cheeks, but my arms are like dead weight, so I don't swipe them away. I remember some of what he said, but then nothing about when we left Anavrin. Lucas's inky hair gleams, and this close to him I can smell the scent of wind and fresh grass, of my childhood friend and memories of the freedom I had once, and it lessens the painful knot in my stomach.

Part of me wishes to curl up into his arms like a scared little girl. Part of me wants to push him away because I believe what he tells me, and it's terrifying. I haven't trusted anyone in so long. But my gut tells me I can with Lucas.

I glance away, unwilling to have him witness emotions I can't even begin to name. Part of my mind, the side that's constantly on alert, warns that I will end up getting hurt. My heart knows he would never injure me. I'm reluctant to pick which is right. Conflicted, I change the subject. "How do we know the beasts will not find us here?"

"We don't." He grabs the pillow, fallen to the ground when we transformed, and hands it to me.

"And what of the farmer and his dogs?" I'm comforted by the familiar soft, quilted material.

"They aren't far away." His hand lingers upon my back sending tingles up and down my spine.

I grit my teeth. "We have to change again, don't we?"

"I see no other choice, my lady." With a deliberate movement, he holds out his hand.

I clasp it, close my eyes, and wait once again to take flight.

10

"You're an old hand at this now, Tambrynn." Lucas's unspoken words are as clear to me as the dark forest below us.

My wings wobble. *"I don't feel like an 'old hand.' It's getting harder to see. Can we stop and rest?"*

"It's the blackest part of night and, unfortunately, we are not owls who see quite well in the dark. However, I can see enough for us to keep going for now. We can rest later."

I arch to catch more wind, and my wings burn from the effort. It's been hours since we left my childhood home and though I have been used to grueling work, flying is different than scrubbing. *Am I to forever be told what to do and how long to do it? When will I be free?* I can't help the bitterness that invades my thoughts. Even though not spoken, I know he can sense my emotions.

"Freedom comes in many forms. Sometimes 'mid difficult circumstances, it is simply a choice one makes."

"How can you choose when you aren't free to do so?" Beyond the forest we've been following is a pasture, its hillside dotted

with sheep. A small shelter pokes out of a rocky ledge. Beneath the stretched canvas lies a sleeping shepherd boy. I can't help but think he's freer than anyone at the moment.

"Are you not free? I'm not forcing you to follow me. I am hoping you will choose to, but I wouldn't make you." I can almost hear a chuckle in his thoughts. *"Your grandmother told me once that bitterness holds no elegance. I now know what she meant."*

I pull back, falling behind Lucas as he flies. *"Are you saying I'm bitter?"*

"I'm saying you have a choice. Stay here and face Thoron and his beasts or hasten to the Zoe Tree and get to Anavrin before he can find us. Which do you choose, Tambrynn?" His words come out clipped.

I don't want to acknowledge the truth in what he said. *"Can we not rest? Possibly find some water? I'm parched."*

"No rest yet, my lady. I know you're unused to flying and that you're tired. However, the cold which chases after us assures me danger is not far behind. We need to keep going."

The clouds have blocked the moon's light for some time. Bright stars glitter in the dark sky. If Lucas is right about the storm, wouldn't we feel it? Wouldn't the animals around us sense it, or have they forgotten things as well? Yet as I look around, the animals rest quietly. Even an owl idly blinks large yellow eyes at us, showing no concern about dangers as we fly past.

Soon I can't keep up with Lucas, and I fall behind.

The first swish of the air next to me doesn't register as anything more than wind. The next does, but belatedly so. An arrow pierces my wing, throwing me out of flight. Instant pain rocks my right shoulder and neck. I chitter in agony as warm blood oozes down my feathers. My right wing seizes, so I try to use the other to keep afloat. I spin in circles, one wing dangling and the other flapping, before falling to the forest. Dead fingers of brambles and bushes slice at my body from every angle.

I crash through a deep mound of prickling bushes. They bite deep into my flesh as I move, stinging, stinging. I scream as limbs scratch at my body and I drop downward, my feathers stripped as I fall. I tumble farther, farther, until at last, I drop, panting on the damp, cold ground.

A form flutters above me and I panic. But it's Lucas, and my heart lifts. He flies past where I am, chirping a mournful tune and calling my name.

Horse's hooves thunder the ground beneath me. My legs are unsteady as I move, heading toward the shafts of light that fall beyond the brambles toward where Lucas flew. I try to call out, but I can't. Fatigue and pain sap my energy, and I collapse into utter darkness.

11

The moon sparkles across the deep blackness of the sky above me when I open my eyes. The forest is an uneven bed of undergrowth, its sodden, earthy scent the only comfort to my aching body. Shivers wrack me as the wind skitters autumn leaves around my feathered form. Is it the storm nipping at me?

"Tambrynn?" A whisper of my name floats upon the night breeze. I turn but cannot find the source.

Maybe I am dead and my soul awaits transport. Will I soar up to the great heavens above, illuminated by its starry splendor as the stories Mother regaled? She always made heaven sound so wondrous. Will the moon allow me to dance with the stars while they sing?

Imploring words beckon to me over and over. *"I am coming, my lady. Do not leave me, not for the moon, or the stars, or the heavens above. I won't give you up to the moon or the Kinsman. I am coming."*

The clamor of hooves grows closer. Pain explodes behind

my eyes with every shock of vibration. My mind becomes muddled. There is only cold and pain.

And I am so tired.

"Call to me, my lady. Please. Don't leave me." Grief and yearning pull at me, tugging me into consciousness.

I know this voice.

My tongue is swollen in my mouth. My *trill* garbles incomprehensibly. I push away the panic, which presses upon my chest, suffocating me, and force myself to take deep, even breaths. I have to focus, but on what?

I sing Mother's poem:

"I went for a walk one crescent moon night,
and saw the stars twirling in a bright, shining light.
The sky was filled with a strange, twinkling song,
so, I begged for the moon to bring me along.
I wanted to frolic, I wanted to play,
I wanted to dance and forever stay,
with the moon, and the stars, and the heavens above,
where the only things near me were shining with love."

"Tambrynn?" His word whispers his relief.

"Lucas," I murmur. He's found me as I knew he would. I close my eyes, giving in to the fatigue and pain.

My body is grasped tight, and I'm lifted high into the air. I am unable to see what has hold of me and my heart beats quicker, so fast I fear it will explode from my chest. Then a saddlebag attached to a dark horse looms ahead. I am tossed into a pouch. The space around me closes in, and other objects poke and press me on all sides.

My breath catches, and I panic. There's no room to stand. *"Lucas? Where are you, Lucas?"* My voice is sharp with high lilting notes edging on panic.

"My lady. I am here. But I cannot save you now. You must have patience. I will follow you and rescue you when I can."

No longer a sweet whisper, his voice is as clear as if he is standing next to me. My heartbeat steadies. I am not alone. Lucas is here. The bag jostles when the horse moves into a gallop. I'm jostled to and fro, and the pain from the wound between my neck and shoulder throbs.

"Please, help me." Desperation makes my chirp garbled.

The ride goes on and on. I feel as if I've been put on a threshing floor and beaten to a pulp. I am beginning to lose hope when, at last, the horse's motion slows then stills completely.

My abductor starts to hum. I struggle to breathe, my beak open and panting. The whole of my body trembles from the jarring ride. The wild thudding of my heart makes me dizzy. My head grows heavy and darkness overtakes me.

Scents of butter and bacon assault my nose before the sizzle fully wakens me.

Food. My empty stomach twists, gurgling. Have I fallen asleep in the scullery? Cook will surely have my head on a platter for it.

I jerk to attention. A wave of faintness makes me lose my balance. I wobble to my feet and glance down at the strange appendages. Confused, I scan the room, tilting my head sideways to get a good look. This is not a scullery. It's a small, cluttered space not much bigger than the Broodmoor's pantry. And it isn't a woman cutting up the vegetables. It's a man, and he looks far too delighted with chopping things to pieces. I gape at him through bars.

Bars?

My movement catches his leering attention, and he turns toward me. A tongue darts between two hairy lips and he rubs his hands together as if warming them. In the center of his forehead is what appears to be a third eye. Unlike a regular eye, it wavers like an illusion or a reflection in rippling water—

there but not there both at once. The eye darts to and fro and then stops as it gazes upon me.

Horrified at the sight of the extra eye, I jerk away, not wanting to get close to him. My exhausted body protests and I only manage to squirm an inch or two. I am powerless to do anything but watch the odd man.

"Ah, my little injured songbird. Good, good. You are awake."

A bush of a graying beard moves as he speaks. He claps his greasy hands and hums while swaying back and forth.

His deep voice rings with a strange accent I've never heard before. Following the path of the bars, I see they are a part of a birdcage.

A birdcage!

It all returns to me in a rush. Disbelief washes away as fury replaces it. I scream my dismay.

"Yes, yes. You are perfectly safe now. All is well. Rest, rest."

Agile for a large man, he dances and hums as he works. The air fills with the odor of roasting meat.

Meat? What kind of meat? Am I to be next? I stand, leaning against the cage on my uninjured side, and totter around looking for a door or a hole. There's a door, but when I push against it, it's locked. This truly is a prison, solid and inescapable. Pain radiates from my right shoulder, and I stop to rest.

"No, no, little songbird. Do not fret. I will not harm you. You're much more valuable than this lark." Beady eyes peer through the bars, and I notice the feathers now. I'd cleaned a dozen just a few days ago for Cook, but being a bird now gives the idea of 'cleaning' one a horrific meaning. The man laughs as if he senses my discomfort, and his breath is sour and hot. I limp to the far side of the cage, away from him.

Where is Lucas? Didn't he promise to find me? My

heartbeat quickens in my chest. I call out, but nothing happens. The gruesome man aims a ghastly smile at me and the wavering third eye blinks. With a fling of his sausage hands, he covers the cage with a cloth and everything becomes dark.

"Lucas, where are you? I'm stuck in a cage! Get me out of here!" My screams are melodious, frustrating me even more. It doesn't take long before I collapse into a heap. No sweat dots my brow. I am parched from panting and am unable to cry. Once again, I'm not in charge of my own life, and the thought burns deep in my soul.

Knocking filters past the fabric draped over my prison. A person enters the kitchen. "Ah, yes, yes. Good lad. Good lad. Come in. We must celebrate. My little songbird has awakened and is in very high spirits. Come, you will see."

Light jars my eyes as the material is yanked from the cage. I glance hopelessly up at the visitor. A man stands beside the disgusting cook. And just like his extra eye, the vision of Farmer Tucker's son—the scar, the cowlick, the stringy balding hair—wavers atop the actual person.

Did I hit my head? Am I seeing double? That can't be? It's two different people. I tip my head side to side, and the person beneath becomes apparent.

Lucas!

12

"Wot a be'u'iful bird." A sparkle of teasing plays in Lucas's gaze beneath his disguise and his lips curve in a sideways grin as he stares at me through the birdcage. The smile, though handsome on Lucas, becomes leering when placed atop the farmer's son's illusion. I blink, but the bizarre image remains.

Lucas pokes a finger through the bars and wiggles it, enticing me.

Indignant, I attack, but miss. I curse the fact Lucas is a voyant and able to anticipate my every move. Though I trust him, seeing him disguised as another is disturbing. Not to mention the double image makes me woozy until I focus on one and not both.

I scream and it comes out as a lilting, chittering birdcall. *"Get me out of here."*

"Isn't it lovely?" The cook beams at Lucas. "I knew my songbird was rare the moment I saw her silver feathers gleaming in the moonlight."

"Yes, indeed. I ain't never seen anything like her before."

Lucas sports a cocky demeanor as he sits down at the table and starts talking to the revolting man. They fill their plates and begin to eat.

Eat! Why is he not saving me?

"I have a strange feeling I'll get a good price for her." The cook talks while eating, and food flies from his mouth. It's as repugnant to watch as it is to hear. I'm to be sold again?

I fume in the cage, glaring, willing them to feel my anger, but to no avail. Neither pays any attention to the furious way I plump my feathers. I give up when the barbs of pain from my wounded shoulder are too much, and my annoyance rises.

I glance at the lark, now sizzling and golden, fresh from the pan. It could have been my bacon-roasted carcass on the plate. The thought is enough to keep my beak shut.

"Well, well, my boy—"

"Call me Richard." Lucas takes a swig from a mug and swipes his arm across his mouth.

"Sure, sure, Richard. It was most neighborly of you to offer your help." Grease glistens down the length of the man's beard. Besides his manners, his worn clothing informs me he is not a nobleman. "I'm unable to chop wood due to an injury. And one can't survive without wood, now, can one?" He waves his sausage fingers in the air.

Lucas shakes his head. "It's all in a day's work."

"I can't pay you much, but you'll find I am a most proficient cook." The burly man lifts his shirt a tad and scratches at the massive belly underneath. There are red stretch marks across its pale expanse and a twisted, bulging belly button with tufts of hair sticking out of a dimple in the center. I turn, sure I would've retched if not in bird form.

Lucas grins widely, as if he knows my thoughts, yet he does not look my way. "Very kind, Mr. Fetmann. I ain't never had a meal such as this'un. Been on me own now for years since me father passed on. Mum couldn't care for us all an' so I took off ta make me own way. So, I'm glad to oblige for the right price."

If Mr. Fetmann is an accomplished cook, Lucas is an accomplished liar. With each passing moment, I wonder at the ease with which he takes on this other personality. Words in a different voice and dialect roll off his tongue effortlessly. Doubt creeps into my mind, and I turn away from Lucas and focus on the man beside him. They continue eating as if nothing at all is amiss.

"I wish I could keep you on." Mr. Fetmann picks at his teeth with the tip of his knife when they've both finished. "Poor, poor. That's my lot in life." He winks at Lucas. "You're welcome to spend the night after you've chopped the wood, and take your leave at first light." With great effort, the cook heaves his rotund body up from the chair to stand.

I glance over at Lucas, hopeful that he will now find a way to free me.

"Thank-ee." Lucas looks at me and then turns with an innocent grin to his host. "You said yer songbird sang be'u'iful last eve. She ain't done nothin' since I come in and she looks ta be injured. Wot say you sell 'er to me for half a bronze token and I'll 'av me own meal fer the road tomorrow?"

"Tempting, tempting." The third eye on his forehead opens wide and the cook glances off blankly for a moment, then blinks. The dazed look is gone. "I cannot. I have something much more important in mind. There's no amount that would satisfy me."

"Wha' about two gold tokens? Tha's more'n fair considerin'. And I promise not to put her in a stew."

I remember my words to Lucas in the cottage about cooking him in a stew. Maybe I shouldn't have teased him so rashly. I'm sure he's only mocking. Isn't he?

Lucas glances toward me, and his true dark eyes sparkle with humor.

The cad!

Mr. Fetmann's eyes light up, but he keeps a solemn face. The third eye stares directly at Lucas. "She's quite a beauty, she is."

"An honorable man such as yerself ought ta have new trousers. Those've got a hole in 'em larger'n my fist. Ye could do that with a coupla crowns in yer pocket." Lucas narrows his eyes at the man, studying his reaction. "Four gold crowns. Final offer."

I turn to glance from Lucas to the man, catching a look at the hole Lucas spoke about. Once I see it, I can't unsee it. A rip splits the center of the back of his breeches forward to the front. My cheeks heat and my skin bristles beneath my feathers in shock.

Mr. Fetmann's eyes take on the blank stare as the third eye opens wide and bulges out, almost as if it wishes to burst out of the man's head. After a moment of hesitation, Mr. Fetmann grimaces and the third eye shrinks back. "Yes, well, well. I cannot."

Lucas shrugs. "I see I ain't persuadin' ya none. How 'bout a nightcap to end this long day?"

He didn't give up trying to save me, did he? He couldn't. But they open the front door, leaving it ajar, and leave me alone in the foul kitchen.

In sadness, I let out a trilling song full of sorrow. After the grief passes and no one returns, I glance around the cage. I need to find a way out while Lucas has the grisly man distracted.

I attempt to push my small body through the bars to no avail. They tower over my small frame so I flutter up with one good wing, but the top of the cage is secure, and even if it weren't, I'm not strong enough to make it move enough to escape. I only manage to rattle my jail, causing some of the clutter to fall from the table I'm on to the dirty, wooden floor. The keyhole of the square lock teases me with its gaping mouth as if it laughs at my fruitless antics.

Below my enclosure, though, I spy a key. It looks small enough to fit the lock, but it, too, seems to mock me.

I'd panic, but what little strength I had is sapped. I wish I had something to eat, some water at least. I crumple to the floor of the birdcage and wait. I may as well be in shackles. At least there I'd get a ladle of water twice a day.

The day's shadows lengthen. The door to the house stands open, and several birds fly in to peck at the crumbs on the table and floor. I chitter, trying to communicate to them, envious of their freedom and bounty, but they only spare a sidelong glance my way before continuing their task. As with the maids in the Broodmoor kitchen, there is no one to come to my aid.

Not even Lucas comes as the day grows long.

I want to stomp and throw things. It frustrates me more because I can't. Soon, even the birds desert the kitchen, and I am left alone in the shifting shadows of the eve.

The key. If only I could get the key! I could fly away forever. Except I need Lucas to change me back. What happens if he never returns and I remain a bird forever?

Curse my luck.

Noises filter in through the opened door. Mr. Fetmann's voice slurs in an unrecognizable shout, and then silence.

The moonlight casts a bluish hue around the kitchen when they finally return. Lucas has Mr. Fetmann's arm draped over his shoulders and is helping him into the house. It's quite a task since he's easily four times the size of Lucas. The man's head is hanging, and spittle dangles from his slack mouth.

Lucas leads him stumbling into the other room. A thump is followed closely by a groan.

Lucas returns to the room as his dark-haired self. Immediately I notice a fresh welt on his cheek. "Ah, my lady. It's hard to get a man that size drunk, but finally, he is asleep thanks to some mushroom dust I slipped into his pipe. Have you been very angry?" His gaze stops on the key on the floor. He bends over, picks it up, and holds it up to show me.

I refuse to answer him. However, I can't keep from eyeing the key in his hand.

"Surely you're hungry?" He picks up a chunk of bread and sits it by the bars on the opposite side of the cage. I have never begged for food, not even on my worst day. I wouldn't start now. Unmoved, I glare at him.

"You don't like being locked up. It's better than the alternative, I may say. I believed you were dead when you dropped out of the sky so quickly." Lucas places a hand on his chest. "I apologize for not keeping you safe. It is my duty, and I failed. I was so close to retrieving you." His eyes shine with unshed tears, disturbing me with their intensity.

He walks over to the cage, the key in his hand. "But Fetmann appeared and it got ... complicated. I sensed some kind of magic on him. When he kept hesitating and the last bit where he attacked me, I knew something was afoot." He rubs the bruise on his face. "It's likely he's been spelled by Thoron to keep an eye out for you."

"I saw a third eye on his forehead. Just like I saw Farmer Tucker's son and you at the same time. Was that some sort of disguise?" I hobble toward Lucas and the lock.

Lucas drops the key as he tries to unlock the cage. "You saw through my disguise? That's incredible, your ability is growing. However, our situation is worse than I thought if you *saw* a third eye on Fetmann. He's obviously been hexed. Whatever Fetmann witnesses, Thoron sees."

His hands shake as he picks it back up. "It's a good thing I decided to disguise myself or I might've completely given us away if you haven't already." The metal scratches into the keyhole before it clicks. He swings the door open.

My heart beats quicker. Worse than he thought? How much worse?

"I'm sorry you had to stay in that cage while I worked out a way to free you. It took much longer than I imagined it would. But it all makes sense now. A seeing spell would allow the person to stay awake for long periods until the body collapses from exhaustion. Fetmann was still quite agile, so he can't have been hexed too long ago. We'll need to hurry." He reaches in, carefully lifts me out, and places me on the floor.

He caresses the wound on my neck, sending shivers across my body. "Return."

I am caught in the familiar whir and changed again. I drop to the floor, and the weight of my human body settles over me like a heavy blacksmith's anvil. It takes me a moment as I struggle to adjust to the heaviness and fill my lungs with air. My neck burns from the wound. I touch it and find it has scabbed over already.

Anger still burns in my gut for having been caged and the whole bargaining business. I never wanted to be sold again. The plates and the silverware rattle on the table. I clench my hands tight to maintain control. Grease on the platter ripples and then stills.

"Very well done, my lady." Lucas bursts out.

I glance back at the room Lucas took Fetmann, fearful he'll wake up.

"He's out good and sound. Between the whiskey and the mushrooms, it should override the hex for a while."

I let out a deep breath. "Good."

Lucas runs a hand through his slick hair. "Let me check the wound, then you need to eat to keep up your strength." He points at the cold remains on the table. Fat is gelled around the bird's carcass, and the pickled cabbage, which I've never liked, curdles the air with its pungent stench.

My stomach roils as I think about the lark. "I don't think I shall ever eat meat again."

I twist my head as he pokes at the wound located right at the bend of my neck and shoulder. "Ow. That hurts."

"My apologies, but I had to make sure it wasn't worse than it is. Flesh wound only. You should still be able to fly, though it might be sore for a few days." He cuts off a slice of bread, slathers it with butter, and pours me a tankard of water.

I eat quickly, guzzling down the cool water, but it does little to fill the ache in my stomach. I turn away from him and rub my injured arm, willing the pain away. I glance over at the cage and frown. How many times have I been locked up in one form or another? Now my father is coming after me with spells and hexes that I can't even begin to understand. Now that the excitement has died down a bit, the last day or so crashes down on me, and my chest tightens.

"I can't do this, Lucas."

13

Lucas's surprise twists into a frown. "I do understand your frustration, Tambrynn, truly I do. But now is not the time to throw a tantrum or jest."

"I'm serious." Hot tears sting my eyes. "I can't walk around without being noticed. I can't fly without being shot out of the sky. What am I to do? You said it yourself, I'm too distinct." I yank a handful of silver hair and shake it at him. "But couldn't you just disguise us like you just disguised yourself with that sickening man?"

"I'm not strong enough to keep us hidden for very long, and even if I could, I fear we would forget who we were. And then we'd be more vulnerable than ever. There'd be no chance at fighting off Thoron or getting to the Zoe Tree and passage to Anavrin."

I glance at the wired cage from which I just escaped. How innocent it looks now that I am more than a few inches in height. How many people has Thoron hexed? Could he curse everyone here on Tenebris?

Hysteria bubbles in my chest, but I've no strength left to stave it off. "If you could've seen that eye, Lucas." I take a deep breath. "I may have some abilities, but they're nothing compared to Thoron's magic. When we faced off in the cottage, I just got lucky." The wind whistles by the open doorway, swirling dead leaves around to settle at our feet.

Bread crumbs dance on the table and I brush them off with a shaky hand. "I almost wish I were back in the scullery. At least then I knew what to expect. But this? It's too much."

My heaving breath comes out in wisps as the air whips around us, reminding me of the night in the manor before he flew into my life. Back into my life, I remind myself. Is it suddenly growing colder?

"Do you see what you're doing? You're controlling your ability to call. You're doing it. Don't let your frustrations get the better of you."

"How can I not?" Tears prick my eyes, and I will them away.

"It wasn't a fluke that you were able to hold your father off in that cabin. Only strong mages can hold off other powerful mages. And you did that without any training. Can you imagine how extraordinary you'll be when you have some proper training?"

Doubt bites at my gut. I want to believe him. "I don't know."

"Think of Nellie. You protected her against that vicious maid. She wouldn't stand a chance against Thoron. We need to leave this magic-forsaken kingdom to protect her and others like her."

I see Nellie's face in my mind. Poor, sweet Nellie. She, like me, had no control over her life. Cook, Adelia, and Farmer Tucker's sons, I can justify allowing some suffering. But not

Nellie. A responsibility I don't want rests on my shoulders. I shrug, but the invisible weight stays.

"Why do you have to be so ... right? It's annoying."

It's his turn to shrug. His eyes glow with a softness I'm unsure I can put a name to. "We have to be brave, Tambrynn."

I sniff and swipe a sleeve across my face to clear my tear-blurred sight. A wisp of a memory trails across my mind of another time he told me to be brave.

Lucas leans in close. Warm breath tickles my skin as he whispers. "Your life has suddenly changed, and not for the better. It's understandable to want to pull back and hide. I can tell you from experience that hiding doesn't make the problem go away. We'll get to the passage and return to Anavrin where you're free to use magic without the whole kingdom working against you. Your mother would want this for you."

My stomach twists painfully at his words. Mother, who had fought so valiantly against the beasts. She wouldn't want me to give up. Hot tears fill my eyes, and once they fall, I can't stop them.

His arms wrap around me, enveloping me in his warmth and scent. Sunshine, wind, and home. My tears soak into his dark shirt as he holds me tight, caressing the skin beside the wound and the sting turns to shivers. A different kind of longing blossoms in my stomach, surprising me. I've never been particularly attracted to anyone, but in this moment, I am to him.

It's not just because he's safe, though he is. His embrace is more comfort than I have known in years. I'd adored him as a child, and he had adored me. But this is so much more. Not even the beasts scare me as much as this intimacy does.

"I wish I could give you peace. I'm not that powerful." Regret dims his voice. "Hunters don't just aim at birds in the dark. It wasn't a coincidence. Fetmann didn't just hear you singing, he sensed you thanks to Thoron's spell. I'm afraid our running won't end until we are strong enough to stop Thoron." Lucas pulls back. "Can you trust me to get you that far?"

I twist my head to look up into his handsome face. "I'll try."

His dark eyes rest upon my lips. "May I kiss you?"

Stunned, I give a brief nod. Emotions swirl inside my stomach.

His mouth is soft against mine, the kiss sweet as honey. The wind, cold before, ignites around us.

Hot pinpricks of excitement and fear zing from my lips, making a passage through my body. My arms stretch around his neck, wanting to pull him closer. My toes curl inside my shoes. His heart beats against my body, speeding my pulse.

A groan sounds from the man in the other room, breaking the moment. Flames of embarrassment consume me. I have never been kissed before. I understand now what all the fuss is about. My thoughts scatter and refuse to cooperate. I sway into Lucas.

He steps away, holding me at arm's length until I'm steady on my feet. However, he does not release me fully. A contrite grin spreads across his reddened face. "My apologies." He croaks out the words before clearing his throat. "We probably need to leave."

My hands shake as I smooth down my wool dress, hoping my emotions aren't showing. Though I've witnessed trysts between maids and farmhands or lords, I've never had any experience myself. The pans and plates on the table shake as my emotions spiral out of control. For safety, I rush outside, hoping the cold air will cool the heated blood pumping furiously through my veins.

Lucas calls after me, and I hear the door slam shut.

"You said we need to hasten." My words mist on the cool night's air. Frost slicks the grass where I step, crunching under my feet. I walk hurriedly as if my attraction to Lucas has sprouted hands that will suddenly grasp hold and choke me. I slip and fall to my knees.

"Tambrynn, are you all right?" Lucas's voice cracks with concern as he slides to a stop on the ground beside me.

Too close. I can't think clearly when he's this close. I hold a hand up to keep the distance between us. "I'm fine. I just needed some air." I struggle to catch my breath. It doesn't take long for my overheated emotions to calm.

Trees line the hills. Their towering forms cast shadows all around the darkened area. I shiver against the cold, against my own mixed emotions.

"You are clearly not fine. Please talk to me. Tell me what you're feeling."

"I can't even begin to explain how I feel in this moment." How have I become such a coward? I've faced the whips of farmers, the beatings of mistresses, and the hostility of many. Yet, I can't handle one small kiss.

His stare penetrates me, peeling away my secrets as if they were petals on an unfurled flower, making me vulnerable. "I was too forward. You're not ready for this yet."

Trepidation pricks my stomach. "I cannot—I know not—what to say. This is all confusing. I—I've never kissed anyone before."

"I know you're confused. I shouldn't have—I should've waited." Moonlight plays on the dark locks feathering across his forehead. He takes my hand and places it over his heart. His shirt is as silky as it looks. "Before I lost my memory, I adored you. I would've died to keep you from harm, but I was gone when your mother was murdered. I was gone when you were taken. And then this world had stolen enough of my abilities that I couldn't save you. It was too painful, and I tried not to feel anything until my memories of you were just gone."

Pain makes his voice rasp, and I reach out to touch his cheek but stop before I make contact. He grasps my hand, and with tears glistening in his eyes, places it against his cold cheek. Sparks fly up my arm, catapulting straight to my soul. He tips my chin upward, forcing me to look at him. His narrow eyes glow though it's dark, and I glance at his lips still reddened from our kiss.

"I realize by all accounts I'm older than you. It's only because I've remained changed for so long that I haven't physically aged. I was twelve when you called to me as a three-year-old." He smiles at my questioning look. "You were in the camp where I was staying, and you called out to me. Maybe because I'm voyant? But Cadence swore it was the Kinsman making me your Watcher, your protector. So, when she left Anavrin with you, I came along to help."

He shakes his head. "I don't recall much when I was lost as a bird. There's only flashes, and only when I was near you. And since I've reawakened to who I truly am, I can't help but be drawn to you. You're generous even when others are cruel. You help and don't condemn."

I dip my head. "Except when it comes to Farmer Tucker's son."

"Even then, you listened to me." He hesitates. "I shouldn't have kissed you so soon, regardless of any feelings I may have toward you. I promise to wait until you're ready. I'll keep my vow of protection over you and nothing more if that's all you desire. If I must, I will care for you from afar as I have been doing all along."

He stands and gathers my shaking hands to help me rise beside him. "This way to your pillow, my lady."

The almost full moon lights a glittering path between the groves of trees, casting a silver glow in front of us. I can hear a faint, high-pitched howl in the distance. My heart stops briefly, and I pray it is just the wind or my imagination.

But I know it is not.

14

Hours later, after I refused to turn back into a bird, I'm exhausted again. "I never knew walking and traveling across uneven countryside could be so tiresome." My voice comes out breathy, like I've been laboring hard. I have a stitch in my side though the path we've chosen is bearable because Lucas scouted it by air first.

"We have been traveling for hours now, and I'm tired, too." He glances around. "Sometimes it feels like this kingdom sucks everything out of me. Though I do recall most people grow tired when they come close to their eighteenth birthdate and they mature into their abilities. Maybe we should take a break."

I lead us to a fallen log and sit down. "Did you?" I ask.

Lucas sits next to me. "As mixed-bloods, we tend to come into our abilities at earlier dates than most full-bloods. It's the reason we're so strong and unpredictable. We scare the eldrin because there's no way to measure our power. They can't control us."

He shrugs. "I was so young when I started changing forms.

And djinn's magic tends to be erratic. I'd get upset and change to a snake because it was something I knew scared my mother. Once I sent an illusion and had my father convinced he was blind. It's probably why my parents deserted me."

I stare at his shadowed profile. "That's awful. I'm so sorry." Though I'd always felt mother's absence acutely, I couldn't imagine being abandoned by her no matter what I'd done.

He grins but shakes his head. "Djinn, as with any mixed-bloods, aren't readily accepted in favorable circles on Anavrin. The Eldrin Council made sure of it. But I was accepted into your grandmother's village where things were better. Not everyone believes we're expendable or worthless. I learned to control my emotions. I owe her my life."

Clouds move across the moon, sending dappled shadows around us. My chest pinches both from longing and envy. Which I know is unfounded since Lucas had suffered so much before I knew him. "I'd really like to meet her."

"You will, I promise. We will find her as soon as we get to Anavrin." He takes my hand in his. It's warm against my chilled skin.

"I hope so. How much farther do you think we need to go?" Ahead of us, the path disappears behind brambles and wild vines.

"If we walk or we fly?" His voice holds a note of humor.

I sigh. "Flying would be quicker." I grasp his arm tight and send him an imploring look. "Please don't allow me to fall out of the sky again."

"I shall do all that I can to keep you out of trouble." He stands and pulls me up.

My shoe gets caught in a hole near the log. I teeter and clutch his arm, unbalancing him.

He tumbles flat on his back. His narrow eyes widen and a dark lock spills across his forehead. His mouth opens in surprise, and he laughs. Memories of my childhood friend rush through my mind. We'd played like this before. I remember how I loved to make him smile.

That free, childlike happiness I haven't felt in years explodes within my heart. I grin.

"Do I glimpse the girl I once knew?" Vulnerability makes him look younger and happier.

My pulse quickens. "I remember pushing you down as a child, and you laughed the same way."

"Yes. You used to get petulant when you didn't win. So, I learned to let you win." He lifts his hand to me in an unspoken request to help him to his feet.

Invigorated with good humor, I step back. "Let me win? You did not!"

"Possibly it was only once or twice." He gestures with his outstretched hand again. "I promised never to allow harm to come to you again. You can count on me."

I pull him up, but not the way he expects. Reaching out my hand, I *call* him, and up he springs with more force than intended. His body collides with mine. He tries to catch me as we plummet, rolling to the ground inches away from the thorny bushes at the edge of the forest. My body lies sprawled atop Lucas, my forehead resting upon his chest. I shake with laughter.

"Tambrynn, are you hurt?" Concern edges his voice and he struggles to arise.

I peek at him, trying to keep a serious expression on my face. Tears stream down my cheeks, but it's not due to the twinge from my neck. I'm unable to keep my humor in check. "You, sir, have broken your oath. You have indeed allowed me to fall."

His hand rests on my shoulder, placed beside the gash from

the arrow. He sighs heavily. "It is my turn to ask you to never, ever do that again. My heart cannot take it."

"I'm unsure I can do that." I can't look into his eyes for fear he will witness my innermost feelings, which are shifting, becoming more solid. He must certainly hear the thumping of my heart even over the sound of the rushing water.

"As much as I am relishing the moment, my lady, may I ask you to please allow me to rise?"

"Yes, of course." I move to sit beside him.

"Ah, there." He hands me the pillow, and we stand. "That's going to leave a ring-sized mark on my back."

"I almost forgot about the ring." I grab the pillow and clutch it to my heart. A wisp of a memory comes to me. I recall seeing a ring on a chain around Mother's neck. "What happened to Mother's ring?"

"It was missing when I returned to find you both gone. She was never without it. Perhaps it was buried with her, or used to pay for her burial?" His lips thin. "I'm sorry, that wasn't kind to ask."

My heart seizes. "I was sent away, so I assume the Commonwealth took our possessions for payment." I hug the pillow close wishing it could be Mother. "I do wonder, though. Why a ring? If it's a key, why not have an actual key?" I sit upon my knees with my gray wool dress tucked beneath me and face him.

He shrugs. "It is said when the Kinsman's first children rebelled, he divided the One World into separate kingdoms and sealed them with a talisman, a special key so they couldn't unite to try and overthrow him again. Only the Eldrin Council, those who were loyal and obedient to the Kinsman, would be allowed access to the keys."

"How did the Kinsman divide a whole world? It sounds like

the fairy tales Mother used to tell me, but I don't remember her telling me that story."

He looks away into the dark landscape. "When I found the sanctuary here on Tenebris, I searched it trying to find them or their journals. Eventually, I found some of the ancient scrolls. One was titled, *The Tale of the Divided Kingdoms*. In the Tale, the One World was a magical place where everything ever known grew in abundance. But though they had everything they'd ever need, some of the children wanted more. They coveted the Kinsman's ability to create something from nothing."

"Jealousy," I murmur. I'd felt the stirrings in my own heart.

He sighs. "Exactly so. Jealousy twists the heart and soul. But the children weren't strong enough on their own to overtake the Kinsman. So, in order to manipulate the natural order of magic, they had to steal another's magic and twist it into what they desired. They did this by murdering several of their kin."

I gasp. "That's awful!" I'd always wanted a sister or a brother. Since Mother had died, I'd longed for a family of my own. It was why I'd wanted to search for my father.

Lucas's dark eyes sparkle and he nods in agreement. "When the Kinsman found out, he called out to the depths of the sea and it reached up with an icy spinning funnel—a brinicle—that sucked in and captured his disobedient children in a frozen prison. They would be held there forevermore, never to be found until the time of reckoning came."

Hairs bristle on my arms and I gaze up at the bright moon. It's a horrific tale. "Reckoning?"

His smile is tight. "The scroll said the Kinsman will return one day and sort out the rest of his children like sheep and goats. Those who follow his holy writings will join him in a new world, one of order, equality, and abundance."

"And those who don't?" I ask.

He winces. "They'll be devoured by their own desires, locked forever in a savage glacial nothingness."

The wind, though gentle, grazes its cold breath across my skin and I recall the blizzard. I wish I had the cloak to keep me warm. I tuck my chin to my knees, warming my fingers. "What of the rest of his children who didn't succumb to jealousy?"

"The rest of the world he divided by a Great Sea, separating the lands so far apart you wouldn't be able to see them on any of the highest mountains. He shut them tight with His mighty hand and sealed them away with magical talismans. That is all the scroll said. But I found some of the cleric's logbook which describes Tenebris as being a 'land bereft of natural magic but having a hunger to devour anything that itself is mystical in origin.'"

"And you believe this to mean it makes us forget things?" I turn towards him and move to brush a strand of hair tickling my cheek, but Lucas beats me to it. His fingers are warm against my chilled skin and I fight the quiver it elicits.

"It took me a while to figure that out. And only after I returned to myself this last time did that entry make sense. But it could explain why there weren't any clerics at the sanctuary. I have to wonder if they eventually forgot their abilities and wandered away. Or they died there guarding the secrets. However, I found no skeletons to indicate that happened."

Trees rustle behind us. Wide-eyed, I sweep my gaze across the thicket. I hear nothing save the stream. There is a rotten scent of some kind floating on the breeze.

Shadows move across the trees at the edge. We stand, and Lucas pushes me behind him.

I hear the snarls before seeing the beasts. There are eight of them, and they look as if they've come through the stream. They're soaking wet and have moss and brambles stuck to their hunched bodies.

They step farther into the clearing and the bright moon highlights their hideous, malformed faces. Their skin is worn, like tanned hide that's stretched too tight over their facial bones. Teeth protrude from the lengthened jaws like the gnarled thorns on the bushes near us. Their elongated fingers with clawed nails are sharp as scythes. Their stench is overpowering. I shudder.

At first, it doesn't appear as though they notice us until the front beast points its nose in the air and takes a long sniff. How they smell anything beyond their own odor is incomprehensible. His head swivels in our direction. My eyes widen and I clutch Lucas's shirt tight.

In unison, they howl.

"We need to go. Now." Lucas reaches back and grasps my hand. I *call* my pillow to me and nod. In a whirl, we are airborne.

15

My wings ache from flying all night, especially the one still healing from the arrow wound. The sun has already lost its brilliant oranges by the time we land on a grassy cliff near a fortress above a seaport town. To my horror, we'd seen several groups of beasts across the countryside as we flew. Some sensed us and mauled the air with their claws.

I blink my eyes against the bright sun. Dying panic also makes me weary, but it's the crowds along the Black Sea's shoreline that make my feathers stand on end.

There anchored along the docks are eight ships of varying sizes and sails. The air is full of people calling out to each other as they load and unload the ships and the constant cries of seagulls. Scents of ocean and fish flavor the air. The chaotic noisiness brings to mind the busy town squares with their pauper blocks where I spent too much of my life.

Droplets of moisture fill the atmosphere, weighing down my body, and I fluff my feathers to shake the salty residue away.

"The Zoe Tree, my lady. The tree of life." Lucas stares at a

grand tree growing along the cliffs on the opposite side of the harbor, towering high above the docks. It's even higher than the stone fortress behind us. The tree stands dark against the golden sunlight, its branches stretching wide across the rocky hillside, unfurled as if the wind sculpted them into hands ever reaching toward the sea.

"It looks just like the tree on our rings." I shiver at how accurate the carving is.

Waves tip white and crash against the rocky hills where Lucas and I explore a deserted fortress that stands as an empty-eyed sentinel atop the Narrow Cliffs. Hardy grass grows in the rocky soil around the crumbling structure. It smells of dust, mold, and abandonment.

"Taborfield has prospered a great deal since I was here last," Lucas states. *"The sanctuary isn't far from here. It's hidden among the cliffs."*

Strange anxiety rolls over me in waves that rival those washing along the shore.

"Is that you I'm feeling?" I ask him. The disquiet is different, stronger than my own.

He twists his head back and forth as he studies me. *"Why? What are you feeling?"*

I reach out with the part inside me I use for my calling ability, trying to assess the nuances that buffet my own emotions. *"Fear and dread. Suspicion and uncertainty."*

"I must admit that's fairly accurate. I hadn't anticipated you being able to sense me in this way." He flutters over to a soft patch of grass near the fortress wall, and his black feathers shine bluish-purple in the sunlight. Stone has deteriorated to crumbs on the ground around the outside surface either from natural wear or from an attack. I'm unsure which since the fortress is aged, unused.

"What does that mean?"

Lucas stretches his wings out and glances up at an open window above us. *"You saw through my disguise. You spied Fetmann's hexed third eye, which shouldn't surprise me since you are half-mage. But sensing me? Normally only voyants can read other's emotions."*

His words are carefully chosen, and I can't help but believe there's something he's not saying. However, I'm exhausted and don't press him on it.

I glance back down at the bustling village beneath our cliff. I've never been to Taborfield. It's one of the few villages I haven't been sent to from the auction block. With all of the chaos and wild carryings-on of the sailors, I'm thankful I wasn't. I fluff out my feathers again, trying to rid myself of Lucas's growing unease. *"What makes you so concerned, other than the crowds?"*

"If I were Thoron, I'd make sure to place hexes on villagers around the Zoe Tree. And with the number of beasts we saw in our flight, I'm sure there are many more waiting somewhere unseen. I hadn't anticipated so many of them. It means Thoron is much stronger than any mage I've ever heard of. Getting to the tree has become more complicated than I planned. We could be captured before we enter the Tree. Or they could follow us into the passage. I don't care for either of those possibilities."

"But will we be at an advantage since we're birds?"

One of the men amidst an encampment near the docks aims at a seagull with a slingshot. The bird falls in a blur of white and gray into the water. Drunken men around him cheer while other villagers bustling around them ignore the spectacle completely.

I'd heard about the crude nature of sailors but had never witnessed it firsthand. My heart beats so fast I get dizzy.

"Maybe if your long, silver feathers weren't so distinctive." He

sends me a sideways glance. *"But I'd say that is not an option at this point."*

I mutely agree with him and glance back at the crowds. One of the women moving along the crowd walks with a stilted gait. Her body moves in a jerky fashion. *"Do you notice the lady in the green dress with the brown shawl?"* I ask.

He flutters onto a rock jutting out of the cliff. *"Yes."*

"Does she seem odd to you?"

He's silent for a moment as he darts his head back and forth to study the crowds. *"Same as the gentleman leaning against the sign. He appears to be watching all who enter from the port, or possibly all who leave. His head jerks around a bit more than normal, though it could be an affliction. We'll have to be careful, though, if we go into the village. No telling who might be on the watch for us."*

Lucas flies over to a low window and enters the gray stone fortress, and I follow behind him. He hops across the empty room. Dirt, cobwebs, and debris dot the walls and plank floor.

I wobble after him, hoping for a soft spot to rest. I didn't want to think about the crowds, the beasts, or my father any longer. *"You spoke about my grandmother saving you on Anavrin. What is she like?"*

He totters over to a corner where moss grows freely, covering the wooden floor. *"She was my salvation. I'd been beaten badly. She made sure my injuries were tended to and, for the first time in my life, I went to school. I learned to read and write, and how to control my abilities."*

He laughs. *"Most djinn are disliked because we tend to create mischief wherever we go. But, being half-djinn, I'm not as impish as my full-blooded kin. If I were, I would've pranked the shopkeeper who beat me."*

My heart aches for Lucas. My beatings are burned into my memory in stunning detail. I understand his desire to retaliate.

I long to comfort him with a touch, but my wings prevent me. *"I'm so sorry, Lucas."*

A few bugs crawl about the damp room, and I'm thankful that though I am a bird and hunger once again clenches my stomach, they do not look like a tasty treat.

He shakes his head. *"It turned out for the best. I'd been there long enough to control my powers when Cadence moved to my village with you. I used to make you laugh by changing into different animals and making funny noises. That was before you called to me in your sleep."*

I dart a glance at him and stumble over a crack in the floor. *"How is that possible?"*

Lucas finds a spot in some dried moss and sits down, situating his feathers into a comfortable position. *"Possibly through my own voyant ability? I'm unsure. We can ask Madrigal when we get back to Anavrin. But you asked about her. She is the most giving person I've ever met. Despite her husband Bennett's prejudice against mixed races, Madrigal insisted the eldrin set an example of charity and goodness. She believed every race has their own virtue and worth. I see a lot of her in you."*

I blush, marveling at Lucas's description of the grandmother I don't remember. *"She sounds wonderful."* I doubt, however, that I could live up to how Lucas describes her.

"Yes, she is." His bird eyes glitter in the dim interior of the fortress. A cool morning breeze rushes through the grasses outside of the stone building and whistles through the crumbling holes in the walls. *"I'm going to rest while I can. I suggest you do the same. We'll need our wits about us when we try to get to the Tree."* Lucas tucks his beak under his wing, and in a moment, his breathing evens out.

I'm exhausted. There's another patch of dried moss to settle on near Lucas. I scratch the moss into an even layer and follow his lead. I tuck my beak beneath my wing and close my eyes.

———

"My lady? It is time to wake."

My mind is thick, slow, and I disregard the voice.

"My lady? Tambrynn!" Lucas speaks with both impatience and excitement.

"Shoo. Go away." I tuck my arm beneath my head. My arm? My eyes open wide. Scratchy dress. Hair in my face. I sit up and run my hands across my body and wiggle my toes. It is refreshing to be human once more. However, without my feathers, the damp cool air sifts down into my bones. I hug my arms around my body as a shield against the biting air.

"Are you quite done embracing yourself?"

"What?" I blink against bright sunlight, trying to clear my thoughts.

"I have astounding news." A smile splits Lucas's flushed face.

Sitting up, I glance around the room. Oh yes, we settled into the fortress. The arched window allows much light in the room, and I glance across the crumbling interior. It could use a good scrubbing. "News?" I stand and yawn.

Lucas's keen eyes twinkle. "There is to be a festival tonight, just a few hours from now. I heard some hustlers discussing how they were going to use their pilfered invitations to the detriment of the party-goers. So I, being the law-abiding citizen I am, divested them of their bounty." He pulls out two cards like the ones my mistresses received for balls.

"Isn't that thievery?" I ask, half in jest.

"Certainly, it is, my lady. But my intentions are pure." He puffs out his chest, looking quite like a human magpie.

I send him a one-eyed glare. "Is this part of your djinn side showing?"

His smile is wide, and his eyes gleam with good humor. "I should never have revealed that information. You're far too smart for your own good."

It is an effort not to laugh. I take one of the cards from his hand. It's thick and made from the finest parchment I've ever seen. My heart tugs and I lean against the hard stone window frame. "I've never attended a grand event like this before."

"Neither have I, except in bird form." He winks at me.

I read the words, set in actual gold, printed lettering:

HEREWITH
You are invited to a
MASQUERADE BALL
to be given at
the Spaw Ballroom,
Nightfall, Thursday Eve, October Twenty-Eighth

I rub my finger over the words, having never seen a printed invitation. The ones I'd had the chance to spy were always handwritten in crisp, inky cursive letters. Servant girls didn't get to enjoy such events unless they worked the upper parlor—the only maids allowed to serve guests. During those occasions, I stayed in my room, without a chance to observe. I wouldn't even know the first rule of etiquette.

The mischievous tilt of his head catches my immediate suspicion. I narrow my eyes at him. "Masquerade Ball?"

"Oh, yes! That's the best part. Well, that, and the fact we can get to the sanctuary through the Spaw." He waves a hand as if that information is of no consequence. "But we can disguise ourselves behind masks. No one will notice your eyes!"

The thought of going out without having a hood covering my face is thrilling. "But my hair. How will you disguise that?"

"Leave that to me. I am a master of disguises." His excitement is infectious.

I think of how much Lucas looked like Farmer Tucker's son when I was in the cage, but as I swipe a hand across my wrinkled and torn dress, I have my doubts. "You'll have to use every trick you know. And what shall we be doing during this festival?"

Lucas grasps my hand and twirls me toward him. "Why, enjoying it, of course!"

16

"Being an unseen observer at your grand manors has paid off with my greatest accomplishment ever. I used this pattern from the last holiday ball." Lucas touches the frayed collar of my gown, and it tickles as it transforms. Gone is the stained, scratchy wool and in its place is a soft, purple costume with a silver-white bodice and pearl buttons.

Just under the beautiful illusion, I see my original attire, but the vision above it is laid out like a reflection upon water.

I'm shocked that it's the same color as my favorite childhood dress. Tears burn in my eyes, but I hold them back, not wishing to spoil the moment with the terrible memory of how it was ruined by the beasts.

Lucas combs his fingers through my hair and the silver strands lighten to a milky white, resembling the wigs I've seen worn by some of the higher society of women. Ringlets bounce and brush my cheeks. My scalp tingles as if his magic is soaking into my very skin.

He raises a fisted hand and, in the blink of an eye, creates a pebble-gray, feathered mask from a scrap of fabric. I touch the exquisite matching embroidered stitches that would put any seamstress to shame. With a wave of his other hand, I have an elegant fan, formed it seems out of nothing but air.

Delighted, I turn so he can tie the mask into place carefully within the curls on the back of my head.

"There," he says. He trails a hand down my neck to the lace edge of the snowy gray bodice. Quivering, I blush and turn away. The sateen skirt is slick under my shaking hands.

It's more elegant fashion than any of my mistresses had owned. Pulling the skirt back, I study the magnificent heels upon my feet. Silver thread forms an intricate heart pattern on top of the shoes. I'm delighted to see that it sparkles.

Lucas's hand is warm upon my back. Shivers dance across my body. "It matches your beautiful silver hair."

I'm touched by his supportive gesture. However, I'm also glad my hair is not silver for once. "What do I look like?"

"Tonight, you play the part of princess, my lady." His teasing holds a genuine, if wistful, tone.

"Then I shall need a prince to escort me." I curtsy low and hide my face behind the flowered fan. The slightest movement of my head shifts the mask, tickling my ears with the feathers.

His wide grin meets my glance. "My turn. Spin around and don't look back until I've instructed you."

My excitement mixes with embarrassment and my heart races. The last rays of sun exchange place with the moon, and the evening air cools my heated face. Lucas shifts, scuffling behind my turned back. I dare not peek.

"Now, my lady, you may look."

Grinning, I close my eyes and slowly face him, careful not to tangle in my skirts.

His rich voice deepens. "Open your eyes and behold your escort."

Inhaling a deep breath, I brave a look. My heart jumps into my throat.

I focus on the image Lucas has created that hovers just over his true physical person. His jacket is a dark blue-and-silver patterned brocade, while the vest underneath holds the same pattern in black. His dark curls are slicked back and tied into a ponytail, allowing me a view of his ears for the first time. A shiny black ascot hides his neck. With a low topper hat, Lucas stands taller than I remember, and I glance down at his shining boots.

"Do I pass inspection?" He swings his arms wide, one hand holding a grand, silver-handled walking cane. A simple black mask covers the top of his face, but his narrow eyes shimmer through the holes. Even his pale skin is transformed to a honeyed color.

I smile in approval. I'd always scorned the mistresses for their theatrics, but truly there's a hitch in my chest.

"Oh, Lucas. I'm speechless." My nose stings from unshed tears.

"Just the reaction I'd hoped for." He winks and tosses a small purse in the air, catching it as it falls. "Coins from the Fountain of Wishes." He holds up a hand at my disapproving look. "I did it while a magpie and only took a few to enjoy the festival. With the crowds in town, there is plenty for the slickers to gather."

The fountains were in every large village and closely monitored as the monies went directly into the local treasury, though what they used it for could only be guessed as nothing ever seemed to improve no matter how many coins were thrown. Only the Village Slickers, who wore special waterproof boots, were allowed near the fountains to wade in and gather the coinage. If anyone was caught stealing from the fountains, they were heavily fined and held in the workhouses until the fines were paid in full.

I quiver, thinking of Cook's words about sending me off to the work-houses. They were hovels, and often the workers died before they ever finished their sentences. "That's risky, too risky. What if someone would've taken a weapon to you? Couldn't you just disguise some rocks or something instead?"

Lucas waves a hand in dismissal. "My disguises only work when I'm there to hold them. Once I'm too far from an object, it returns to what it was. It was busy enough I wasn't seen. I probably could've cleaned it and The Fountain of Luck out without anyone noticing."

I hesitate. How many fountains did Taborfield have, and how many people were going to be there? "How will we ever fit in? I'm afraid we shall stand out everywhere we go. And what if I get separated from you? Will I turn back into my true self?" I twist the fan in my hands. "Maybe we should just wait until everyone is asleep, and then we can leave?"

"They have men watching the entrance to the hill and the tree at all times, and with your plumage, I fear you would be spotted. If I promise not to let you out of my sight, and make sure you have the fun you've deserved but never experienced before, will you come without further complaint?" He places my trembling hand in the crook of his elbow. "Do you trust me?"

I nod, smiling, glad for the support of his arm as my legs are shakier than a newborn foal's. The reticule, created from my pillow and ring, lies upon the window's stone edge, and I grab it as we depart.

We stroll out of the broken-down fortress side by side. The air is crisp and clean as we step around the crumbling building. Overgrown brush and boulders flank an old, worn path that winds down the cliffs into town.

Music and voices drift over the landscape as Lucas guides me across an iron bridge where we hand an attendant our invitations. I hold my breath for a moment, certain the man will know I am an imposter, but he nods and waves us inside. Anticipation heightens my awareness and excitement builds within me. I don't remember ever being this eager and happy.

My heart twinges, however, at the beggars along a fence line outside of the Spaw's grounds. They call for money or food to anyone who ventures close by their perch. Most of them are women, no doubt widowed or abandoned, and too old for indentureship. If they refused to board and labor at the workhouses, there was no place for them to earn an honest living.

My hands itch to hand out the coins Lucas took.

"We cannot save them with only a few coins," his gentle voice whispers to me. "And we don't want to draw more attention to ourselves than we need to." He nods at me, understanding shining in his dark eyes behind his mask.

I frown but acknowledge he is most likely correct. I stiffen my back and continue past them at a safe distance.

A banner placed at the entrance describes The Spaw. It was built along the Narrow Cliffs over a natural healing spring and boasts an impressive view of the coast.

Ladies and gentlemen casually stroll along the sea walk, dressed in all manner of finery and costume. My heart soars to be among the crowd with a distinguished guide, one that each time I glance his way takes my breath away. It's not only because of his attractive disguise. I'm certain there were other ways to await a chance to enter the Zoe Tree. His gift of attending the Ball in such an exquisite manner touches me deeply. It is the most thoughtful indulgence I've ever received.

Inside the stretching Spaw grounds, musicians and acrobats fill the landscape in front of several imposing buildings. The scent of roasted hog, seared fish, and sweet bread makes me salivate. My first time being able to mingle and enjoy instead of serving and hiding among the dark corners! I grip Lucas's arm and grin up at him. My heart is overflowing.

Steam rises from a couple of different cracks in the surface around the grounds. Several couples stand around the fissures, kept safe by red ropes and signs that read, 'Danger, Hot.' A colorful wooden advertisement details where the actual healing pools are located behind the buildings.

"Your eyes are shining, my lady." Lucas's smile is as wide as mine.

"It's thrilling, is it not? I may need to be pinched to believe it." I never imagined in my grandest dreams anything as festive as the colorful entertainers or being one of the beautifully dressed ladies walking arm in arm with their handsome gentlemen. Several women with white wigs are scattered among the throng, though their masks aren't as elaborate as the one Lucas crafted for me.

With a jerk, I spot a woman with a third eye. It's a wonder her head has not detached from how she glances about, not only at the crowds but in the sky as well. "The lady with the black mask and gray dress to our left. She's cursed." I whisper.

Lucas glances at her and then past her as if he is just looking around. "Yes." He turns and leads me off the boardwalk and through the entertainers instead.

My earlier good mood plummets and I tense. I search every face from the clown on a unicycle to the juggler and beyond, suddenly wishing we could just get this over with.

"You will seem suspicious, my lady, if you don't stop peering about like that." He leans over and speaks low into my ear. "Take a breath and act normally. Our disguises are more than adequate. You said so yourself earlier when you thought we would stick out in the crowd. But we don't, so relax."

I loosen my grip on his arm and inhale slowly, then exhale slower yet. "My apologies."

He squeezes my hand. "None needed." This time his smile is genuine. We come to another boardwalk and step up on it.

As we walk, I don't see any other hexed individuals or any signs of my father, so I begin to take in the scenery instead.

The Spaw, a massive brick building looming over the seaside, creates a stately and regal air. My stomach flutters with excitement and trepidation. Sweat slicks my hands as we walk up the white wooden stairs, and I have to concentrate so I don't trip or fall.

Lucas gives my arm a reassuring squeeze and I smile back at him. His eyes are illuminated by the glowing stained-glass windows lit by flowered, carved glass sconces. My stomach tightens with desire, and my breath hitches in my chest. I pry my glance away from him to take in the view of the bluffs which drop to the dark beach.

Lucas points to a place beyond the Spaw. The setting sun radiates a brilliant orange-gold on the trees and rock walls that jut high above the crashing waves. "There, below the Spaw, hidden part-way down the cliffs, is where I found the sanctuary. There are a dozen winding tunnels nearly impossible to get to unless you're djinn and can fly in. Luckily, there were lanterns someone must've used before me stored behind a stone wall. The inner sanctum itself looked as if it were carved by hand, not by the Kinsman."

He takes a deep, shuddering breath. "This is where I was when the beasts attacked you and your mother. I have regretted leaving you every day since then. Maybe if I hadn't left, Cadence would still be alive."

My heart twists. "There's no true way to know that. You

might be dead as well. I'm unsure why I was left with only a scratch while Mother—" My throat clogs, and I'm unable to finish what I was going to say. I clear my throat, but it tightens.

Lucas slides his arm around me. "I'm so sorry, Tambrynn, I don't mean to sadden you. Cadence was a wonderful woman, and she loved you more than her own life. I only mention it in case we need to hide, or possibly go back and find the maps I recall seeing. They would help lead us on our journey back to Anavrin in the passageway once we make it to the Tree. I should've grabbed them at the time, but I sensed the attack and left straight away."

The band around my throat lessens and I take a deep breath. "Are you sure we will be able to make it to the Tree tonight?"

"If not, we should make it before dawn, though I believe tonight the men will have more than the Ball to distract them." He smirks in a way that I know he is up to something.

"What might that be?" I almost whisper, curious.

"Let's just say some keys to a particularly large shipment of whiskey ended up in the wrong hands. Being a bird who can eavesdrop and pickpocket has its benefits." Lively notes from the music grow louder as we continue toward the Spaw.

I nudge his arm playfully. "You truly live up to your djinn heritage." I'm warmed at his affectionate grin, which lightens my anguish. He truly is handsome, much more than any other gentleman I see around me. My heart skips, and I have to look away to control the rush of desire that flows through my body.

We wait behind a row of masked ladies and gentlemen in line on the promenade, which opens up to a concert hall. I slowly glance around, both at the faces and then at the scenery, once I'm assured there are no hexed costume-goers near us.

I've never seen a place as imposing as this, though I've

worked in many manors. My eyes widen, imagining the work needed to keep it clean and in order. Standing taller, I remind myself that I'm not here as a servant. Not tonight.

A large orchestra plays upon a circular platform, each man dressed in a cream jacket, white shirt, and cream breeches. Behind them, tall doorways allow a view of the sea rolling as far as the eye can see. The gleaming floor is full of twirling dancers, with several standing along the edges of the room watching and talking in small groups. The crush of bodies heats the cooler night air.

Lucas presses his hand to the small of my back. My cheeks warm at the intimate touch. Confusion settles in as my heart races at his closeness, making me breathless. This is such foreign territory for me. I don't know if I can survive a whole night of being this near to him. We make our way past the barriers and onto the floor crowded with couples spinning in time to the music.

"Shall we, my lady?" His whisper flutters the feathers on my mask.

My heart flies to my throat. What am I thinking? The only experience I had was with a broom in an empty room when no one was looking. "I don't know."

Lucas lifts my downturned face. "Trust me. Just hold tight, and I shall lead the way."

Too stunned for words, I allow him to take my hand in his, and we walk to the edge of the dance floor. He places my free hand on his shoulder, smiles, and nods. I hold my breath as we join the colorful swirling stream.

"You're doing wonderfully." Together we blend as one, moving in and around the others. It's a simple step, and my legs take over as if I'd always been dancing. The whir of the spinning makes me feel as if we are flying. In truth, I prefer this sensation to the other.

Exhilaration bubbles in me. I gaze up into Lucas's dark eyes. Everything fades from my sight except him.

Until I catch another wavering third eye over Lucas's shoulder. I stumble and struggle to find who it was until I see the attendant standing near the orchestra as we swing by. It's him.

Lucas is quick to catch me and steady our steps. "Tambrynn?" He holds me much closer than before, protectively.

I shift slightly back and nod my head toward the well-dressed custodian. "The man by the stage. He's hexed." We flow with the dancers and are now across the expanse of the dance floor on the other side of the platform.

As we turn, Lucas glances up and over at the man. "He isn't looking at us. I think we're safe."

Finally, the orchestra's last note lingers in the air. A waltz starts up and Lucas quickly guides us across the far side of the ballroom and through a hall to a quieter sitting area. The waltz's chords fade the farther we move inside.

Waiters walk amongst the crowd, holding shining silver platters with drinks and delicacies. I take the thick napkin a server offers and place two of each of the golden pastries and a couple of the sweetmeats. I can't help the groan at the first bite of pastry. Buttery and flaky, the crust bursts into a cheesy delight on my tongue. I quickly dig into the rest of the delicious food, savoring each bite until they're all gone.

Lucas laughs deeply. He takes his own assortment of the offerings. His moans draw the attention of a group of four moving between rooms.

My face heats, and my hand holding the now-empty napkin trembles slightly until I remember I'm in disguise.

"Here, this may calm your nerves. Let's find a table and sit." Lucas trades our soiled napkins for drinks. He grabs a mug of sassafras and a glass of punch off a tray. I take the ruby red drink, and we move to a small table in a dark corner facing out toward the rest of the room.

Lucas gulps his refreshment down before we sit. I take a cautious sip and the punch bubbles tickle my lips. I'd been given sherry once years ago as a prank, and I remember gagging on it. I found out later one of the nastier maids had wanted to see the "witch" get drunk, but luckily, I hadn't cared for the alcohol. The juice is quite fruity, without any hint of liquor, and much more to my liking. I drink half before I realize it.

Lucas takes in each person in the room and I follow his gaze with my own, trying to find any other signs of my father's magic. I sigh and sit back against the carved wooden chair when I find nothing of concern. We sit for several minutes in quiet contemplation.

Our knees touch as Lucas scoots closer to me. A golden vase with fresh-cut red and white roses rests atop a linen tablecloth. I inhale their potent scent and before I can stop it, I burp slightly. "Oh, excuse me."

"Would you like another punch?" Gaiety fills Lucas's deep voice. He sets his mug on the other side of the table.

I sit up and fan myself. "I think one is more than enough, thank you." Every sight, sound, and scent intoxicates me. I think back on the young mistresses' dreamy looks when talking about balls and parties. Their unadulterated enthusiasm seemed childish and silly to me when I had so many other real things to worry about, but now I understand.

Lucas moves closer to me. My breath catches in my throat, and I lean toward him in response. I run a hand across his square jaw and stroke my thumb across his smooth chin. I glance up and catch the look of desire on his face. "May I kiss you, my lady?"

I nod and close my eyes. His lips sweep across mine. An explosion of heat flares in my veins and blood rushes through my body. Lucas pulls my chair toward him, deepening the kiss. I can taste the spicy flavor of the sassafras on his lips. His hand makes its way to the nape of my neck where he caresses the tender skin.

Passion ignites inside me like fire on kerosene.

He breaks the kiss and leans his head to mine, a touch of sweat on his brow. "You must know I never thought this would happen. After I came to my senses from being changed for so long, I had hoped, but I was never sure." He motions a hand between us. "Tell me you feel it, too."

"I do feel it, though I have to wonder if there's more than just punch in that punch." My voice is breathy, as if I'm winded.

He chuckles. "The alcoholic drinks are being served in another room. I noticed it when we danced by." His dark eyes find mine. "When I came to, my first thoughts were of you. And now, I didn't want to let you go when we were dancing." He puts a finger across my lips as I start to speak. "And don't tell me it's just the dress. I've already admitted I have feelings for you." His words whisper across the curls on my nape, sending fresh bumps across my skin.

Boldness overcomes me, and I have to ask. "What was it you said again?"

His hands caress the sides of my face. "I'm in love with you, Tambrynn."

If I were not already sitting down, I would swoon.

17

Lucas's declaration sinks into my skin like water on parched soil.

He presses his lips against my forehead. "I'm not trying to pressure you into saying anything or reciprocating something you aren't comfortable with or feel. I know we've only just reunited, and your memories have only recently returned to you. I've had the opportunity to ponder my own affections as I've followed you. You're no longer the child I knew. My feelings have grown. But I don't expect you to feel the same for me."

I draw a quivery breath. "Lucas, I'm unsure. Everything has changed so quickly. It's only been a couple of days since I was lost in the storm and found the cottage—and you. And then there are all of these emotions." The vase on the table rattles, and my fear ratchets.

He takes my hands in his, and the rattling settles. "I know you're scared. Believe it or not, I am too. I promise you can trust me even if it ends up that you don't feel the same way. I will ever endeavor to care for you no matter what. I hope you know that by now."

I can no longer hold the tears back, and moisture dampens my mask. "The only person I remember loving was Mother. Every other time I got close to someone after she died, I was sent away and had to start over again. Then you came, and I remembered you. You were my closest friend. I do admit to being infatuated with you before—" I cringe, thinking of my father and how he took Mother's life so easily.

Rage and fear battle in my heart, but Lucas's steady grip centers me. "If Thoron had found me before you, I don't know if I would've survived. I do know my feelings for you are becoming stronger each day we're together. Whether it's my former crush or that I'm connecting to you because you've helped save me? I love you, but I don't know if I feel the same thing you do. I couldn't endure it if something happened to you, though."

"You don't have to worry. I'll do everything in my power to make sure nothing happens to either of us. We'll get through the passage, to Anavrin, and we'll find your grandmother." He wipes away a tear that escapes my mask and kisses me, gently. For the first time in years, I feel safe, cherished. The distrust I held for nearly everyone, and all of my misgivings, evaporate with the soft caress of his lips on mine.

When my pulse steadies, I concentrate on his declaration. Questions fill my mind. "Tell me about Anavrin."

He gazes past me, his expression happy. "Anavrin is beautiful. The colors are brighter, the air is invigorating. The water is clean and clear, unlike the murky waters here. The trees and the mountains are taller than anything here. You'll see when you get there that Tenebris is like a shadow of Anavrin's beauty. I miss it dearly."

"But you said you lived on the streets, yet you still miss it?" I play with a button on his jacket, which curiously, is streaked to look very much like a feather.

"After your grandmother found me, my life changed. The village she built was incredible. I was free for the first time in my life." Lucas smiles. "I learned so many things I never had time for before." Excitement radiates from him. "There's so much I want to show you."

"It sounds wonderful." The room grows crowded and warm and the music has ended, possibly for a break. I snap the fan open to cool myself.

A servant with a tray of punch passes by, and Lucas grabs two goblets. He hands me one. "Let's celebrate. We are almost home, Tambrynn."

I don't know whether to be relieved, scared, or excited. As I sip from the glass, I notice a gentleman with a grotesque bird mask bending over someone's shoulder. He turns and sweeps a glance across the room. He holds a glass with amber liquid. On his hand, I recognize the ring he wears. It's the same one I've kept hidden for years. But, how? The man with him turns and focuses on me as well. There is a third eye on the second man's forehead.

I dip my head and sit my empty punch goblet on the table, my hands shaking as I do. Could it be my father? "Lucas?"

Lucas cautiously glances up. He tenses before dropping his head close to mine. "Act like nothing's amiss."

I twist in my chair closer to Lucas, away from the men. "What do we do?"

Lucas speaks quietly into my ear. "We need to find a way out of here now. Hopefully, he won't have noticed us in our disguises or sensed when your ability slipped for that moment." He stands and holds out a hand to me. I take it, and he guides me in a meandering path through the people who weren't lucky enough to get a table.

As we pass through the doorway, I send a furtive look over my shoulder. The two men are no longer standing there. "Lucas," I whisper, "they're gone." He nods but says nothing. A wave of tingles washes over me before we reach the promenade, where several people gather in groups talking and laughing around the lush lawn.

I glance back a couple of times as we walk, but I don't notice either of the men nor the attendant following us. A salty gust rushes over us, and I notice my white curls are no longer white but yellow. Glancing down at my dress, I see Lucas has changed it to a deep carnation pink. Lucas's blue and black ensemble is changed to red and brown, and his black hair to a rich mahogany.

Lucas's hand tightens on mine. "I told you I was handier than you might imagine, my lady. Hopefully, no one noticed it as we walked from one room to another."

Sweet relief washes my doubts away. "You do surprise me." Outside it is much cooler, and I step closer to Lucas for warmth.

He leads me nonchalantly, as if we were on a garden stroll, to the cliff's edge. There are several groups of two or more gazing down at the sea along the line of the stony bluff that runs in front of the Spaw. Their conversations and laughter lift and carry on the gentle evening breeze. The moon reflects off the dark, frothing waters that spread out beyond the ledge as far as I can see.

Lucas points at a rocky isle not far from the sandy coast. "Smile and laugh as though we are discussing something interesting."

I smile, but my laugh comes off a bit flat. "My apologies. I'm not much of a pretender."

He grins back at me, and it's more genuine than mine. "I'm nervous, too."

The smile on my face loosens until it is natural, and I relax again. He glances behind us. "I had hoped there wouldn't be as many people hexed by Thoron in attendance. It might be wise to cut our entertainment short and find the sanctuary before heading to the Tree. I don't know if he knows the whereabouts of the sanctuary, but it would be nice to get the maps I saw there years ago. That is, if they are still there. Come."

He leads me past the grassy lawn into a border of dying brush-weeds and trees which create a sparse-looking forest. I'm thankful my skirt is slick as it makes walking through the denser foliage easier than it would have been otherwise. Several feet inside the trees, it gets darker and the trees thicker. Lucas stops.

"Ready, my lady? Stay close to the rock. It might help your silver plumage blend in." He takes my hand.

Feathers replace the silky folds of my dress, and we're in flight.

Across the Spaw grounds, revelers continue, unaware of two birds flying above them. As Lucas requested, I stay close to the gray rock of the cliff as I follow him in a tight flight past several ledges that lead to a cave opening halfway down the stone wall. Wind buffets our bodies as we fight against it to fly. Lucas was right. There's no way anyone could get to it without being a bird or having yards and yards of rope strung from above or a ladder taller than the tallest manor I'd ever seen hitched up from the rocky beach.

Once on the cave's ledge, Lucas changes back. Gusts brush damp sea air over us as he stands and puts me down in the shelter of a rocky nook. "I'd like to see if you can change yourself back, now that you've gone through the transformation so often. Just think of your normal form and let the tingles rush over your body, don't fight it."

I gulp and think about my girl form. No longer foreign, the tingles run from my toes to the top of my head. Disappointment stings as I notice the beautiful gown and patterned shoes are gone. My feet are snug inside my worn leather slippers, and my rumpled dress chafes my skin. I'm unable to stop a grunt from escaping as I brush a hand across the scratchy wool fabric. My hair, now loose, whips around my head. Wind from the rushing waves swirls around the opening where we stand. I bend down to pick up the pillow so it doesn't get carried off with a gust.

With a single touch, the pillow melts away into sand, leaving the ring in my palm. "Put it on so we don't lose it in the dark cave." Lucas grins, his curls blowing with the wind. "And you're still beautiful no matter what you wear."

Goosebumps spread across my arms at his words, and it's more than the rush of air circling around. I rub my hands across my arms.

Lucas walks deeper into the cave and picks something up in the darkness, but I cannot see what it is until he lights a lantern. I shiver slightly in the salty breeze. Lucas holds the lantern up. "There's not much kerosene left, but if we hasten, it should get us to another one I left farther in. If it's still there."

I raise my eyebrows at his last words, barely spoken, as if he's unsure. I take his outstretched hand and glance around the cave, taking in the dark, jagged rocks at the top of the opening. It's like we're walking into the throat of a stone monster. I shudder and clutch Lucas's free arm.

"It's said these sanctuaries are built among where the dragons used to nest. When they died off, the clerics would use their lairs since there were numerous tunnels and spaces to hole up. It's more likely to be superstition twisted into a grand fairy tale. I often wonder how the eldrin found the caves in the first place, unless they came upon the hot springs first and discovered the caves from there. However, my searches found no such entrance."

I run my hand over a wall marbled with gray and black stone. Almost as if it had been burned by a fire-breathing creature. I shake my head at that thought. It would be a simple thing to spin a tale of dragons from it.

Chalky dust clouds the air as we shuffle through a channel that looks as though unused for quite some time. The dust we walk through is deep here. Though it's dry, there's a damp chill that makes me huddle as close to Lucas as I'm able.

Every once in a while, Lucas lifts the lantern to a wall and I see marks on the rocks. The air grows warmer the farther we walk until the creeping dampness no longer makes me pinch my shoulders. We follow the side where an eight-pointed star is carved into the rock.

"Did you leave a trail when you were here last?" I ask as I step past the strange star.

"Some. There are four symbols, each leading to different parts of the caverns deeper inside the cliff. One leads to the heated water the Spaw now uses for their healing baths. Two lead off to open ceremonial areas. The star one leads to the sanctuary, so when I located it, I went back and marked each turn so I could find it easier next time."

He's quiet for a moment as we continue. "It was the last path I followed when I came here before. If I had located the sanctuary the first time, I may have made it back to you in time."

I squeeze his arm. I've had years to grieve Mother, but it always feels new each time I think of the attack. My anger turns toward my father, who was truly the one at fault for all of my sorrow. "I had many nightmares after Mother died. In each one, I would try to go back and save her, but I never could never reach her, even in my dreams. I can't help but think you might've been injured had you been there. Where would that have left me?"

He squeezes my hand between his arm and his side. "You're right." His voice is tight and his lips twist sideways. He holds the lantern higher as we move through the tunnel, which narrows so that we are only able to walk one by one. "I just always felt so responsible for your safety because I'd promised Cadence I would help her keep you hidden, safe from Thoron and any of his gruesome creations. At that moment, I'd let all of us down. Even Madrigal, who had given me the best chance to live a normal life. I had her granddaughter's life in my hands." His shoulders tense. "I will endeavor never to let any harm come to you, my lady."

I tug his arm and look into his face. It's creased with pain so bare I can almost feel it for him. I place a gentle hand on his smooth cheek. "I believe you, Lucas. Together, we'll keep each other safe. And we'll avenge my mother's death. But you don't have to call me a lady."

That gains me a grin that melts my insides like butter in a hot pan.

"I do when you're half-eldrin royalty. Your mother, grandmother, and grandfather held high places in the Eldrin Council, the rulers of Anavrin. Neither your mother nor grandmother thought you should be shunned, but your grandfather, being the chief eldrin, would have been the one to make that choice. He'd decide whether to shun you as a half-breed or accept you in a lower eldrin role, one much like a servant. If he went against the Council's laws, his position would be in jeopardy. But you are still eldrin royalty."

I dismiss the royalty comment while indignation churns in my gut at the thought that my grandfather would've rejected me to a life of servitude rather than lose his position. Holy council or not, it stings. I can't imagine anything being more important than having people you love—family.

Would I always be subject to rejection?

18

I'm glad for the darkness which hides my tears from Lucas when he swings the light away from my face. I swipe a sleeve across my damp cheeks. They're gritty from the dust we kick up as we walk. It scratches my skin.

Lucas is unaware of my emotional breakdown as he continues to speak. "Your grandfather Bennett died confronting Thoron for conceiving a child with Cadence, making his granddaughter a half-breed. For him, a high-cleric, it was detestable, and he wanted recompense from Thoron. Thoron immediately attacked him, and Cadence, coming to her father's aid, tried to shield him with her magic. Your grandfather died in the attack, but the spell also hit Cadence. She feared she wouldn't carry you to full term, but she did. You were born at night during a full moon where the stars shone brightly. She said you were the most beautiful baby ever." His chuckle is low and throaty.

I wipe my sleeve across my runny nose. "And thus, my stories of the stars and the moon." I smile despite the sorrow in my heart to learn of my grandfather's disapproval. "Thank you for telling me about what happened. I never thought I'd have a true family again."

"I hope you consider me as close as family." His words are soft and spoken over his shoulder at me.

"I do." My words are low enough that the silence of the tunnel almost devours them whole. But Lucas squeezes my hand, and I know he heard me.

"Anyway, these tunnels. When I found the papers in the sanctuary, there was a book that labeled this symbol as the Star of the Kinsman. A holy hieroglyph, it said." He laughs briefly. "That's a fancy phrase the clerics use. The eldrin consecrate their surroundings in worship to the Kinsman with oil made from the Star of the Kinsman plant. I've heard it smells like the great Heavens when it burns."

"Great Heavens? You mean where the stars are?"

"Yes, it's where the Kinsman is said to live." He points up. "But only the eldrin know for sure. They are the keepers of the holy secrets."

I touch the hieroglyph, and it hums beneath my fingers before flaring a bright silver, engulfing the tunnel with blinding light. I jerk my hand back to cover my eyes and the brightness disappears. I blink quickly, trying to regain my sight. The lamplight seems dimmer after the flash. "That hummed like my ability does, only a bit stronger. More like the rumble of a dozen horses pounding the ground."

Lucas, uncovering his eyes, quietly stares at me with an unreadable look on his pale face. His eyes gleam with the lantern's flickering flame as he touches the symbol. "I don't feel anything."

"No humming?" I ask. I'm afraid to touch it again. The hum was enough that I worried it would collapse the tunnel, burying us underneath rocks forever.

He looks closer at the symbol and back at me, his eyes

narrowing. "Nothing. Do you realize the Star looks very like the pupils in your eyes? Almost animalistic."

"It does?" At first, I'd study my eyes in water or silver trays to try to fathom the secrets to why they looked different. After a while, I stopped looking because of the suspicion and negative attitudes of all who saw them. It had been so long since I'd glanced at my reflection that I wasn't sure if I remembered what they truly looked like. "What could it mean?"

"I'm unsure." The lantern sputters and Lucas tugs my hand, walking quickly past the star.

"How far is this sanctuary?" I ask as I stumble over rock debris behind him. Dust plumes in the air, pricking my throat.

"I don't quite recall, but it can't be too far." As the lantern dims, Lucas guides me forward until we reach a split in the tunnel.

He grabs another lantern with some kerosene hanging from a nail driven into the stone. Three tunnels each go off in different directions. He rips a piece of cloth from his shirt and lights it with the dying lantern wick, transferring the flame to the new lantern.

We head down the tunnel, following the etched star symbol. It's deathly quiet except for our footfalls. I'd been in plenty of dark cellars and attic rooms which were small and uncomfortable, but these stone walls are constricting like I'm being swallowed alive. I take a deep breath and flex the hand I'm not clenching tight to Lucas's shirt.

The narrow tunnel suddenly opens to a massive chamber with tables, shelves, and chairs. Dusty papers and books are scattered everywhere, from the floor to the tables, and even some on rock ledges in the wall. The lantern light bounces off what look to be gems in the walls, reflecting the light so it is brighter than any of the tunnels, and I breathe easier.

Our appearance scares a small bird. No, it wasn't a bird, but something that looked like a serpent with wings. It snarls out a crow and darts into the hallway we just came from. "What was that?" I ask.

"Unsure. But let's find the maps and get out of here." Lucas places the lantern down on a table and scrambles through the papers, scrolls, and books. "It's here on a table somewhere. Look for a map that's labeled 'Zoe Tree Passage.' It will help us navigate the passage between kingdoms so we don't enter the wrong one."

I go to another table and shuffle through several sheets of paper with symbols similar to the ones on the tunnel walls. I search carefully, as some of the papers are brittle and start to crumble when I touch them. They're all layered with dirt. "How old are these?"

"As old as the divided kingdoms. Hundreds of years." Lucas moves to another table and flips through papers and books. "Here's the Tale of the Divided Kingdom." He brushes off the cover which has several symbols much like the ones we saw on the walls.

"What does it say?" I ask, sorting through piles of scrolls on a chair. I breathe in the grime. My eyes water a bit, and I sneeze.

Lucas smirks at me. "It tells of the One World and how the Kinsman formed the kingdoms. It does say that Tenebris was intended to be left without magic." He flips through the book, which begins crumbling into flakes, so he stops. "It doesn't say why or how, just that the Kinsman gave this division to those who spurned the use of magic. There's something not right about it, as the clerics noted. I didn't get the chance to read much on the others. I looked up Tenebris first before I had to leave."

"Is that why no one here believes in the Kinsman? Because

there's no magic?" I ask, flipping through another book. It's in a language I don't know and also fragile.

His brows furrow. "The clerics mentioned the apathy and forgetfulness causing a degrading in the society as a whole or something. They were worried the people would turn away from the Kinsman." Dust clouds puff out as he searches another table. It's his turn to sneeze.

I chuckle at him.

He sniffs. "It looks as if someone has been here since I came last. I can't find anything I read before, except for this book." It's the book that crumbled.

"You don't think the eldrin have come back, do you?" I ask as I continue my search. Some are hard to read because they're so faded, and the luminous light isn't as good as having a true lamp to read them by.

"I don't know, but it doesn't feel right." He glances around at the glowing room. It's silent save my movements. He turns back and continues searching, a frown on his face.

We continue looking for what feels like hours, although it can't truly be that long, until we end up at the far end of the chamber where the shelves hold thick tomes. I remove one and something drops to the rocky cavern floor. "Lucas? This was behind a book." I trail a hand over a metal tube with a rolled-up map inside it. Lucas unrolls it. It's of Tenebris. I recognize several towns, though there are many more not noted on it. Could it be that they didn't exist back when the map was drawn?

Lucas hands it back. "It will be similar to this, but it will have the Zoe Tree label on it." He pulls out all of the books near the bottom.

I wave at the dirt billows rising as the books fall to the gritty ground.

Lucas pulls out several sheets rolled into one large

bundle from behind the bottom shelf. He unfurls several smaller maps rolled inside a larger one and turns to smile at me.

"Got them. It looks like maps of several kingdoms. We'll take them all." He rolls them up tightly and hands them to me.

————

The moonlight is bright to my eyes after being in the cavern for so long. It's high in the sky, making the time around midnight. Though I should be tired, the fresh salted air and excitement of starting a new adventure renews me.

The sensation of being watched tingles over my scalp. I glance around, peering closely at some trees which have managed to grow along the cliffs. I see nothing and hear nothing save the waves and the wind. "Do you sense anything? Something watching us?"

Lucas stops and studies our surroundings. "I don't. But just to be sure, stay close to the rocks as before. Luckily it seems the wind has died down so it won't be so drafty as we fly. Follow me, and I'll take the least observable path to the Zoe Tree." He holds the tightly rolled maps he'd taken from me when we exited the caverns, having doused and left the lantern where the first one had been behind some rocks close to the opening in the cliffside.

I nod. Lucas's change is immediate. I close my eyes and think of flying as a bird. Tingles flow over my body, and when I look again, I'm eye to eye with Lucas in his magpie form. He twitches and flies off.

I follow behind him as near as possible, flying close to the rocks. We swing out past the Spaw, where masked ladies and gentlemen continue to dance to the lively notes coming from the musicians. The crowd has thinned out slightly. Those who remain are quite animated, as if they've imbibed too much alcohol. We're all but invisible to the party-goers.

We fly in the opposite direction from the fortress, swinging a wide path away from the boats docked along the harbor— too far to be targeted by anyone sitting among the docks. The singing there is as lively as the songs coming from the Spaw, except these are liberally sprinkled with bawdy tales of women and whiskey.

"My plan seems to have worked." Humor laces Lucas's words.

"It does indeed."

The sea ripples beneath the silvery glow of the moon. Once in a while, a fish shadow slinks beneath the water as if they are dancing as well. It's not far to the other end of the cliffs where the tree reaches out over the rocks toward the water. The tree's size becomes intimidating the closer we fly.

The tree is at least the width of two carriages around at the bottom with long, thick branches that unfurl in all directions in the shape of a mushroom on top. It is a most impressive tree, stretching long branches several more carriage lengths to reach the ledge which drops straight down to the sea.

"We're almost there." Lucas curves toward the cliffs beneath the tree, keeping close to the rocky ledge.

Luckily, in my bird form, my mouth is not hanging open to show my wonder. *"It's the most extraordinary tree I've ever seen."*

"Yes. Cadence told me the Kinsman split the Zoe Tree, a tree as big as a mountain and reaching so high in the sky it touched the clouds. This tree is only a portion of the original tree, a placeholder, she said. There's a path between each tree that allows the Kinsman to travel from kingdom to kingdom. In the end times, when the Kinsman returns, he will bring the portions back together to reform the original tree, and the One World will be reborn again."

"I can't imagine a tree bigger than this. And the Kinsman visits each kingdom? How can that be when so many bad things happen

all the time?" The notion of an all-powerful being deigning to walk among his lesser creation seems absurd to me.

"Though Cadence told me this, I have to wonder if it's a tale the eldrin tell to keep the other races in line. The clerics were always warning of the Kinsman's wrath."

We reach the Zoe Tree. Its bare branches stretch out, swaying, reaching as if trying to grasp hold of the moon. It grows windier the higher we fly. The tree's branches creak and knock together.

I land upon an enormous lower limb, lush with leaves not yet turned with the season, and wait while Lucas circles the tree. The tangy scent of tree sap wafts from a hole another bird has pecked in the thick bark nearby. The wood appears to be intact, though the glistening river of hardened sap makes a winding path as it flows down the tree.

When Lucas finally lands, it is below me. He changes back to his human form before his feet touch the rocky ground. Dark curls flicker around his head. The branch I perch on is a head's length above him. The tree's bulk blocks the majority of the wind.

Lucas tucks the rolls of maps in his belt. "Are you going to sit there all night?" His smile makes my heart do a flip-flop.

I flutter down to him and try to change before I land as he did, but unlike his graceful landing, I fall onto my backside. I have to twist to stand and my cheeks flush.

"You do fall more now than I recall you did as a child." Lucas's lips quiver with the laughter he holds back. "Do not be too disheartened. It took me years to be able to do what you've done in days, my lady."

I stand and brush myself off, though more of the debris is probably from the cavern than my fall. Luckily the breeze cools my embarrassment before I face him fully again. I thrust my unruly hair behind my shoulders, wishing I still had the curls

Lucas created for the Ball. "I've never been accused of being graceful."

He tucks my thick hair behind my ears, trailing his hands down my face to rest on my chin. "I disagree. You are quite graceful in your bird form, now that you're used to it. We'll practice on your landings once we make it to Anavrin."

I lose myself within his dark eyes. He takes my hand with the ring and holds it up. "Are you ready?"

His ring is identical to mine, as I knew it was, but it is strange to see them both together. I follow the direction of his gaze and freeze. A glowing light appears at the base of the tree. "Oh, my!"

Lucas grins at my astonishment. "My lady, step from one world into another."

19

Light glimmers in the center of the massive tree. Lucas presses his hand against the bark, and I follow his example. The tree cracks lightly, its thick gray bark breaking. Wide as the length of my hand from my palm to my fingertips, it opens into a small double doorway broad enough for one person to step through and tall enough most people wouldn't have to bend over.

Lucas grabs the left side while I take the right and, together, we pull the tree bark open. Like the door on the chicken coop, it sticks slightly, whether from disuse or because it is an actual tree that opens magically into a doorway, I'm unsure. I shield my eyes against the radiance blasting through the breach. Lucas does the same. When I reach out to touch the light, my fingers disappear up to my wrist. I yank my hand back to my chest.

"Your mother said it was another dimension." He laughs at my confused expression. "Like my illusions. It's a reality that rests apart from the one below or above it, but it is there at the same time." Lucas reaches out and touches the light. "It won't hurt you. See?"

I try again. It's bewildering that though I no longer see my hand, I can still feel my fingers moving on the other side of the blinding brightness.

Lucas glances around, concern creasing his usually smooth face. "We need to move quickly. It's dark enough for this to be seen by anyone for quite a distance."

Hesitant, I move forward. The bark frame is thick and I press one hand to it as I step inside to an immeasurable space. It's larger than I could've imagined, not that I would've ever dreamed of something so incredible. I poke my head back through the doorway to peer back at the massive tree and the cliff's side, lit by the light pouring out from the inner space. The difference is almost dizzying, and I can't help but glance back and forth until Lucas clears his throat. "Sorry. It's just so fascinating."

"I do agree, but we mustn't dawdle." Lucas assists me as I step back into the passageway. Once we let go, the door creaks shut, sealing behind us. I long to open it back up once more, but Lucas has already stridden past me into the passage. He spins around with a smile on his face. "We finally made it! The only one I know that has another ring to gain entry is your father, and I didn't see him or his beasts. Dare I say I think we're safe?"

I can't help but grin at his delight.

Inside is breathtaking. Green vines with thick stems curve several feet above us, creating an opulent canopy. Lush grass cushions my footfalls along a path toward a mossy bridge. The wooden handrails are carved to resemble the vines. A sparkling, clear stream trickles just below it. We stand on the grassy area between a slight incline that leads up to the bridge and the edge of the stream.

Lucas walks forward and bends down to cup the water in his hand. Each droplet glimmers with a shining light. "Cadence called this the River of Life. There is no beginning or end. It crosses into each kingdom where the Zoe Tree grows, keeping the trees fed and viable, and thus keeping the passageway open."

I kneel beside Lucas and reach out. The stream is refreshing and cool to the touch. I see my reflection and cringe at my gritty, gray hair tangled in wild waves around my head. "Oh, no." I run my hands over the disorderly mess. It will be impossible without a good comb to clear the knots.

"Lean down. The water has healing properties that should help with your hair."

I send him a disbelieving look but do as he said. I sit on my shins and bend my head over the stream. The water is lightly scented.

Lucas sets the maps aside and dunks my frazzled tresses into the water, letting the cool wetness soak in before he scrubs lightly.

"Have you done this before?" I ask. Goosebumps rise across my arms as my head prickles with the coolness of the water and his gentle touch.

"There was a small skirmish, a battle of sorts, before you, your mother, and I entered the passage last time. We had gotten quite dirty and scratched up. As soon as we reached the river, your mother jumped in, clothes and all." He laughs. "I remember thinking she'd become crazed, until I witnessed her wounds healing, her clothes instantly cleansed." He squeezes out my hair and lifts my head. "So, I jumped in after her. The water tingles, does it not?"

I run my fingers through my untangled hair. It reflects silver in the water. "It does." I can't help but stare at my changed reflection.

Lucas stands and holds out a hand to me.

I grin at him and take it. "Do you know how to swim?"

A gleam enters his eye as he helps me to stand. "I do, but if I remember right, it's not that deep, at least not until the edge of the bridge where it deepens into a gyre. You certainly wouldn't want to swim there."

"What is a gyre?" I ask.

"It's like a funnel that I'm guessing drops off to another Zoe Tree in another kingdom. Cadence wasn't sure where they would lead, so she warned me to stay away from them." He shrugs.

I study the water under the bridge as I wring out my hair. It's darker, almost stormy-looking, and I nod in agreement. I turn and bound awkwardly into the river downstream from the bridge, clothes and all. Cool water slaps at my face as I fall forward into the clear stream. It's invigorating, and I turn and splash the water toward Lucas. He watches me from the shore, an amused look on his face.

"Oh, to be rid of that salty seawater and all the dust from the cave!" I spin in a circle, water sloshing in every direction, clouds of grime mixing with the clear stream drifting toward the bridge. "It's glorious!"

Lucas jumps into the water next to me, sinks, and then shoots out of the water. His hair, which had been dusty from the cave, has turned a bluish-black, instead of the dark inky black I recall it being before. His skin, though still pale, flushes a healthier golden color.

We chase each other in the stream for a few minutes, splashing and laughing until I catch a flash of something dark moving over us and I stop to look. My arms prickle, and I rub my wrinkled hands across them and realize they are glowing.

"What is it?" Lucas stops. Water rushes over me in a small

wave while his hair and face are dripping wet. His shirt is soaked, drooping, and I catch just a flash of his chest.

I'm distracted from my luminous hands as my pulse races. I tuck them under my arms and try to hide my thoughts and my suddenly heated cheeks.

It takes me a moment to push aside errant thoughts of seeing Lucas's chest to answer him. "I thought I saw something, like a bird flying, only bigger." I spread my river-chilled fingers across my face, cooling them. I'm torn between a growing desire for Lucas and fear that Thoron has followed us into the passage.

Lucas twists in a circle, searching the infinite emptiness that has no clouds, no sun, and no moon. It is odd to behold, but not in an alarming way. The air is warm enough to be comfortable, and there's no breeze to chill my damp skin.

"I don't see anything," he says.

I'm grateful that the heat has finally left my face and I can look at him once again. Though the blue light has left my hands, I'm still slightly shaken. "This has been exhilarating, but we should probably stop dithering and find the doorway to Anavrin."

It's his turn to blush slightly. His smile is crooked, with a hint of regret. "You're right. Of course, we should."

Glad my dress is wool, and less prone to getting soaked, I'm still quite wet when we step on the grassy beach. I slip off my shoes, preferring to walk in my woolen stockings alone until the leather dries enough not to squeak. When I stand up, I get a full view of Lucas's bare back and my breath catches in my throat. He's wringing out his shirt back into the river. His sinewy muscles bunch as he moves, causing my heart to flutter wildly.

I turn quickly, a hand on my pounding chest, trying to quiet my thrumming, desirous heart. I'd only ever viewed bare chests or backs when I was a child on the farm years ago. It had always been older gentlemen who had pot-bellies, hair across their shoulders, and were sweating profusely—nothing to prepare me for seeing Lucas with half his clothes off.

"My lady, are you all right?" he asks.

I take a deep breath, trying to calm myself like when I'm trying to control my abilities. I run my shaking hands through my long hair for something to do with them. "I'm fine. Just looking around." My voice cracks, and I'm forced to clear my throat.

I sense Lucas behind me before he steps into my line of sight. He's glancing around the passage. "It is quite stunning, isn't it?"

I'm still working to appear as though nothing's wrong when he turns toward me, a mischievous gleam in his eyes and the grin on his face letting me know he's completely aware of my discomfort. His shirt, thankfully, is back in place, and the acceptable amount of skin is now showing. He carries the maps, picked up from the side of the river, and luckily, they did not get damp.

"Where do we go from here?" I ask.

He unrolls the sheets and, after studying it for a moment, points to the bridge. "It's only three doors that direction if I've calculated correctly." His eyes squint into the distance and he motions for me to go ahead of him onto the walkway.

My heart rate slows, allowing me to think clearly. "Is that bad?"

"Not at all. Last time we went past several more doors before we found Tenebris." He huffs out an indignant laugh. "We were unable to secure a map when we left." He carefully rolls the papers back up. "It's why I wanted to visit the caves. The eldrin keep all of the relics including the maps to the doorways of all the kingdoms there."

"How many doorways do you remember?" My shoes still drip as they dangle from one hand as we walk, leaving a glistening trail upon the sandy strip of land beside the river. From the side, I notice wooden steps leading up to the walkway. Water rushes lazily by now that our splashing has ended.

Lucas squints as we walk side by side up a wide stairway to the arching structure. "There were seven or eight doorways we passed, maybe more. We were in quite a state when we finally reached the Zoe Tree on Anavrin. Cadence, with Madrigal's help, borrowed the rings so we could enter the tree. Needless to say, the clerics did not take kindly to Madrigal's assistance."

My stomach dips with alarm. "Would Madrigal have been punished for helping us?" A breeze that holds a myriad of different flowery scents greets us as we step upon the plank base of the bridge. The dark wood itself is well-worn, and I wonder how many have crossed its path before me.

Lucas steps over to the elaborate handrail and gazes down. The water has indeed grown deeper. It darkens to a deep blue and then opens into a blackish funnel straight underneath the bridge. I grow lightheaded and step away from the side.

"Punished, yes, but the eldrin don't discipline their own as they do with others. She would probably be stripped of her title and relegated to a lower-ranking trade. Purity, pride, and honor are everything to the eldrin. They use shame and humiliation to maintain order in their ranks."

I rub my fingers across a smooth curl in the handrail, my heart twisting at his words. "Which is why my grandfather would've shunned me."

Lucas nods his head in agreement. "It's all he understood. Eldrin don't marry for love, nor are they moved by emotion, so when your mother became pregnant by someone of lesser standing, it was an insult to your grandfather personally and a disgrace publicly." He steps away from the edge and walks toward the bridge's center.

I follow him, frowning. "But you said Madrigal built the villages and helped you. They must have some emotion, some care for others."

He's thoughtful. "They have feelings, yes, but they take their nobility seriously. Too seriously, if you ask me." He shrugs. "From infancy, the children learn to put honor and idealism ahead of their emotions. They don't play as other children do. They are made to be studious in all they do." We reach the end of the bridge and descend the stairs.

Large trees and rocky hills rise on my left, and colorful flowers and bushes full of fruit on my right. Hills jut out before us with grass so green it almost hurts my eyes. Through it all runs the river, sometimes narrow enough to step over. It snakes into the distance as far as I can see in all directions.

There are several paths, much like the animal trails in forests, just wide enough for one person to walk through. Memories of walking with Mother to gather mushrooms and berries flit through my mind and squeeze my heart. "I can't imagine not being able to play as we did in the forest behind our cottage. I always felt safe, though Mother was constantly watchful." I smile sadly at Lucas. "I now know why she was always so careful and attentive."

His chuckle is light. We follow a path that's the widest one to our right. "Those were the best years of my life, better than the village beneath the mountain even. You're right. We were allowed to be children for a short time. It was wonderful, wasn't it?"

My cheeks stretch with a smile. "It was." Plants I've never seen before grow unheeded, dotting the ground in a wild mix of colors and scents. We come across a strange-looking tree, the limbs spooling from the center in arm-like branches. Ivy grows thick across the trunk and limbs. Blue, star-shaped flowers bloom in abundance among the waxy leaves. A scent sweeter than ten pastries fills the air. "This is like the star on the cavern walls, isn't it?" I ask, lifting one vine to look closer at it.

He eyes the tree and pulls the maps out. Besides the first tree labeled "Risan" are stars. Lucas plucks a flower and hands it to me. "It's the Star of the Kinsman. The first doorway past Tenebris."

"Truly? It does smell wonderful." The star is blue, darker on each of the eight-pointed tips, and then fades to a silver-white on the inside. My fingers stick with the milk that leaks out of the stem.

"Yes, they're quite rare. Like I said in the cavern, that sticky sap is mixed with other ingredients to create oil the clerics use. It was also sold by peddlers on Anavrin as a healing ointment." He wipes my fingers off with the hem of his shirt.

The grass and foliage thin out, replaced by spikier plants growing out of dirt and rocks. The river cuts a curving path, and though the plants aren't as lush, there are still many different kinds of flora to behold.

Our path leads to another tree, almost as large as the Zoe Tree. It, too, is in full bloom with orange flowers in bunches of three. They are a pleasing scent but not as strong or sweet as the star tree. Lucas glances again at the maps. There's a bundle of three circles and the title "Pallasea" next to it. "Anavrin should be the next doorway."

"So, these trees are doorways to other kingdoms?" I rub a hand across Pallasea's thick bark.

"Yes, and the relics are magically linked to each doorway. That's why this and the last doorway did not light up for entry. If we wanted to enter a different kingdom, we would've needed a different relic, according to the kingdom." Lucas lifts his hand with the ring. "Anavrin should light up when we reach it, much like the tree in Tenebris lit up when we were close by." He leads me past the tree, and we walk for several minutes without speaking.

"What different kinds of relics are there?" I ask.

He shrugs. "I don't know. The clerics keep them secret. These rings were synchronized with Anavrin and enabled us to enter Tenebris, but I'm unsure how it was done. It could be eldrin magic, something I never knew. Cadence only shared with me the basics in case I needed to return with you should something happen to her."

My heart twists. Another shadow flits past the corner of my eye. I jerk to the left to try to catch what it is and bump into Lucas. My hands tingle and flicker with blue energy. "My apologies, I thought I saw something again." I shake my hands to stop the tingling, but though it lessens, it doesn't go away completely.

Lucas stops and looks over the endless landscape. Trees dot the land sporadically in every direction. Some grow in great clumps, while others are large and stand-alone. The river cuts a meandering path through it all like a blue string. There's no sound of wind, flutter of wings, or scurry of small feet anywhere. Even the water nearby is calm and silent. "Do you notice there are no sounds of animals here?"

Lucas narrows his eyes to slits. "Now that you mention it, that does seem a bit strange."

I turn in each direction, fighting a sense of dread. As my anxiety heightens, my hands glow brighter. "Was it this quiet when we entered the passage?"

20

Lucas is serious as he glances back at me. His eye twitches. "I was too busy to notice. And our first time, it was a harried trip. I only recall Cadence being nervous at how long it was taking us to find Tenebris, though she kept reassuring me that everything was all right. But I must admit I feel prickles along my bones just now." He rubs the back of his neck with his free hand.

The light which seemed to come from everywhere dims. Fog swirls in great clouds, and an icy wind billows through the plants, bending them low.

Lucas unrolls his map again. He checks the markings against our surroundings. The wind makes it hard for Lucas to keep the parchment still. I clutch his arm, desiring his steady warmth.

"Would we not have noticed if anyone else entered the Zoe Tree?" Panic rushes through me. "Should we return to Tenebris?" My throat tightens and my words come out in a strangled whisper. My grip on the leather shoes tightens. They're not soaked now, so I slip them back on. Though the path had been smooth, there were bushes with thorns and rocks here and there, and my stockings won't give me much protection if we need to run.

Lucas frowns as he studies the map. "We're too far in to go back. Anavrin's the next doorway, so it's close." He tucks the maps in his belt again and grasps my hand in his. It's sweaty, revealing he's as disconcerted as I am.

The air crackles around us. The breeze whips my hair around and the silver ends sting my face. They're still damp. Though, with the wind, it won't take long before they're dry and a tangled mess again. Without my hood, the best I can do is loosely braid and secure it inside my collar.

Hand in hand, we continue.

The dusty landscape turns lush once again and the new overlarge, shiny-smooth leaves dance in the wind. The trees are taller, wider around, and grow in clumps of threes or fours. Hair on my nape prickles, and I can't help but sense there's something besides us here. My hands still twitch with a halo of blue and my gut buzzes like a hive of disturbed bees.

An explosion bursts in the air, and I'm airborne without wings. Brush breaks my fall onto the rocky path as I land. Cuts sting across my exposed arms and I grimace against the pain.

Lucas, likewise, is knocked off his feet beside me.

A mighty winged bird squawks above us. No, it's not a bird. The body is long, and the tail is not feathered. There doesn't seem to be any plumage on it at all. In the space of a blink, it's gone. Completely gone.

"What—?" I hear a zing and then catch a flash of red. Out of instinct, I raise my hands an instant before Lucas yells in pain. Fire, like hot coals, sweeps through my body.

I scream, and a sphere of blue surrounds us, not unlike the light that protected me at the cottage. However, Lucas is on the ground, twitching and writhing, his arms across his chest.

Light, like a rope, is wrapped tightly around him. There are no ropes on me that I can see, but the burning lingers in my muscles.

Waves of cold air swirl in the warm atmosphere. Rain mists around us, and lightning cracks above.

I kneel and reach out to touch the light-ropes, but whatever it is snaps at my hand. It scalds my skin, leaving a blister behind. My hands brighten, and as they do, the pain disappears. Lucas continues to convulse. I glance around but see nothing, no one.

"Lucas?" I yell to be heard over the wind while jerking my head back and forth to see what the danger is. He doesn't answer me but keeps whimpering. My shaking hands are now bright blue. Fear, hot and heavy, churns in my stomach. My eyes are over-warm and I blink, but the sensation doesn't go away.

A shadow steps out from behind one of the immense trees. There's a wide grin across my father's cruel face. Behind him are four of the beasts. They stand heaving as if they'd just run a great distance. Foamy drool drips to the ground from each of their menacing jaws.

Fury replaces my terror.

"Thought you'd escape me, didn't you?" Thoron's hands radiate red light like a flash of lightning, and it whirls around them in a spinning ball. Darkness, which flows over him like smoke from wet wood, wavers over his body.

My heart sputters. Gusts whip at us in every direction now, and I struggle to stand. I wonder how he got here before us, but I'm more concerned about Lucas. Rage blooms in my gut. "What did you do to him?" I yell to be heard, my jaws clenched. It's all I can do not to uproot trees and crush him and his ghastly beasts.

Lucas yells, but his words are incoherent as his body

twitches. His eyes open wide, wider than they've ever been, and all I can see are the whites.

Bone-deep dread makes me shake. I've never wanted to strike out at someone as I do at this moment. There's a storm inside me that matches the storm gusting through the passage and it's growing. I clench my hands into fists, my fingernails digging into my palms.

Thoron grins at me and raises one brow. His dark eyes are hard, calculating. His hair with the gray streak thrashes around his head. "Just a simple hex."

Beside me, Lucas stops twitching so I glance down. It's not only that he's stopped twitching. He's lying lifeless in his bird form on the ground. "Lucas!" My lungs seize and I grab him. I can feel his heart still beating in his chest, but he's not moving.

"Undo it. Now!" Wind buffets Thoron almost as if I sent it to knock him over. However, he stays standing, a frown upon his face. My hands tingle like I've laid on them too long.

Thoron lets out a condescending laugh. "I think not, dear daughter. Give yourself up, and I'll free your admirer." He stands in front of the tree as if we're having a normal conversation about the weather.

I knew Thoron would be the kind of person who would use Lucas to manipulate me. There've been so many in my past who tried to make me obedient by threatening something I care about. What Thoron doesn't know is that I'm not afraid of him. The only thing I'm terrified about is what his hex is doing to Lucas.

Lucas flutters in my hands, his sleek feathers soft against my skin. *"Don't do it, my lady. You can't trust him. He's a liar."* I'm relieved to hear Lucas speak and hurry to communicate before Thoron flings more magic our way. *"I have no intention of doing anything that man asks. Are you all right?"*

"I can't seem to change myself back, but other than that, yes, I'm fine."

His tone doesn't convince me.

Thoron lifts and swings his hands rhythmically as he chants something too low for me to hear.

"Can you tell what Thoron's doing?" I clutch Lucas gently to my chest, wishing for a way out that won't injure him further. The balls that swirl around Thoron's hands connect and grow into a much larger ball of red, crackling lightning. They light up the gruesome beasts which stand idly behind him.

"No, but it can't be good, especially if he isn't trying to sic the beasts on us. He probably wants you unharmed, at least physically, for whatever he has planned. The doorway isn't far. We need to move closer to the other side of the tree he's standing near. I can see the outline of the doorway to Anavrin on the other side."

Thoron throws the ball at me before I can catch a glimpse of the doorway, so I duck and roll, keeping Lucas tucked close to me. I'm careful not to crush him, but I'm not very graceful. My hair crackles and the heat of my father's hex singes the ends, but my blue, glowing sphere stops it from more harm. *"Should I change to a bird?"*

We're closer to the doorway and Lucas furiously darts his head about. There's nothing nearby to use as a weapon. Nothing but trees, dirt, and plants. *"I don't know if we can open Anavrin's door as birds."*

Another ball of red flashes and hits my sphere. I turn in time to see it bounce off. I grin as Thoron has to dodge so it doesn't hit him instead. Now's my chance. I stand and run past the tree, Lucas still in my hands. Two more hexes hit the sphere. It must be weakening, though, because the last one pinches at my back like the bite of a whip.

"I don't know how much longer I can keep this up." I pant as I run between shiny-leaved bushes with thorns and thick-barked trees. Their branches whip around in the wind, which turns icy, and fingers of lightning crack from above. One of the strikes lands near us. Startled, I step too close to one bush and it catches my dress. I stumble, dropping Lucas. I'm on my knees gasping for air, my dress still snagged in the thorns. The thorns are half the length of my fingers and clutch the fabric of my worn dress like a fist. Dirt clouds the air and gets into my mouth. I choke and spit it out.

The doorway glows like the one from Tenebris, outlining the opening. It's two trees away from where we are on the ground. They have massive trunks two-carriage lengths wide. However, the entry is close enough to hasten to if I can distract Thoron. I grasp at anything that comes to mind.

The next hex Thoron throws at us makes my skin prickle like needles under my skin. The sphere still protects us, but I don't think I can take another hit. Lucas is ahead of me on the ground, fluffing the dirt from his feathers where he rolled after I fell. With determination, I yank my dress free from the bush, ripping the bottom hem irreparably. I stand and turn to face my father. My eyes heat up again as anger rushes through my veins.

"Stop!" I raise my hand to pick my father up like I had Lucas. It would usually be invisible, but this time my calling flashes like a blue hand. Thoron swiftly bats it aside. It hits one of his beasts which yelps and is knocked hard to the side. The beast lands against a tree trunk but also into some thorny bushes. It yelps more as it thrashes against the bush. The other beasts hunch as if waiting to be beaten. Thoron sends a red-whip toward the fallen beast, tightens it around the neck, and pulls. The beast's head snaps and the body droops to the ground, a heap of claws, fur, and scarred leather skin. A glowing cloud hovers above the beast before swiftly flowing into my father.

Horrified, I take several steps back—toward the doorway. My chest pounds. I have to get away from this evil man! Or, I determine deep in my soul, destroy him. I wish I could, in this moment, but I'm not strong enough.

Thoron's snarling mad now, much like his deformed beasts. He swings his arm low and red flashes toward us. It's another rope, and it's coming straight for me.

"Look out, Tambrynn." Lucas's voice booms in my mind.

My blue circle of protection is almost gone, so I throw myself sideways, trying to avoid it. "Please, Kinsman, save us," I scream.

The blue light around me dissipates as Thoron's hex strikes the sphere before I get halfway to the ground. Pain explodes all over my body. I lay twitching. Darkness creeps over me like ants crawling on my skin, and fingers of agony press against my mind. I raise shaking hands to my head, willing the torment away.

Fire explodes near us. Thoron screams. My limbs grow weak and the hold on my head intensifies.

"Focus, my lady. I remember your mother saying focus is the key to using magic. You can send whatever hex your father has back on him if you concentrate on it."

I nod. I focus my inner ability on the foreign magic. It's red and malevolent, like Thoron. The fire nearby crackles, its smoke clouding the air. I flinch when my blue energy grasps my father's vile spell. Suddenly, Thoron's magic slips, and I envision the hex spinning back toward him. I hold that picture in my mind, gather what's left of my ability, and imagine flinging it back toward Thoron.

When I open my eyes, I see the hex, surrounded by blue light, flying from me toward my father. Strangely, his clothes are smoking as if they'd been lit on fire and then extinguished.

My returned hex is too quick for Thoron to avoid, and it

hits him square in the chest. He barks out a piggish squeal as he's knocked backward and into the tree he was hiding behind when he first attacked us. His beasts whine and dazedly glance about, almost as if coming out of a trance. One shambles off quickly. The other two fidget as if they don't know what to do.

It starts to rain pellets of sleet. *"Lightning, fire, and ice. I think the passage is unhappy we're using magic. Let's get out of here before it gets worse,"* Lucas implores.

I don't wait to see if Thoron gets back up. I grab Lucas, and with my head down and free arm protecting him, I sprint to the doorway. Something hisses behind me, and pain explodes all over my body, slamming me against the wooden doors.

My head throbs. My hands are empty. I've lost Lucas. Dull ringing echoes in my ears, but the storm is coming full tilt at me. I put my hand against the doorway to stand, and the wood cracks beneath it. It splits open into two doors like before.

Lucas wobbles before me, fluffing his feathers and tottering around. Without hesitating, I pull open one side of the doorway, toss Lucas through, and jump after him.

PART TWO

21

A bright moon in a sky full of stars shines down on us as we tumble out of Anavrin's Zoe Tree. There's a mild breeze ripe with the scents of saltwater, fish, and something like a dung heap. The doorway is slowly closing behind us, and I know it won't be long before Thoron follows us into this new kingdom.

It's dark, and my eyes take a moment to adjust to the moonlight. Shadows of trees, as well as leafy bushes, surround the Zoe Tree's hill. Just like on Tenebris, the tree spreads itself out wide, as if reaching for something. Rushing water echoes, but I don't see much beyond the dusky horizon.

The ringing in my ears is curiously gone, but my body still aches as if I'd just been physically beaten instead of being hit with magic. "Lucas, are you okay to fly? Do you know which direction we need to go?"

He staggers around the base of the tree. *"I recall we took a boat from the mainland to this island."*

Panic grips me, and I take in the new kingdom while

glancing back at the doorway. "An island? How are we supposed to get off? Can you fly?"

His wings spread out, and he jumps. He hovers, his wings faltering, before dropping to the ground. He tries again and almost makes it high enough to reach my head. *"I might be able to, but not right away."*

The tree trembles. "Well, we need to get out of here before Thoron manages to make it through the doorway." I concentrate on changing, but no tingles come. Nothing happens. "I can't seem to change either. What'd Thoron do to us?"

"I'm not versed in hexes, but perhaps it will wear off now that we're in Anavrin."

How long would that take? I pick him up. There's a path from my left side that crosses in front of the tree and spans down to my right and out of sight. A forest runs the length of the hill where we stand and ends on a rocky edge. Branches from the Zoe Tree reach across the area in both directions, towering over us inland and toward the ledge.

I shuffle to the cliff, my shoes pinching my feet and the cuts on my arms throbbing. Though it's night, there are still birds diving into the water, seemingly for a tasty fish meal. These are certainly not the Narrow Cliffs, but the drop-off is too perilous to try to climb down. "Does anyone live on this island? Should we take the trail?"

"Thoron may assume we'd take the path since it would no doubt be the easiest way away from the tree. There were a few mixed-race fishermen. See, the beacon light from the watchtower in the distance? It keeps sailors from running ashore in the shallows which surround the island. The nomad fishermen kept their boats there before. Possibly we can borrow one and make it to the mainland before daybreak, though I'm unsure what time it truly is."

A flash splits the darkness and I duck, afraid it's Thoron.

However, it's just the beacon. It moves in a slow circle atop a dark tower, much like an enormous, one-sided lantern. Heart beating hard and fast, I study the terrain. There are hip-high, long-leafed plants and trees with tall trunks that end in massive, finger-like leaves on the tops.

Dirt and rocks dance at my feet and the ground rumbles. The doorway glows and then goes dark. We need to hurry.

"My lady. Can you try to change to an animal, say a dog, perhaps? That would give us a chance to travel through the foliage and allow you to scent and see better."

I carry Lucas as I rush to the least brushy area. I grimace at his suggestion. "I can smell the fish and whatever else the wind is carrying fine as a girl. Besides, you would need to be able to stay with me if I can't hold onto you."

"When you get past the edge of the trees, try it. I'll hold onto your fur with my claws and beak if necessary."

"I'll try." The Zoe Tree shudders again, and I'm sure I hear the door creak open. I hurry into the brush, knowing that the beasts might be able to pick up my scent no matter what I do. Moonlight and shadows dapple across the foliage, but it's bright enough to avoid most of the plants and I can identify the scaly trunks of the trees.

I put Lucas down and close my eyes. I picture the raggedy dog that one of my masters owned. It wasn't much to look at, but it was the smartest dog I'd ever known. Much smarter than its master. But no tingles come. Nothing signals any kind of change.

I open my eyes and look down at Lucas. It's dark and his form blends into the scenery. I hear yelling behind me. It's Thoron, though I've come far enough that I can't make out what he's saying. "I'm not able to, Lucas. Are you sure you can't fly?" At least one of us could get away.

"I can try again." His wings flutter in the leaves.

My hands glow blue. Thoron must be getting closer. I stuff them into my armpits to hide the light. Lucas continues to flit around for a moment before my impatience forces me to catch hold of him.

I scramble through the forest, trying to make as little sound as possible, but failing. I'm not even sure if I'm going in the right direction. Possibly I should've tried to climb down the cliffside instead.

The thick leaves are as sharp as razors, so I hold my arms above my waist to keep Lucas from getting sliced to pieces. Large flowers pop out of the knife-edged growth here and there, a kind of dangerous beauty. Luckily, my stockings keep my legs safe from the offending foliage. I hold Lucas in one hand while trying to clutch at anything to keep my balance as I fumble around the thick vegetation. The ground is uneven, with roots that curl slightly above the soil from the strange-looking trees. This can't be a forest. It doesn't resemble anything I've known before.

I gather my ability and push my will into my next words. *"I wish we could fly!"* Warmth radiates from my hands. It flashes and dies. Lucas twitches in my grasp, and fear sinks into my bones. I wrench him back to my chest, cradling him as shame and fear kindle in my gut. Oh, Kinsman, what have I done?

"I'm sorry, Lucas. Please be all right." His trembles intensify. I stop and clutch him tighter, afraid he's having some kind of episode. He stills, his meager weight heavier on my heart than my hand. The scent of flowers mixed with the rank air almost chokes me as I wait. Tears sting my eyes.

There's a rustle in the trees behind us. A howl pierces the air and scatters several birds. My instinct is to run, but if Lucas is hurt, would I injure him more?

My fingers continue to tingle and glow. I wish I had some

gloves to cover them, but since I don't, I clutch them, and therefore Lucas, tightly to my chest.

"Oh, Kinsman, please help us!" I whisper as I stagger through the foliage, the forest angling down into a valley. It's dark enough now that it takes me by surprise and I stumble into one of the trees. My left side throbs from what is surely another bruise. I stop to catch my breath and listen.

A crackling roar startles me. Is that one of the beasts? It can't be. It sounds different. Bigger.

Wind kicks up around me. Patchy clouds disappear as the beacon light circles around, but nothing indicates an approaching storm. I cradle Lucas carefully, but he starts to jerk and move. My heart stutters for a moment and I fear he might thrash around and out of my hands. "Hold on," I murmur.

A shadow moves over the trees above me. Another shrieking rumble makes me hunch down out of fear.

"*What is that?*" Lucas sounds groggy.

"Are you okay?" I whisper, relief loosening the pinch in my shoulders.

"*I think so. But what's going on?*"

"I'm unsure. Don't move. If I drop you, I might not be able to see you well enough to pick you back up."

"*Tambrynn.*" An unfamiliar voice speaks into my mind. It's neither male nor female in tone, but it's powerful enough to send pain shooting through my brain. "*Stay down.*"

I cower, more from discomfort than fear, and chills race across my skin. The air holds incredible power, like when lightning strikes. I don't recognize this voice, but whatever it is, it's powerful. I flatten myself to the ground, curling my body around Lucas.

"*My lady, what is it?*" Lucas asks. He twitches in my hands, so I loosen my grip.

"Did you not hear that voice?" Faint wisps of acrid smoke prick my nose.

Before Lucas can answer me, a blast of fire explodes, igniting the sky in a straight route from whence we came. I brave the blazing heat to catch a glimpse of an immense creature with wings that span farther than I can see. Flames spew from its monstrous, pointy head. The orangish-gold underside of it glows like cracks in the glass of a lantern.

High-pitched, horrid screams erupt behind us. The creature circles, and I glimpse its tail swishing. It's bigger than any animal I've ever seen and eclipses the tops of the trees with its size. The beacon light catches its red, orange, and gold body, making it appear as if it is fire itself come to life.

"What is that? Can you see anything?" Panic laces Lucas's words.

Leaves and limbs crack and rain down not far from where we hide. Ash and shattered debris from the trees float in the dim light. I turn to view the line of fire.

Three beasts flail about, their flesh and hair aflame. Nausea twists my stomach even before the smell hits me. Burning flesh. The flames are mirrored in Lucas's dark eyes. I turn and heave on the other side of the tree we lay next to. It has been hours since we'd eaten at the ball, and there's little that comes up. Even so, bile burns my throat.

Smoke clouds the area, choking the air and me with it. Brush and bushes are alight with flames. I sweep Lucas up and dash through the valley and back up the next rise. Thoron is nowhere to be seen, and my hands no longer glow blue.

"Tambrynn." The voice returns. *"It is safe. Thoron has retreated. For now, anyway."*

"Kinsman?" Even as I say it, I doubt. However, who else would be able to speak into my mind except for Lucas. And it wasn't him.

"*Kinsman I am not. My name is Audhild, the dragon of the Gray Mountains.*" The shadow returns, the formless creature sailing over the trees. It blocks the moonlight so I cannot see it clearly. "*I have been sent to ensure your safety.*"

"*Tambrynn, who are you talking to?*" Concern edges Lucas's voice, almost drowned out by the power behind the other voice.

"The creature says its name is Audhild, a dragon of the Gray Mountains. They, he or she, said Thoron is gone." Though the name is unfamiliar, it is stated so clearly, I will probably not forget it for years to come. The shadow disappears again.

"*Gone or dead?*" he asks.

"Just gone."

Lucas grunts. "*As for that dragon. Are you quite certain?*" He jolts in my hand. "*They're not supposed to exist anymore. And I've never heard the name Audhild before. I wonder why you can hear it and I cannot.*" Lucas flits up, floats, and drops to the ground. He does this a couple of times until I catch him.

Chills bloom across my arms at how large the creature appears compared to Lucas. Lucas's magpie form would be like an ant trying to stop a trotting horse. "Stop, please. You'll wear yourself out."

I watch the shadow as it circles the trees in a snake-like pattern. "What are you, and who sent you?"

"*I am fierce. I am ice and extinction, fire and death. I am guard and guardian. Dragon is my genus. My master is one you cannot see or hear. I have been sent, however, by the beggar-thief of the Shrouded Mountains. I have a gift from him to help you on your journey. Catch.*" The dragon flies closer, revealing its great golden belly. It's rough, as if lined with stones of varying sizes. It unfurls a leg and drops something from its wickedly sharp-looking claws.

I reach out in time to catch it. It's a braided cord with a

stone woven in the center. I'd joked to Lucas about slaying a dragon. But instead, we'd just been saved by one. Mother's fairy tales never said dragons were benevolent. "What is this? And why would a beggar-thief send you to save me—us?"

"The necklace was your mother's. Put it on, and don't take it off. It saved her when the mage attacked before you were born. It will protect you. My debt to the beggar-thief is now repaid. Thoron has been held off for a brief time. You are free to go." Audhild's snaking path lengthens, going higher and farther away, allowing the moon's light to shine through the trees again.

The necklace hums in my hand, an iridescent blue-green, though it's too dark to make out much of the details. "But that isn't answering my question."

"It is not for me to answer that question. You will find the beggar-thief in the hidden refuge of the sacred mountain. Flesh unto flesh. He shelters himself much like you've been hidden. If you go to him, he will not turn you away. He will be your strongest ally." The shadow disappears like smoke in the wind, there and then gone.

"Wait! What does that mean? I don't understand." I clasp the stone tight in my palm.

There is nothing but silence and the crackling of the dying fire left behind by the dragon.

22

The full moon is centered in the sky, which should mean it is high-eve. At least it would be on Tenebris. Without Audhild's shadow, and since a swath of the limbs and leaves had been torched by the dragon's fire, it is much easier to see through the heavy treetops.

Lucas flutters at my feet. *"My lady, what is going on? Where did the dragon go?"*

I glance back where the beasts lay like charred logs, their bodies smoking and scorched beyond recognition. It's an easier sight than before, to be sure, but it does nothing to ease my churning stomach.

"Audhild's gone. We are on our own." I put the necklace on and bend to pick up Lucas. The gem is warm against my skin, though I only held it a few moments, and its humming turns into a contented purr. I place my hand over the warm stone, curious.

"What was that you just put on, my lady?" He pecks at a knot in the woven cord.

I rub at it, the rough cord over the smooth rock. *"The*

dragon said it was Mother's. That it protected her from Thoron before I was born, and it will protect me now."

The feathers on Lucas's dark, bobbing head gleam dully in the moonlight as he studies it. *"Truly? It must be a talisman or a sacred amulet, then? Can you sense any magic in it?"*

"It hums much like a purring cat. It is curious the dragon would have something of my mother's to give me upon our arrival, isn't it?"

"Do you not believe the dragon?" Ending his study of the necklace, Lucas fluffs his feathers and settles into the palms of my hands. *"The old tales say that dragons don't lie. But I recall stories about dragons being just that—stories. So, yes, it is interesting to learn that they exist after all this time, and one turns up now. With gifts no less. Did Audhild say why?"*

I trudge through the forest away from the tree, toward the watchtower, hoping to find the boats Lucas spoke of. "I feel nothing dark coming from the necklace. The dragon spoke in riddles for the most part. It saved us because it owed some beggar-thief of the mountain a favor. Do you know who the beggar-thief is?"

"I don't recall hearing about a single beggar-thief of the mountain. Many of us, part djinn mainly, were beggars and thieves because of the hierarchy dealt down by the clerics. This must be someone new, or I would've heard tell of them before."

I stumble over a fallen log, catching Lucas before he rolls out of my hands. Luckily, the trees before us become sparser as I make my way through lush bushes, and it is easier to see what is underfoot.

A flash blazes over us, traveling in a circle. "What an interesting light."

"An old nomad tinkerer created the light from the unique fire rocks found in Bloodthorn Forest. The rocks travel down the Hevell River to this sea. Legend has it they are pieces of bones from long-

dead dragons that used to live in the forest. I'd never believed that until now. Having witnessed how large Audhild is, it may be true."

"Nor would I have believed in dragons if I hadn't seen it with my own eyes. I have to wonder if Audhild is the only one, though I must say I don't know that I want to be the one to find another." Shivers race across my skin at the thought.

"At least he was on our side. Head toward the light, and hopefully we'll find the boats."

It isn't long before I'm able to trudge my way out of the forest. The dirt becomes rock, and finally, we're out of the dark shadows of the trees. The watchtower is situated on a cliff not far from where the forest line ends. Atop the tower is a bowl holding a blue-green fire. The bowl appears to be suspended by a chain from the roof of the building and a silver platter slowly circles around the flames, sending out a pure white light.

I glance at the stone now, which emits a faint radiance. It is green-blue, much like the fire in the watchtower, and has a rusted-colored center with brighter thin red veins that thread out through the gem. The cord is braided black string woven around the stone, tied to capture the gem, and then wound into the necklace itself.

Between and below where we are and where the watchtower stands on a rock bluff is a flat beach area. There are five smallish square buildings along the shore which line up with five sailboats of differing sizes, nothing big enough for more than a few people at most. There is, however, a rowboat turned over on the sand not far from the other boats. It's much smaller.

I've never rowed in a boat before, nor have I ever been on a sailboat, and the masts looked to be more complicated than I can maneuver. "Let me try changing once more." I set Lucas down and close my eyes. A light barrage of tingles sweeps over my feet, but when I open my eyes, I haven't changed. I sigh, defeated.

"Perhaps you're too weak. I cannot change when I've been taxed too far." Lucas offers, sympathy lacing his words in my mind.

"Are you sure the boats are the only way of getting off the island? Can you try to change once more?" I know I sound weak, but I can't help it. The thought of taking a boat out in unknown waters has my hands sweating.

Lucas stands still, his neck feathers lifting with the light breeze coming off the shore. Seconds pass. *"I'm sorry, my lady. I can't change, either."*

I curse my father silently. "What if we stay hidden here until daylight?"

Lucas hops around the edge of the hill we stand on. There are few bushes and trees that grow here, though a couple of trees lean out of the hillside and over the sea. *"The fishermen take the boats out before sunrise and don't return until just before sunset. Though the rowboat might not be taken out to fish, it might be used to get from one spot on the island to another. And I don't trust that Thoron has retreated far, no matter what the dragon told you."*

He is right, of course. I don't necessarily trust Audhild either, even if the massive creature did save us from my father and give me my mother's necklace. I scoop Lucas back up and survey the edge of the hill we stand on. Eventually, I find a narrow, worn path down the side of the hill, meandering to the beach. Though the sea spray isn't as salty as the Black Sea on Tenebris, the air is ripe with the rotting smell of fish. It is the same rank odor I smelled before.

The fish bones and discarded scales piled around the thick, wooden tables near the buildings would be why. Buzzing bugs swarm around the waste. There's also a cat chewing on one particularly large skeleton. Its golden eyes glimmer at me before it growls and runs off with its meal. I've never seen such a slovenly display in any of the places I'd worked. Not even Farmer Tucker's kitchen, which had often been ransacked and left a mess by their sons, was this disgusting. I pucker my lips and hold my sleeve against my nose as I quickly move past them.

The rowboat looks almost as if it's sculpted from one massive tree trunk instead of hammered together with nails. It's heavy and has two benches with two oars that are smooth and darkened around the ends of the handle from wear. I'm relieved to see they're short, as if carved for a young child, so they may be easier for me to handle.

"What happens when we get to the mainland? How do we return the boat?" I ask quietly.

"*Why are you whispering?*" Lucas chuckles, and it comes out as a small *cackle*. "*The fishermen live across the island. There's no one around that I can tell.*"

"You may be used to thievery of sorts, but I am not." I raise my voice, but not by much. I don't want to be caught trying to abscond with someone's property. My hands shake more. "And you didn't answer my questions."

"*We will leave the boat tied at the harbor on the mainland. When they search for the rowboat, they'll find it and probably only miss it for a day or two. It will be fine.*"

I don't completely believe that, but I toss the oars in the boat and push it down to the rocky sand and into the water. Lucas hops over to me and I lift him into the boat to get settled before I try to enter. I glance around the sides, wondering how to do so without getting wet. Maybe if I got the boat to the edge of the water instead? I pull it back and step in. After I settle down to sit, I attempt to push us into the water. It doesn't work.

"I think you'll have to get into the water first." Lucas teeters back and forth on the opposite bench.

"But I don't know how to get in that way," I snap at him. I know it isn't Lucas's fault that we're in this situation. And it's mostly because of the exhaustion and unease of doing something I'm not familiar with. I sigh. "Sorry. Not your fault." I silently curse my father again and push the boat out farther into the rolling waves. Though the tide is slow, I can't help but be nervous. This is nothing like the serene river in the passage.

The water is up to my calves when I try to climb back into the boat, hands on the side and head first. It rocks and almost tips over. Lucas screeches and flaps around. I drop back down into the water and walk the boat back to the shallows. The boat rocks again this time, but I manage to get in and swing my legs over. My shoes, legs, and bottom of my torn dress are soaked now, but I'm in the boat and that's all that matters.

The boat moves gently back and forth as the tide pushes us back toward the shore. Now that I'm actually in the boat, I notice metal clamping hooks for the oars. I line the poles up on either side and place one into the curved metal. As I try to set the clamp to hold it in place on the first, the second one drops into the water. I scramble into the water to grab for it, and the boat heaves with me. Lucas clucks in protest.

I squeal when I land waist-deep in water, barely managing to keep the boat from tipping over completely. Luckily, I grasp hold of the floating instrument. The necklace sits crooked, the gem resting on my shoulder, so I tuck it inside my tunic for safekeeping. My silver hair reflects in the water, and the light from the watchtower flashes over us. Red rocks and shells glitter in the sand, making the water a pearlescent blood color. It's eerie, and I wish to be done and on the other shore.

Cold water seeps across my chest and wakes me up a bit. An old hand at getting in now, I make it over the side of the boat and slowly roll in. I catch my breath, drag the oar into the boat, and check to make sure the other is still beside me. My wet hair is a mess of tangles as I brush the clinging tresses from my chilled face, and only then do I remember. I haven't given much thought to my hair or eyes since the Ball. Lucas is right to leave while it's still dark. I want to groan, but I don't.

Carefully this time, I place the left oar in and clasp it. Then I lift the other one into the clamp and lock it in. I take a deep breath, proud that I manage that small feat. However, the boat is now sideways to the shore. I work with the oars to point us away from the island. Pushing one and then the other on the sand, I row the boat out of the shallows and into deeper water. My arms are already straining with the effort. "How am I going to do this?"

"The trick is to keep them even. If you pull too much on one side, we'll go around in circles." Lucas's dark bird-eyes glitter at me.

I hold back the impulse to stick my tongue out at him and pull them toward me, praying they're even as he said, but I hit more of the sand. We're not deep enough yet. I shove harder against the sandy bottom, and then we're bouncing much more as the waves come one after another toward the shore.

My heart races. Swimming in a docile stream is one thing. Trying to swim in the dark toward a shore I cannot see would be another. "Oh, Kinsman. Please help us!" I cry as I take my first pull without hitting the sand. We're propelled a couple of feet. I think I'm finally getting the hang of things when I push past a rope and a buoy, which also happens to line up with a wooden dock not far from where I row.

The wind hits me and as I yank on the right one. I pull harder to compensate. We spin halfway around. I jerk the left one back and the boat tips with my action. A wave, bigger now since we're in deeper water, hits the rowboat. It pushes us farther up and sideways. Lucas squawks and topples into the water. The boat rights itself as the wave rolls by, but there's another headed straight for the boat.

"Lucas!" I yell, trying to find where he landed. Water rushes over the side of the boat, tipping it over.

Seawater fills my mouth and nose, and the cold seeps deep into my bones and cramps my muscles. Sheer panic sweeps over me as I sink, unable to touch the bottom of the sea.

23

I flail in the water, my lungs protesting as I hold my breath. Then all my air escapes in a scream as something wraps around my legs. It clamps hold of me and instead of dropping down, I'm flung in the opposite direction with incredible strength and speed.

My head bobs above the water not far from the overturned boat. I choke and cough out the brackish water, flinging my arms out in panicked splashes. Something moves beneath me, bouncing me, steadying my strokes, and I am finally moving toward the boat instead of just splashing around. I recall stories of sea creatures big as ships, and I swing my arms in harried arcs until I reach the boat.

"Lucas!" My throat and nose are sore from the salty water. I cough more to clear my lungs. My teeth chatter as the chill from the water settles into my body.

"I'm right here, my lady." Lucas fluffs his damp feathers. He's calmly perched upon the overturned bottom of the rowboat. I'm sure he wasn't there when I surfaced.

Something, most likely a fish, brushes by my legs and

circles around me. It's either a giant one or a fabled sea creature I'd heard about that feasted upon sailors. My scream comes out ragged and I kick out to get it to go away. Holding the side of the overturned boat, I glance around only to realize I can't see anything in the dark water.

"My lady, are you having a fit of some kind? A muscle spasm, possibly?" Lucas darts back and forth on the boat's bottom.

It takes me a minute to find my composure once more. "I'm fine." I pray silently that I haven't lost the oars, or I will be swimming back to shore for sure. And I'm unsure I could manage if I experienced another brush with whatever was in the water with me again. "You'll have to find another place to stand if I'm to turn this hollowed-out log over."

Lucas fluffs his feathers out again. *"I flew up here from the water. I may be able to stay in flight until you get it turned back over. Otherwise, I'll have to perch on your head."*

I don't hesitate. I want nothing more than to get out of the water and back into the boat. "Let's hope it's the first, shall we? Here I go." Luckily the side I'm at has the oar held by the clasps, so I grab hold of them and heave the boat. I call to the last tingle of ability in my gut and *push*.

I fear it's not enough as water haloes around me and the boat teeters at the halfway point. I groan, fearing I don't have enough strength or ability left to try again should it fall back over. Lucas flies, claws out, at the top side, and luckily, it's enough to tip it over. The boat swings and falls quickly right side up, smacking the water and sending saltwater splashing into my face.

I rub the excess water from my eyelashes. Water pools inside the boat. I pull myself over the side slowly, careful not to capsize it once again, and flop half on one of the benches and half on the wet bottom. I'm gasping as if I've been running, and I lay there catching my breath.

"Are you all right?" Lucas totters across the bottom of the boat and flutters up to the bench I'm sprawled across.

"I can't do this." I twist myself around to sit and stare out at the dark waters glinting with moonlight. The waves aren't batting us around quite so much this far out. Something tickles my cheek and I jerk to brush it off. It's a strand of seaweed, and I clutch a hand to my chest. It's then that I comprehend I've lost the necklace.

"Oh—oh no!" I cry out. Between whatever was in the water swimming next to me, the fishy smell still wafting from the tables on the beach, and losing my mother's necklace, my stomach seizes in my distress. I retch into the water, purging myself of the small amount of saltwater I've ingested. My heart thumps painfully in my chest as I throw the offending piece of seaweed back into the water as well. I slump and restate breathlessly, "I can't do this."

"I'm sorry about the necklace, my lady. There's no way to retrieve it now. It's too dark. Unless you want to go back overboard to try?" It's not as much a question as a statement.

Below me, I am sure I see something swim by the side of the boat. Fear clutches my heart and I sputter. *"No, thank you."*

Lucas hops up on my lap and gently rubs his beak on my arm. *"If it helps, I did row you and your mother across this same bay when I was but eight years old. You can do this. I know you can."*

I pat his sleek head and then stop. He's not a pet or an actual bird. Well, he is, but—I'm so adrift right now, in more ways than one. Not so long ago, I found out magic exists. Then I learned my father was evil and would kill me if given the chance. And finally, I traveled to a new kingdom only to find a fire-breathing dragon. He gave me a gift from my mother, and I lost it in less time than it takes to drown.

I've prided myself on being capable despite all of the persecution from others about my hair, my eyes, and the strange events that happen due to my uncontrollable ability. I tried never to give anyone a reason to think I couldn't live up to whatever my post required. Yet here I am floundering with something that seems so simple. Just row a boat. Once I start to giggle, I can't stop, and my stomach aches when I finally manage to control myself. "I'm going mad."

"I know everything here is foreign and, since I am unable to change, this is exceedingly more difficult than planned. Rowing a boat isn't a familiar task. But I know you can do this, Tambrynn." The moon makes his blue-black feathers glow, highlighting the white bib of feathers beneath his chin. *"You didn't even lose a paddle when it tipped. That must be a good sign."*

My chuckle is sardonic. "I don't believe in good signs. Only bad ones."

His laugh is sincere. *"Like when you saw me at the manor? I know you thought me to be an omen of bad luck."*

The boat bobs gently, and I'm tired enough to want to curl up and sleep. "Well, you repeatedly were. I always ended up moving from one employment to another when you showed up. At least until that last time." So much has changed since the carriage wreck in the forest. I bury my head in my knees, hugging them as if doing so will help me regain my sanity. I take a deep breath and let it out.

I think of Mother and her able, positive attitude. She'd encourage me to do this. I close my eyes and recall her voice, so strong and sure. My heart fills when it comes to me readily, just as I remember it. A smile tugs my frowning lips upward. I lift my head back up, bolstered enough to try again. "Okay. Let's go. How far is it to the mainland?"

"Not far. Go straight and it won't take long to see it."

I grab both of the oars and, after a moment to rally my determination, begin to row. I start slowly, like a rusty hinge on an old door. I work to keep it even. However, when I pull too hard on one side without meaning to, just like Lucas stated earlier, the boat heads in the other direction. I groan each time because it takes more effort to work back in the same direction.

Something bumps the bottom of the boat, twirling it back the way it should've gone.

I gasp and clutch the oars tight in my hands, but I can't detect anything around us or in the water. I glance behind me to gauge how far we've gone and whimper when I see it isn't as far as the burn in my arms indicates. Lucas stands on the bench in front of me, his bird-eyes sharp, scanning the waters on both sides of the boat as it creeps across the rippling water.

Eventually, I succeed in getting in a rhythm like I would when I'd scrub or clean out chimney flues. Though my arms ache, I'm used to pushing through the pain to get the job done. Or at least I used to be. We make progress as the flashing light from the watchtower widens and dims as it sweeps over us.

After what seems like forever, the dark outline of a small pier with a few boats appears. A small village slumbers beyond the pier with only a glimpse of a couple of lights or fires hidden behind windows. "Is this it?" I ask eagerly but breathlessly.

"Yes! I told you it wasn't far."

I don't argue with Lucas over what constitutes far. I push harder, longing to reach the other shore. The silhouette expands as we grow closer with each stroke I take. Light from the watchtower no longer flickers in the corner of my eye, and I'm heartened that we are almost there.

Until the water closer to the shore becomes choppier. My arms protest now with trying to keep the strokes even and strong. Numbness bites at my fingers and my wrists ache with the effort. Even my shoulders are cramping.

Lucas hops back and forth, agitated. *"We're drifting, my lady. We need to go to your right more, or we won't reach the harbor on the mainland. We don't want to end up stuck in the Sunken Forest along the shore."*

I heave and pull against the tide. "What is that?" I ask through gritted teeth.

He hesitates. *"It's a section of forest submerged below water. Very dangerous."*

Now he tells me this? "Shouldn't the tide be pushing us toward the shore, not down the side of the shore?" *Like it had on the island.* I don't speak it aloud, though. Rowing alone is enough effort.

My strokes weaken. The next pull is slower, shallower. I'm so tired. The current pushes against us and we drift sideways. I stop to catch my breath and groan when the front of the boat turns to point in the wrong direction. My arms, burning from exertion, lay useless at my sides. We are at the mercy of the flow now.

We move quickly along the shore in a diagonal line, both toward and alongside it. Something catches and scratches against the underside of the boat, startling me. We'll be lucky to make it to shore with all of the debris I see poking out of the water. Several trees lean out over the water as if waiting to dive in. The Sunken Forest widens as we drift away from our destination. I haven't the strength to swim ashore, let alone take care to keep Lucas from drowning.

Not that I want to end up in the water again. The thought of the fish that touched my leg and the bump on the bottom of the boat heightens my fear. "I recall stories of man-eating fish in the sea on Tenebris. Are there any such creatures here on Anavrin?"

"Worse, my lady."

My pulse races as my imagination takes control. "Lucas, what do I do? I cannot row any longer." My voice is hoarse though I haven't been screaming. My mouth is dry, however, from breathing heavily through it and from the salty water earlier. Water splashes over each of the sides now as the boat rushes along the shore. The dark shapes of branches poke out of the water, giving me visions of monsters with tentacles and sharp teeth.

His head bobs back and forth. *"If you could grab hold of the tree limbs, maybe we can crawl our way across the shallows until we reach a spot where we can disembark. Just ... just be careful what branches you take."*

"Why?" Panic forces my voice higher than normal, but Lucas doesn't answer.

I swing the oars inside the boat, the clasps holding them in place, and sit on the side closest to the shore, trying not to tip the boat over. A branch is coming to my left, but it's on the wrong side, so I let it pass. We're carried along, and I see another limb to my right. I reach down and grab it. The branch lifts out of the water, but it's attached to something with clothing.

It's not a branch but an arm that appears to be reaching out to me. It's part of a decayed body wearing a dark jacket with buttons. I scream and drop the arm. Have the dead been unleashed to greet us? The body sinks slowly back into the water. I rub my hand down my dress, wishing to be rid of the sight.

"What is it?" Lucas flutters over to the side where I'm holding my sleeve over my mouth to keep the screams that are building from escaping and drawing any unwanted attention toward us.

My heart is pounding in my chest, and though I'm chilled, sweat breaks out along my forehead. Hot tears gather in my eyes.

"Tambrynn?" Lucas reaches out a wing and his feathers brush softly across my arm.

I thrash my head back and forth. Though we've bumped along the submerged logs and timber and we're past the dead body, it takes me a moment to speak. "It wasn't a branch." I squeeze my eyes tight, unable to say what it was.

Lucas dances across the bench and jumps up to the side to look over. His head turns one way and then the other. *"I was afraid of that. Was it—?"*

"A dead body." I choke out the words.

"It is as I feared. We need to get ashore, but not here. It's too dense. No telling what else is in the water. It's shallow enough to try and use one of the oars to guide us down the shore a bit." His voice, though in my mind, rings with urgency.

I take the oar and unlatch the hook. I'm glad it has a larger, rounded end so I can grasp it easier in my shaking hands. I'd do anything now to not end up back in the water. It's still too deep to touch the bottom with the oar, so I use it to push against what truly are sunken trees, but progress is painfully slow.

Exhausted, both physically and emotionally, I close my eyes. "Please, Kinsman," I mutter the quick plea for help. A warmth gathers inside of my gut—my ability! It had been missing since Thoron threw the first curse at us in the passage.

I reach out one of my hands and *call* for a strong limb. TREE limb, I amend in my mind. Within a couple of seconds, a rough object touches my hand. I open my eyes and see a bark-covered limb. My squeal is a mixture of relief and joy. The branch is lodged solidly in the seabed, and I *call* for another and another until we are in shallower water and I can navigate along the shore.

Night lightens to day. I can now see the landscape better. Trees similar to the ones from the island grow here and there along the shore but are joined by taller, thicker trees, more like those that grew on Tenebris. I'm overjoyed to see something familiar. There are thick-leaved bushes and plants that cover the shore in spots, but there's also grass greener than anything I've seen before. The hill cliff next to the boat slopes down until it becomes a flat space to land the boat. Blessed relief rushes through me.

The valley is wide enough for three boats to land if necessary before the land rises into hilly banks again. There are ridges and drag marks that show this isn't the first time boats have landed here. I steer the rowboat using the oar with what remains of my last strength, and finally the boat bumps onto the sandy shore. Birds wake and begin their morning chatter. Many are chitters or songs I've never heard before. Several fly from one tree to another or flock to the dewy ground to hunt for their morning meals.

I tumble out of the boat, landing in ankle-deep water. It's clear enough to see down to the sparkling rocks and sand. I take a reassured breath and drag the boat as far as I can ashore, which isn't too far, but far enough that it hopefully wouldn't end up afloat again.

I flop down to the ground, more tired than I recall being in a long time. My arms are like the clear bone jelly bought from the herbalist's shops, all jiggly but having no apparent substance.

With a flicker of wings, Lucas lands next to me.

"I never want to do that again." The sand is still cool, but the sun warms my upturned face.

"I'm so sorry I couldn't be of more help. I thought my heart was going to explode each time you screamed." Lucas shifts next to my side.

"I think mine did when I pulled that body up." Chills race across my skin and I shiver violently.

Rustling sounds from the direction we'd just come. When

it's accompanied by a loud gurgle, I sit up to see if we've been followed.

Above me stands the strangest creature I've ever witnessed. Face like a frog and covered in various shades of green algae, moss, and seaweed, it's as big as a small man but much rounder. I scramble backward. "Wha—wha—?"

"Watch out, my lady! It's a froggen."

24

Lucas flutters into an assault on the frog-like creature with his claws out and wings flapping furiously. However, he hasn't quite returned to his full strength, and the froggen bats him away easily with one webbed hand. Lucas rolls tail over beak along the grassy sand.

The froggen's wide mouth turns down in a frown, and I discern the seaweed covering the lower part of its face is actually a beard.

I crawl over to Lucas and pick him up. "What is a froggen?" I whisper.

"I've never heard a good story that included them. They rule the water kingdom and long to war with the eldrin to rule over the land as well. They're not trustworthy." Lucas puffs out his feathers and shakes them out.

A dragon and now this. How many other creatures would we come across? I turn to face the froggen, not wanting to leave my backside vulnerable. My stomach churns.

It stands in front of me, one webbed hand spread across its yellowish belly, while the other arm is crooked behind its spotted back. Dangling from its hand is my necklace. The toes on its webbed feet are long and rounded at the ends. Yellow-green, bulging eyes squint at me as if sizing me up. The perusal stops as it stares into my eyes. It shows no shock or surprise.

"Hail, silver mage with the star eyes." It, a male from the sound of its deep, sticky voice, bows low. The top of the bulbous head shines wetly. "It is I, Siltworth of the Sunken Forests. My clan graciously welcomes you home ... and as a token of goodwill, I return the talisman you lost." When I hesitate, he tosses it at my feet and bows his head in a strangely formal manner.

I grab it and twist the long cord, tying it off to shorten it so it won't fall so easily again. I glance back up, and Siltworth is still bowed slightly.

Holding Lucas in my arms, I force my exhausted body to stand. I curtsey without taking my eyes off Siltworth. "Thank you, good sir."

With a flourish, he moves his hand and raises his head. "Of course."

"How—how do you know I've come home?" I ask.

Lucas chatters in disagreement. *"It is not safe to speak to froggen. I really must discourage it."*

Siltworth's bulbous eyes dart back and forth at Lucas. Can he understand what Lucas is saying? "Your return has been foretold," he states. His deep voice is croaky, and I have the urge to clear my own raw throat.

I don't know what that means, but Lucas is circling Siltworth, his feathers ruffled.

"My companion," I wave my arm toward him, "is quite dismayed by your presence. Tell me, do you mean us harm? How did you find us?"

Siltworth tips his head down again. It resembles a lump that juts from his wide, plump body. "I beg for your benevolence, my dear lady. Your wise companion is right to be on guard. Please send him my apologies for the problematic situation he finds himself in as my kind are quite familiar with it." He bows his bloblike body toward Lucas though his eyes never move from me.

My mind spins. Is he a djinn like Lucas? "You are familiar with what situation, sir?"

He opens his wide mouth and a pasty tongue darts out across his thin lips. "Though most creatures that reside on Anavrin are not magical in body or spirit, only by gifts or proxy, I can assure you I am verifiably authentic—as are you. My eyes detect a shape hovering beneath this bird's feathers, is that not so?"

Though he doesn't seem to be a threat, I am unwilling to give away anything about Lucas.

"Your reluctance is understandable, even if it is quite unbecoming. You may find Anavrin to be much different from where you were raised. I can't imagine living without magic." He shrugs his broad, splotched shoulders. "But I can assure you that you are in no danger from me. We share a common enemy." His eyes glimmer red for a moment, then fade back to green-gold. His flat nostrils shut and then flare back open.

It is unnerving to see his eyes light up, and I have to wonder how he knows so much about Tenebris. I move to step back but hesitate. Hadn't Lucas said that my eyes glow? Hadn't I noticed the heat when I gathered my ability? I refuse to be like so many others who had shied away from me because I look different. I tamp down my emotions and face him without flinching. "And who might that enemy be?"

His eyes flare red again. "The death mage, Thoron, of course. He mutilates the sanctity of magic with his *Mortuus Irrepo* hex. It is an abomination. I trust you feel the same way?"

The fiery intensity in his eyes dims, but the fierceness does not leave them.

"My lady, speak carefully." Lucas calls at the strange-looking creature in front of me. Siltworth merely glances at him with disinterest.

"You mean his beasts? The ones he kills and then brings back from the dead." As with my former employers, I wish for no misunderstandings or miscommunications, nor do I desire to be drawn into some sort of dispute between my father and anyone else as I've just arrived in this new kingdom.

"His Sluaghs, yes." The seaweed-looking whiskers twitch with the drawled-out words. "That and more. The dead should be left to their peace. Is that not so?" His voice lowers with the last sentence, and I sense a double meaning. His intense gaze and stance make me believe there's a trick to his words, some sort of veiled innuendo I don't understand.

"Slew-aws?" I test the word out.

Siltworth's eyes narrow and his thin lips thin even more. "Yes, his undead servant army. Sluaghs." He croaks the last word.

I recognize a condescending tone when I hear it, even one from a strange frog creature.

Lucas hops over to me. *"Do not agree to anything, my lady. Don't trust him, no matter his dapper manners. I assure you no creature on this kingdom should be trifled with. Especially fully magical creatures, which can be as dangerous as your father. Most likely Siltworth has been following us this whole time."*

I recall the brush of something in the water, the seaweed, and the bump against the boat. I work to keep my face impassive. I nod once to let Lucas know I understand him. "I do feel the magic he uses in that hex is an abomination." In all of his magic, but I don't state that out loud without understanding the froggen's motives better.

"So, we are of the same mind?" Siltworth presses. He leans forward slightly, his webbed hands interlaced innocently in front of his algae-covered body.

He's too eager, and my exhausted brain is unable to outmaneuver him. I place one of my hands to my head. Acting ill had gotten me out of a few tight situations before, and I pray it will again. I smile tightly. "I have only just returned to Anavrin, sir. I must beg release from this conversation so my acquaintance and I can find a place to rest and recuperate. I do hope you understand?" If comportment is as important as it seems to him, I hope he will take the hint and not press me further.

His wide mouth shifts downward ever so slightly. A twitch trembles across one of his bulbous eyes. It is as I thought. Civility is important to him for some reason, but he's not happy about it. He nods his head and spreads one arm wide in another bow. "My apologies, dear lady. We will meet again to continue this conversation soon." With a leap, he is in the water. There's no splash or ripple where he enters.

"Not if I can help it," I murmur.

"That was close, my lady. We need to move inland and find shelter."

I wave a hand in the air. "What was that all about?"

Lucas teeter-walks away from the water. *"It is best if we take our conversation somewhere else. Froggen hearing is too good this close to the water. And I couldn't help but feel he can hear me. Please, my lady."*

"Fine." I scan the woods on the right side of the opening. Lots of trees, but after having Siltworth appear out of the water, I'm unsure if it's safe. The area to the left is more of a pasture with trees growing sporadically. Neither is ideal, and I'm too tired to think it through. "Which direction should we go?"

"*Trees. If you can change, my lady, we would be safe higher in the trees.*"

I close my eyes and concentrate but am unable to change. My necklace warms, but the hum I always get with my ability is missing. "I can't." I sigh. "Agreed. The forest will give us the best cover, for now, and shelter us from the sun."

The sun is beginning to heat the air, and I miss the warmth when we step inside the timberland. Between still being soaked with seawater, and the shock of seeing the body and the froggen, shivers rattle my teeth.

The trees are tall here, but the lush vegetation makes it harder to navigate a clear path. We travel for several minutes before my legs cramp and my shoulders grate as I walk. I sit on a toppled log, put Lucas down, and try to rub the kinks out.

"Tell me about the froggen while we rest." My voice cracks and I wish we had some fresh water to drink.

Lucas fluffs his feathers as he settles onto the log. "*There's a childhood story that tells of a mage who was in love with a noblewoman, a renowned singer, who in turn was in love with a djinn. When the woman spurned the mage, he put a spell on the djinn and turned him into a frog. However, because the other man was already a djinn, the spell only worked halfway, turning him into a frog-man. At first, the only thing the frog creature could say was 'froggen,' and so that is what he was named.*"

"That's awful." I rub my tired eyes.

He continues. "*When the noblewoman realized what the mage had done, she was heartbroken. She knelt by the sea where they had often met and wept. She sang such a lonely song, it's said that even the trees wept for her. The froggen heard her distress and gave her a pearl he'd found in the depths. He enchanted it into a necklace so she could change into a sea-creature whenever she wished so she could visit him beneath the waters.*"

"*The noblewoman hadn't realized the pearl had magic and,*

when she put it on, she was immediately changed into a water creature as well. She was furious at him for tricking her. She was even more furious when she couldn't remove the pearl."

I recall being furious after Lucas changed me. "I completely understand her anger."

Lucas stares out across the forest. *"Yes, well, let's just say you were much more understanding than the noblewoman. She slew the froggen, and then she found the mage and begged him to change her back. The mage was disgusted by her appearance and refused. Soon after, the mage was found dead. He was soaked and had seaweed stuck in his throat. When they opened him up, he was full of seawater and sand. He'd drowned in a field outside of his home, miles from any sea or lake. Some say it was the woman. There was no other explanation."*

I brush my hand across his soft back, and he hops into my lap. "So, what does this all have to do with Siltworth?"

"That woman built an underwater empire. Her kin have been known to sing men into the water to their depths, which is probably what happened to the poor soul whose body you found when we were rowing for shore. True to her original heritage, though, they are a noble breed among the merfolk. They are ruled by decorum. You see how politely Siltworth behaved. However, froggen have been at war with evil mages and eldrin ever since. They've fought for dominion of the shores and surrounding areas for years. You are part eldrin and part mage. Maybe not in magic, since mages are only mages because they use dark magic. However, you are descended from one, you share his blood and his magic. If Thoron were to die, what's to stop the froggen from coming after you?"

25

A rustling sound startles me, and I jerk my head up. I'd fallen asleep leaning against the log not long after Lucas's story about the froggen. I wipe spittle off with my sleeve. Lucas's head is tucked beneath his wing on my lap. The necklace is a heated ball against my chest and I move it so my dress is between it and my skin.

I glance around, trying to figure out what it was that woke me. Long shadows from the stretching, leafy branches on top of the trees wave back and forth with a gentle wind. It's still daytime. I can't move without waking Lucas and I don't want to disturb him. The air is warm and my eyes grow heavy again.

Hushed voices draw me from a pleasant slumber. I'm too comfortable to open my eyes, though the necklace is heating through my dress. I shift it grumpily aside to dangle upon the wood I lay against and settle back in to fall asleep.

Something hard clamps around one of my wrists, and I jerk awake. Around me stands seven grumpy-looking men, one of whom has placed a shackle over my right wrist and is hurriedly reaching for my other.

Blue light crackles around my hands and with a single thought, I *push* the man with the metal shackles away. He flies back into two of the others, knocking them down. The four still standing are shouting and pointing at me. The three on the ground grumble and call me names.

My movement wakens Lucas. *"What is happening, my lady?"*

"I wish I knew," I say to him. Sitting him down on the log, I stand and grimace at my sore muscles. The shackles are heavy, and I rub my free hand up and down my arms to dispel the chill. At the last minute, I grasp at my neck and am comforted to know the necklace is still there. "What is this all about?"

The smallest man steps forward, a frown on his grizzled face. He eyes the stone. If the wrinkles and leathered skin are any indication, he is old, but his build is not one of an elderly man. He is diminutive but fit, and his bare arms are muscular though quite hairy. The men all look similar as if kin. They have heavily-lidded eyes, bulging noses, and all but one sports a mustache or a beard. Sleeveless tunics are tucked into dark trousers held up with suspenders. Their smallish feet are encompassed in heavy laced boots.

He points a bent finger at me which must've been broken at one time or another. These are not fine gentlemen but laborers of some sort. "You are trespassing." The accent is one I've never heard before, all hard consonants with long, lilting vowel sounds.

I glance around. "Trespassing? I see nothing here but trees and overgrown foliage. And how did you find me anyway?"

Lucas flies into an assault on the grizzled man. *"They can't lock us up for sleeping in a forest."*

The man bats Lucas away, but not before Lucas claws his arms and cheek. However, one of the others aims a sling-shot at Lucas. My heart thumps painfully, remembering being shot out of the sky on Tenebris before Fetmann found me and locked me up.

"Stop!" I shout. I take a deep, calming breath and grasp the shackle with my free hand. The hum of my ability answers my unspoken request to unlock. The metal is thick and strong, but no match for my frustration. Light flashes around my hands, and with a clank, the metal breaks free.

"*You are getting stronger, my lady!*" Pride fills Lucas's voice. He flutters to my shoulder.

I rattle the offending chain, and the broken band jangles. "I'm not a slave to be shackled. If I am trespassing, as you say, I do apologize. I'll be on my way. If you'll just point me to the village beneath the mountain?" I toss the restraints at the feet of the men.

All seven of them hurriedly huddle and whisper furiously to one another

"Who are these people?" I ask Lucas aloud. A couple of the men shoot me a suspicious glare. The stoutest points a chubby hand at me, and I believe I hear "silver," "stars," and "evil magic" being thrown around.

I sigh. It had been enough days without my hair or eyes being noticed that I'd almost forgotten how strange I must look to anyone new. I remove Lucas from my shoulder and run my hand across the soft feathers along his back, cradling him to my chest. It helps to quiet my frustration.

Lucas tilts his head, his dark, bird-eye gleaming at me. "*They are clearly not magic users, so they're either a tribe of nomads or some strange mix of djinn. However, I've never seen djinn form tribes before, even among mixed-races, unless things have changed that much since we've been gone.*"

"Do nomads look like this?" I ask, curious.

"*I don't recall. I only met one or two of them when I was a child, and I never paid them much mind. No one does, since they don't have magic and aren't a threat to other magic users. And they're rather hermits, living within their villages either in trees or mining caves."*

The men end their conversation and turn to face us. None of them look happy. The smallest man rushes up to me, so I take a step back. "You are trespassing, violating the eldrin accords by using magic, and you broke our manacles which requires recompense. You must answer for your crimes." He jabs his thumb, pointing in the direction behind them. "Come."

Lucas stiffens, and I tighten my grasp on him. *"Don't trust them, my lady."*

"I won't." I stare at the men. If I tell them I'm from a different kingdom, would they believe me? "Look, I don't know your laws."

They all gasp at my response.

A stodgy man with the longest beard tsks. "I told you, she's a mage! They don't know the first thing about rules or the accords. Just look at her! But don't look in her eyes. She'll suck your soul out, I promise you." Spittle flies from his blubbering lips.

I hold my hands out, hoping to placate them. "I'm not here to hurt anyone. I just need to find someone. I'll leave without incident. No harm done, I promise."

Red-faced, the small man takes another menacing step toward me. "Oh, yeah? What about these?" He's short enough that when he holds the manacles up at me, they only reach my chin.

Irritation burns in my gut. *"You* were trying to shackle *me.* What did you expect would happen?" They obviously weren't going to give up without some kind of amends. But I was in no mood to surrender to them.

I don't wish to hurt him, but I will if I need to. I raise one hand and step back. Something beneath my foot cracks and the smile on the man's face alerts me that I've just made an err. Air whooshes as a rope net encircles and lifts me high into the air. It jostles me around and when it settles, I scramble, trying not to crush Lucas as I flounder in the swaying trap. The stone in the necklace burns against the tender skin at my chest, but I'm too tangled in rope to move it. Warmth floods around my eyes.

Lucas drops through one of the holes. He flutters inelegantly around the net before settling on a branch above where the trap is tied.

The one with the slingshot aims and releases. Two others pull out more slingshots from their back pockets. Several metal balls are loaded and shot within moments. I'm astonished and then annoyed with how quick they are.

Lucas shrieks. *"They're trying to shoot me!"* He darts this way and that on the limb as he dodges the first ball.

"Stop!" I scream, irritation burning like fire in my veins as I yank on the rope. My eyes dry against the heat pulsing behind them. I need to get out of this stupid trap! My hands light up once more and the ropes disentangle around me, creating a hole big enough for me to drop through. I land on my hands and knees where I'd just stood. However, my back is to the men. I twist to face them.

"Get her!" one of the men yells.

I grasp the dirt and leaves in my fists to quell my anger. However, blue energy zags out from my hands and travels into the ground toward the men. It hits them and they jump to and fro, yelping in pain. The stone at my neck is a fiery ball, which thankfully isn't burning me though I feel the sting of the heat.

The earth beneath us all shakes.

A couple of the men recover and back away, glancing

around furiously, before turning to run in the opposite direction. Four men remain by the time I can gather my wits.

Lucas lands next to me. *"Well done, Tambrynn. That should make them think twice before trying to capture you again."*

"They don't look like they're giving up." The hum inside me is gone. I try to call on my ability, but there's nothing there. I glance around for a stick in case I have to fight the rest of them off.

"Who are you talking to?" the smallest man demands. "Are you woo-hoo crazy?"

A clap, like thunder, interrupts my retort. Light flashes and smoke clouds the forest as a cloaked man appears off to the side of us. Unlike the cantankerous old men, this man is tidy, trimmed, and handsome. From his radiant, yellow hair and pointed ears, to his embroidered white cloak, down to the tips of his booted feet, he oozes confidence. And annoyance.

"Who is using magic and breaking the accords?" His drawn mouth is lined with two almost imperceptible wrinkles—his only imperfection.

The small man points to me. "Sh—she did, Councilmaster Nyle." Fear reflects in his beady little eyes.

Beside me, Lucas chirrups. *"Beware, Tambrynn! He's eldrin, and he doesn't look happy."*

Councilmaster Nyle looks more sensible to me than the small men. Maybe I can reason with him. "These men were attacking me. It was unprovoked, I promise you. I just wish to be on my way." I take a step to the side to move around him. White-hot pain similar to a heated poker starts at my neck and rushes down my spine. I stiffen. A blue halo forms around me and the pain releases, leaving me bent over and panting as the burning sensation disappears from my bones. However, the pain remains on a spot just under my jaw. The necklace dangles as I bend and pant from the discomfort.

Lucas flies at the eldrin whooping. Nyle puts a hand up and he falls to the ground.

"Lucas?" I ask in my mind, but there's no response.

The Councilmaster narrows his blue eyes at me. "Are you a mage?" His gaze flickers over me, sizing me up.

He reaches out a hand to touch my hair and I swat it away and stand up.

"No. You are a filthy mixed-blood," he spits the words out like he's tasted something rotten.

Indignation and fury rush through me at his arrogance. I could use a shower, but I am not filthy. I've been much more soiled and smellier. I pick Lucas up and cradle him in my arms, recalling the numerous times I'd been scrutinized and judged. I tilt my chin upward, the skin which burned below my jaw pinching, and grit my teeth as I speak. "I am nothing to you, sir. I only wish to be on my way. If you please."

Inside me, I gather what energy is returning into a ball. No doubt this man won't let me go. The confidence I'd seen in him earlier is nothing more than a privileged insolence. Just like every employer, Cook, or Adelia I'd come across before. Only worse because he has magic to use against me.

"You will come with me." Nyle's words are spoken without anger or malice, but they poke beneath my skin like crawling ants. There's a tugging sensation that comes with the 'request' like a noose hooked around my throat.

Again, the stone necklace heats. Warmth washes through my body in answer and the pull evaporates. The spot on my jaw tingles and I press a hand there and feel a raised lump, almost like a scar. Had the eldrin's magic done something to me?

From the corner of my eye, I notice the four remaining men stepping back as if to leave.

"No. Stop," I say, and I *push* my ability into the words.

The eldrin stiffens and the men stop moving. Their eyes dart around anxiously. Indeed, my ability is much stronger here. I don't even have to hold my hand up to keep someone in place.

"Tambrynn?" Concern fills Lucas's groggy voice, but I refuse to look away from the eldrin in front of me. *"Did you know there's a mark on your skin just above your neck?"*

"Do not use your black magic on me, Mage." Councilmaster Nyle's nearly smooth face is now creased with anger, but he doesn't move except to spit his words out. He resembles a toddler with dribble on his lips and chin. A very petulant toddler.

If I weren't so annoyed, I'd laugh at him. Something tells me he wouldn't appreciate the humor in his situation as I do. "I'm no black magic user, sir. It seems you, however, have done some magic on me. Just so you know, I will defend myself if you try to manipulate me again." I hold his glare without flinching.

His hands are fisted tight and grasping the edges of his fine cloak. An ornate golden ring on one finger glistens in the shifting light. It's similar to my and Lucas's rings, but it has a mountain carved into the top instead of a sprawling tree. The gold on the ring matches the gold of his hair. I finger my ring, assured it's still in place.

"I've heard about the eldrin here. You think you're invulnerable, but you're not as powerful as others I've come up against. Trust me when I say you don't want to have this fight." I release the hold I have on him with a single thought.

He lands elegantly with one knee and a fist to the ground. He stands and flings back his cloak with the flair of a king. When he raises his hands, he holds a white ball of energy. With a flick, he sends it flying at me.

Lucas squawks and I raise my arms to protect my face. The

white ball is met with a blue shield that now surrounds Lucas and me. It's the same, but stronger, as when Thoron tried to attack me in the cottage. The magic bounces back at Nyle. He flips, booted feet over long, golden hair, into the trunk of a wide tree which resembles the pine trees on Tenebris. Limbs and needles rain down on Nyle, who sits dazed on the forest floor.

"We need to get going, my lady, before more eldrin show up."

"That would be great if we knew which direction to go," I mutter, annoyed. None of the men were helpful at all. The froggen was more helpful than the nomads *or* the eldrin. A glance around tells me the nomads are completely gone. No flash of clothes or crack of tree limbs gives them away. "How'd they get away without me seeing them?"

Nyle shakes his head and some needles stuck in his hair drift to the ground.

I pick up Lucas and, walking around the dazed eldrin, turn in the opposite direction I believe the nomads left. I don't wish to run into them again.

Nyle holds a hand against his head. "You can leave if you wish. But you're marked now. The council will find you and charge you with attacking me, a Councilmaster, with your unauthorized magic. Your sentence will be death."

I keep walking as I recall Mrs. Calvin's threats. "Can't be worse than the hell hounds on Tenebris, can they?"

"The eldrin are quite adept at magical torture, my lady. And that mark on your neck must be some magical tracking device."

My stomach twists. I hadn't planned on making enemies of the eldrin this quickly after arriving on Anavrin. Now I'd be running from them *and* my father. Not a comforting thought. "We need to find my grandmother and remove this tracker before they find me again."

26

I walk until the sun is high in the sky. The trees have given way to lush meadowlands edged with dark gray mountains and what looks like forests not far in the distance. On Tenebris, fall was creeping toward winter, but here it is warm and sunny, akin to summer.

"Do you recognize any of these mountains?" The air is scented with the sweet perfume of flowers and loamy soil that brightens the fertile area. Colorful petals in shades of oranges, yellows, reds, and purples peek out from the brushy grasses. I stop to pluck a purple one as I take in our surroundings.

Lucas has been flying low to the ground, sweeping the area, and then returning to me to rest before circling the area to scan once more as we move.

The colors here are brighter, *more* somehow. It's like I rubbed sleep from my eyes and can finally see clearly. Since it had been dark out when we arrived, and I'd been too busy earlier with the little men, I'd failed to recognize how much more brilliant Anavrin is than Tenebris.

"We traveled for a day and a half nonstop to get to the island

with the Zoe Tree when we left the mountain. That was in carts, so unless we can both fly, it might take us up to a week to reach the village. And that's if we know where we're headed, which we don't."

I pluck the petals one by one from the flower, contemplating. "Is there any way of getting a map of Anavrin to show us the way?"

"Yes, if I could change back, or we come to a larger town, or if we run into someone who knows Anavrin well enough to make a crude map. Do you feel strong enough to try changing again, my lady? It might be our best chance."

I toss the stem of the flower into the tall grass. "I can try." I close my eyes and locate the low hum in my gut. My mind probes it, trying to test how strong it is before I try. I've been stronger, but it might be enough.

With a thought, the hum spreads through my body. Tingles sweep over me. I open my eyes and find that the grass is now over my head. I have indeed changed. *"I did it!"* My words lift into a lilting song.

Lucas hops around, studying me.

I turn. He's seen me before. Why is he so rapt now? *"Is there something wrong? It's not the tracker, is it?"* My long tail feathers tickle as I spin in a circle, following Lucas. The sun glimmers off my silver feathers, but they aren't just silver now. A rainbow haze shimmers on the feathers I can see. I crane my long neck, but I can't see much more than my tail.

"I don't see the tracker on you in this form. It's just—" He hesitates. *"You're magnificent. You even have a crown now."* Lucas flutters his wings as if pointing to my head. *"That most certainly wasn't there before."*

I stop turning and study him. *"But you've not changed."*

"I am stuck in the form your father spelled me in. I fear I may never change unless we can find a solution to his hex or he changes me back himself. Anyway, let's see if you can fly, shall we?"

My feathers are heavier than I remember. I glance down the stretch of my right wing and realize I'm bigger, too. *"Why do you think I'm different from before?"*

"I believe I'm right about Tenebris leeching our abilities from us. Certainly, Anavrin is quite stunning compared, don't you think? I didn't appreciate how much until this moment."

"I did notice the difference." I ruffle my feathers and, with a wide swing that brushes against the tall grasses and flowers, launch myself upwards.

I'm up and flying, and though I'm not quite as steady as I'd like, I'm elated to be traveling more easily.

Lucas joins me in the air. *"You're doing great, my lady. Follow me. I'll see if we can locate a town to find directions."*

We make swift progress until Lucas spots a stream cutting through the woods along the edge of the mountains. He dives to land beside a wider section of the water not far from a thicket of saplings. It's clean and clear, running slowly downstream. There's a sound of splashing, but I spot no fish, no frogs, or creatures. Could it be coming from near the timber line further up the meadow?

The sun is warm upon my body, but I'm unable to sweat and am becoming overheated. Flying down, I jump in and splash water over my feathers to cool down while Lucas dips his beak in the water.

When I'm done cooling myself and getting a drink, I bob my head around for a closer look. The trees are more like the ones I'm used to on Tenebris, though I wasn't versed in them.

There's more splashing and I glance back at Lucas to see if he's still reveling in the cool water, but he's not. Looking around, I can't find the source of the noise.

"Do you hear that?" I ask.

"Hear what?" he inquires back.

"The splashing." I teeter toward the sound, past several

trees with grayed bark, finding nothing. A high-pitch scream and laugh rings through the air. More wet sloshing noises resound, and though the stream ripples as if from movement, there's nothing there. *"What was that? I don't see anything."*

Lucas flutters over to me. *"I don't hear anything save the swish of the breeze across the flowers. There's not even any birds calling out."*

"There's something strange here." I continue to move upstream. There's more screaming laughter and I hear voices, but they're too faint to make out what is being said. My skin crawls, and I fluff out my feathers to ease the sensation. Out of the corner of one of my eyes, I notice a wavy haze in the air, so I head that way. The voices get louder, as does the splashing, until I'm only a few steps away from it. It reminds me of Lucas's disguise when we went to the Spaw, seeing the disguise with the real image beneath. I'm curious to see what it is.

I change back to my girl form, readying for the weight that suddenly surges through my body. Iridescent feathers are replaced by skin and scratchy wool fabric. I end up on my hands and knees, so I stand.

Faint notes of music, splashing, and laughter trickle lightly in the sun-warmed air. At first glance, I see nothing there. Upon closer inspection, I notice a wavering light—there but not there—similar to a vague impression of the sky and clouds reflecting on the water. It's the length of two large horses standing nose to tail and just as tall as a horse would stand.

I turn my head and, out of the corner of my eye, spy an image of shapes frolicking in what looks like a stream. Children? Twisting back, I only see the wavy image behind a vision of the meadow around me. An illusion?

I reach out a hand to test it, my ring winking gold in the light. As I touch it, a loud pop makes me jerk back, and the wavering air shatters like broken pieces of glass that rain down to the ground, only to disappear like smoke in the wind.

Before me is a group of women sitting in the stream. They all blink in surprise. They're smallish, thick-haired, and their facial features remind me of the seven men who tried to shackle me earlier.

"Oh, my golly-goodness!" one of the women exclaims. "Thank you, Kinsman! Oh, thank you!"

Their rounded bodies roll about, trying to get out of the stream and up a waist-high dirt embankment, until every one of them stands outside of the brook, dripping, wet, and dirty. They inspect each other and laugh in thankful delight, though they're covered with mud and grass. One glances my way, and the laughter dies on her lips. She reaches out a hand and catches the arm of the woman next to her, who pays her no mind until she pinches her.

Their clothes drip around them, leaving wet, muddy puddles on the ground with every movement they make. There are nine of them, small but robust in a plump, well-fed way. None of them have the same hair color, but the familial kind of resemblance is unmistakable. Their dresses are similar under the muck, woven in individual colors and patterns. All of them are barefoot, their skin wrinkled as if they've been in the water far too long.

And all of them stare unblinking at me.

I run my hands over my hair, wishing I had a hood to hide it. But I have nothing, and my dress is beyond repair at this point. I pick at my dress's collar, thankful my necklace is safely tucked away beneath the wool fabric. I stare down at my feet and notice the leather has torn on the inside of my right shoe near the worn heel.

"Who be ye?" the oldest-looking woman asks, her eyebrows furrowed.

Her accent is the same as the small men who tried to shackle me. She bites her consonants and drags out her vowels in an interesting combination. I'm immediately on guard and keep my gaze averted so they don't notice the star pupils.

"Tambrynn, mistress." I curtsy, unsure what the greeting customs are here, and I don't wish to invite their ire.

A brunette woman speaks up. "Oh, you're a fine one, then? Look, girls. A silver-haired *lady* with manners."

"And, see! She's marked by the eldrin. I never seen an elegant criminal before." A red-haired woman points at me. Several women break out in raucous laughter at her words.

My first instinct is to cover the painful spot on my jaw with my hand, but I manage to keep them at my sides. I knew whatever that eldrin had done was not good news. I need to find out how to remove it and change Lucas back soon. *"What do I do?"* I ask him while keeping my gaze anywhere but toward the women.

"These women resemble the men from earlier," Lucas responds. *"I'm positive they're nomads. From what I know of them, they don't trust any magic-kin."*

Two of the women move closer to me. The red-head reaches for my hair which, though tangled, lays loose around my shoulders and down my back. I jerk my head back and sidestep away from her. The movement makes the mark on my jaw sting, and her scrutiny makes me uncomfortable.

"Sorry. I don't like people touching my hair." Hopefully, they won't be nosy enough to ask about it. However, with how they scrutinize me, I'm fairly certain they will.

The older woman steps out from the group. She holds a long limb, a walking stick by the looks of it. It's a whitish wood, well-worn, and a knob on the end makes it look like the end of a bone. I hold back a shiver. She stops directly in front of me. "Who be ye? And what'd ye do to get yerself marked?"

I stifle the impulse to curtsy again. It is obviously not a custom with them, and though it's a deeply ingrained habit, I'm no longer indentured. "Tambrynn. Pleased to meet you."

"Are ye? Ye look more afraid than happy," she states dryly. "And ye didn't mention why yer marked."

"I did nothing except defend myself." I stare straight into her unflinching green eyes.

She gazes back at me for a few tense moments before she speaks again. "Don't we all?" She chuckles and the others join her. She straightens her back, which pops and cracks, and clears her throat. "Pray tell, what day is it?"

For a moment I'm taken aback. "I—I'm unsure."

The brunette turns her mud-splotched face up at me. "Are you sure you're unsure? That sounded like a question to me." Beneath the grime, her face is tanned as if she works in the sun. She only stands as tall as my chest, and she's the tallest of them all. The other women stare, waiting for my response.

I glance over at Lucas who is flying a circle around us. "We, I mean I've been on a journey." I wait for someone to understand, but they don't so much as twitch. "I'm afraid I've lost track of time."

The brunette spots Lucas. Her eyes narrow as her wide lips purse. "You got yourself a pet?"

I don't glance at Lucas though I want to. I don't want to give him away if they turn aggressive. Luckily, I'd learned long ago the value of hiding the truth from my employers. "I don't know what you're referring to." I hold her look with an unwavering one of my own, relaxing my face to feign a schooled innocence.

"Well, I'd be careful about strange animals around these parts. Never know what's hiding beneath the surface." The brunette wiggles her chunky fingers and stares at my hair. "Where'd you say you were journeying from?"

What do I say? Their gazes turn sharper as I hesitate.

"Tell them you're from Anatolia. It's far enough away from here that they may not know much about it." Lucas's voice sounds like he is right next to me, though he's fluttered far enough away I can't see him. *"It's on the border of the Meridian Peaks along the Sea of Marmara. There's a mix of races that live there. You may fit in."*

"Anatolia along the Sea of Marmara," I answer her. The sun is starting its descent and I have to wonder if the days are the same length here as on Tenebris. Had it only been this morn when I ended my sailing journey and met with the froggen?

"Huh," mutters the old woman. I can tell my answer doesn't satisfy her. "Never seen a silver-haired fair one before. Or a half-breed for that matter. Especially not one with hoo-ky looking eyes." She raises a gnarled finger and circles the air in front of me with it.

A howling wind rushes over the pasture, bowing the tall grass and wildflowers low and rustling through the gray-barked trees. With a flash and crack, Councilmaster Nyle appears. Another couple of cracks split the air and two other regal-looking people, a man and a woman, stand behind him.

"Enforcers!" one of the women screams.

27

The red-head squeals. "Watch yourselves, ladies! He's brought Amira and Garrett with him this time."

They rush away from the eldrin and back toward the stream, leaving pools of mud among the crushed wildflowers where they just stood.

The two eldrin who stand beside Nyle resemble him in many ways. All of them are tall, golden-haired, lithe, and have flawless faces. They're as stoic as the stone statues adorning the Fountain of Wishes on Tenebris—a bit too faultless to be real. Their crystal blue eyes scan the scene before them without giving any emotion away.

Nyle's gaze rests on me, cold and unmoving. "I warned you that we would find you, mage. You are found guilty of breaking the accords, assault upon a Councilmaster, unauthorized use of dark magic, and failure to comply. You are sentenced to death."

Surprise and then anger bloom inside me. I'd done many things, but nothing that would require my life. Not even the butcher knife that left Cook mole-free would warrant that. I narrow my eyes at him, contemplating. The necklace beneath my dress warms as if aware of my unease or danger, I'm unsure which.

Energy prickles at my skin from an unseen power that radiates around him like a cloak. Though it's not uncomfortable like Thoron's power, I know better than to think it's harmless.

The old woman barks out an angry-sounding grunt. "Marked or not, aren't ye enforcers supposed to have a summons sent from the Council to capture someone? Or did ye change the accords *again*?"

Nyle's stance is tense, like a pressed coil waiting to spring. "I don't answer to you, nomad."

He's nothing but a bully, just like all of the rest I've dealt with. The only difference is that this time I can fight back.

"*What are enforcers?*" I inquire of Lucas.

"*Enforcers dole out punishments to those who have disobeyed the Council. However, Nyle is the Councilmaster and therefore more dangerous. Keep your focus on him. Tread carefully, my lady. I am close by. Change if necessary.*" Lucas's words pinch at my mind, which worries me. I'd shrugged Nyle off before. He may not be as easily confronted this time.

I gather what ability I can until it buzzes like an angry hive inside my gut. I consider changing to a bird but don't want the eldrin to witness it and therefore know what I can do. Nor do I wish him to know my form. It might leave the small women vulnerable.

My gaze flicks between the other two eldrin. The female wears a fine moss-green cape with gold vines stitched at the collar. The male wears a simpler tan one, though the fabric is as fine as the female's. There's only a dull hum that radiates from them, the female being the stronger of the two. They must not be as powerful as Nyle.

I stand tall, shoulders back, and hold Nyle's gaze with a steady one of my own. "I am innocent of your charges. I've done nothing but defend myself against those little men and then against you. I hardly think that requires a death sentence."

The women behind me titter at my words, though I can't hear enough to know what they're saying.

From behind his back, Nyle produces a wooden staff with prongs on the end. It resembles a twisted pitchfork. The tines enclose a swirling purple ball of crackling magic. Intricate shapes carved along the handle emit a soft light. His hand holding the staff is covered by a silver-blue glove.

The other two eldrin move to stand with their legs spread apart and hands out in a menacing fashion.

Fear skitters down my spine and my fingers brighten to a glowing blue. My eyes warm and the necklace warms. My ability spreads throughout my body, heating me like a log on a fire. It's not painful, though. It's more like coming in from the cold and placing your hands over the flames. Nyle's perfect face wrinkles with a frown. Is he intimidated? I almost smile at the thought.

"Do you know what that pretty stick of his does?" I ask Lucas.

"No, but he's wearing a gauntlet to hold it. That's not a good sign. It must be powerful."

Nyle tilts the scepter, and the waning sunlight glimmers along the texture of the glove. A wave of magic spews out from the glowing light orb in a purple haze. It hits me like a breeze and washes over me, rumpling my clothes and whipping through my hair. The spot on my neck where the stone resides tingles. I see beyond the wavering light encompassing me to Nyle and his two companions. The three rush toward us. Their movements are blurred as if they are going so fast I cannot see their exact actions. They don't understand I'm unaffected by whatever magic Nyle's using.

"Watch out, my lady."

Nyle points the scepter at me. More of the hazy energy flows out of the ball.

I *call* for the scepter. Blue magic streaks between us and jerks it from Nyle's hand, dissipating the haze. The scepter sails to me with the glove still attached, and just as if I'd planned it, turns so the glove settles neatly over my hand. Loose at first, it shrinks and conforms to my size and shape in an instant.

Prickles rush across my arm before an intense heat flushes through me. A puff of warm air lifts my clothes and hair. My necklace is raised and settles back down to rest on the outside of my dress. I close my eyes and there's no darkness, only a bright, radiant light that reminds me of the passage.

I snap my eyes open and everything has stopped. There's no quiet babble from the stream or the sound of bird cries from the trees off in the distance. Nothing moves. A sense of rightness settles in my chest.

I blink again and everything swings into motion, sound crashing around me.

"It can't be!" Nyle roars, his face transformed and ugly in his anger. A memory of Thoron's expression in the cabin flashes through my mind. The similarity is uncanny. He darts toward me.

I swing the scepter and catch Nyle on the shoulder with the prongs and ball. A powerful explosion blasts him backward, his body twisting in the air and landing face down on the meadow, unmoving.

The other eldrin, Amira and Garrett, have darted past me toward the small women who hunch in the middle of the stream once again.

"Don't let them grab the young ones!" the brunette yells at

the others as they all hook arms and form a circle around two younger girls. Have they had to rally against the eldrin before? As I recall, Lucas said the nomads had no magic to defend themselves with. Familiar anger ignites inside me at the injustice of the imbalance of power.

Amira reaches the group first. Head and shoulders taller than the nomad women, she grabs the youngest girl out from the center of the group and hauls her over their linked arms. The women try to stop her, but Garrett is there on the other side, reaching for a second girl.

I *call* to retrieve the girl wriggling and squealing in Amira's grasp, but the eldrin taps her chest. She wears a similar corded necklace woven around a pearl stone. A bright light flashes, and they are both gone as if they were never there.

"Wha—?" I drop my hands. Shock burns through me and my ability heightens from a buzz to a throb in my gut.

The women's circle tightens. Unable to successfully reach the second girl, Garrett grabs the old, grayed woman by the collar of her dress. Quick as a younger woman, she takes her stick from under her arm and thrusts it into his stomach in a move I'd be proud to make. He crumples in on himself with a growling whoof. As he's bent low, she swings the stick and lands a solid crack on the back of his head.

Behind me, Nyle moans. Since the old woman seems to have Garrett under control, I circle back toward him. He rubs a hand across his bleeding nose, and when he sees the red smeared across his hand, he shrieks. Crouched low, he darts straight for me. Somewhere in the distance, I hear Lucas cheep, but I concentrate on the threat in front of me first.

I *push* Nyle, think better of it, and then grab hold of him with my ability. I lift him off the ground to just above the tall grasses. "You will not hurt me or these women." I *push* my ability into the words, focusing on his mind. He struggles against my hold, his flawless face creasing and growing dark. "Do you understand?" I shake him just enough to make my point.

He struggles some more, but I tighten my hold on him. He grimaces then gasps. "Yes."

Sounds of a skirmish ring behind me, but I can't concentrate on Nyle and look at them. My arm is shaking and I'm afraid I might drop him before I'm finished. "You'll leave here and not come back for us." Again, I infuse my ability into my words, the last of the humming *pushed* into those words. "And you'll remove the tracker you put on me."

He struggles, spitting and sputtering.

"Agree before I break your proud little neck."

"Yes," Nyle yells as he jerks his head around like he doesn't agree.

I squeeze again.

"I said yes." More spit flies out of his mouth, a dangerous ferocity glittering in his icy blue eyes.

My energy diminishing, I drop him to the ground. He lands with a grunt, his body heaving as he sucks in great mouthfuls of air.

"Remove the tracker," I order him, my hand still in the air as a threat.

"Fine." He motions with his hand and my jaw is wracked with pain.

I cry out and cradle my chin, glaring at him. The raised area is gone. "Go or I can't promise what I will do to you." I lift the scepter and point it at him.

Wide-eyed, he glances behind me, no doubt to his companion, who sounds as if he's being beaten. He smacks a raised spot on his chest, possibly another necklace, and like Amira, in a flash of light, he's gone. When I turn around, five of the women sit upon Garrett, lying on his stomach on the ground with one eye red and swollen. The oldest woman has her stick an inch from his face.

"Took ye long enough," she states. "Smart thing getting that mark removed. However, I still don't trust ye. All that power ye have? Seems to me yer one of them what with that special necklace around ye're neck. Wouldn't be part of all that Cleric infighting, now would ye?" She nods at the eldrin on the ground.

Garrett grunts beneath the weight of the women. One has hold of his head and is bending it back far enough to reveal a similar corded necklace. The other four have hold of his arms and legs, bending them as I'd seen farmers do when wrestling with their cattle for branding.

"I'm no eldrin," I state simply. Something keeps me from telling her about the dragon giving me the necklace. I sit the scepter down and try to remove the glove, but it doesn't come off. I tug again, but it doesn't budge. This can't be good, can it? *"Lucas?"*

"Is that so? Then why were ye able to steal the Eye of Fate scepter right out from the Councilmaster's hand, along with the gauntlet? If yer no eldrin, what are ye? A mage like he said?"

Garrett grunts, his eyes glaring at me though his head is bent back enough to almost snap it off.

The old woman smacks him on the cheek with her walking stick. No doubt it will match his bruised eye on the other side soon. "Oh, ye think we don't know about ye're magical tricks, ye cleric scum?" She grabs the necklace around his neck and yanks. His head jerks when the cord breaks. He thrashes, but the women holding him keep control. "We're aware of the holy relics and all of the dark magic tokens ye use for ye'selves. How far ye have fallen to have taken our dearest Colly for no reason. Ye surely will be damned!"

She turns to me. "So, ye've just been traveling, eh? Marked by the eldrin and powerful enough to make them remove that same mark. In my book, that's an impossibility. Seems to me ye've got a story I'd like to hear."

She's too perceptive and, it seems, a bit too determined for comfort. Though I'd stayed to help, I'd saved them at least once. It didn't look like they needed me any longer. It was time to find Lucas and leave. "I'm nothing and no one. It looks like you have things under control, so I'm going to be on my way now."

The old woman's scowl suddenly turns into a smile.

"That's not happening." A gruff voice behind me mutters as something locks around my free wrist.

The scepter lights up, sending a blast out that almost rips it from my hand. A shackle hangs from my arm, the open-end dangling. With a thought of 'destroy' in my mind, the locked metal band turns orange and melts off me without injury to my skin. The rest of the shackle rests among the smoldering metal blobs on the ground. I rub the skin above my hand, thankful for the new ability to melt metal. Clearly, Lucas was right about me getting stronger in this kingdom.

I turn and find the seven small men who had confronted me in the forest. They're all on the ground, dazed by the blast. They stand between me and the thicket of trees, which explains how they got here without me noticing. Red scratches on one's arm and cheek prove he is, in fact, the same man Lucas attacked before. A couple of the women who aren't still restraining the last eldrin hurry to their aid.

The small, grumpy man slaps their helping hands away and stands. He adjusts his suspenders with gusto, the snaps reminding me of the sound of whips. "That's two restraints you owe us now. Well, what's happened, Arrin? Where've you all been? We've been looking for you for days."

The old woman tilts her head and narrows her bulging eyes. "We were stuck in an illusion until this one came along. Somehow, she broke it, and just as we were celebrating, the eldrin showed up. They took Colly."

"It's all her fault," the small man sneers at me. "I knew she was evil the moment I saw her."

I inwardly groan. Not again. Just then I spy a bird clutched in one of the men's hands. "Lucas!" I drop the scepter. In a flash, I *call* out to him. Lucas sails toward me, his wings spread wide, his head lolling to the side. I catch him as carefully as I can. A wild rushing like wind fills my ears and fury burns in my veins.

"What've you done?"

28

Tears drip down my face as I cradle Lucas to me. He's so still, but I can feel a faint heartbeat within his unmoving warm body. Hope blooms in my heart, but it's not enough to crowd out the anger. "What did you do to him?" I spit it out through clenched teeth.

"Your companion there? Shot him outta the sky." The man with the slingshot sneers. His hands are fisted at his sides. "Only took one try." His dirt brown beard curls up around his lips in a vicious smile.

My ability fizzles inside of me, not strong enough to do the damage I wish to do at the moment. I'd done too much already. If I could carry Lucas, I'd change to a bird right now and fly off, away from these infuriating, miniature people.

"Why do ye have a bird for a companion?" The old woman's voice is pitched higher than before as she glances between Lucas and me.

The brunette woman gasps and points at me. "I knew it! I saw a bird flying around us earlier. She's a djinn just like the one who trapped us."

I step to the side so I can view all of them and have none of them at my back, the scepter laying at my feet. "He's my Watcher."

Several scoff at me, mostly the men. The women have more open faces, though skepticism is clear in their gazes—all except one.

The old woman shakes the stick at the grumpy man. They both appear to be the oldest present. Possibly they're the leaders or elders of their group. "She's wearing the gauntlet, Nobbert. No djinn or mage could do that. She could be telling the truth."

"Did you hit yourself on the head with that infernal stick, Arrin? She's not. She attacked us in the forest." The old man stabs his finger in the air. Not only are his words heavily accented and choppy, but his movements are equally abrupt and condescending.

I'd like to smack Nobbert with Arrin's stick. "After you tried to shackle me when I was asleep. Are you ashamed of being bested by a mere girl?"

Lucas flutters in my hand then stills. I gently rub his feathers.

"What about the prophecy?" Arrin asks.

Nobbert leans forward. "Superstitious nonsense."

"Then why were ye trying to shackle her, a girl asleep out in the forest without cause? Our kind don't do that." Arrin sneers at him. "I've never seen anyone like her in looks or ability. So I'm telling ye, she is." She thunks her stick on the ground.

Frustration builds until it sends heated prickles on my neck. I hate it when others speak about me as if I'm not there. Garrett's icy blue eyes watch me closely, unemotionally, just as Lucas described the eldrin to be. I don't trust him at all. "What are you both talking about?"

"Ye," Arrin shrieks.

"Nothing," Nobbert yells at the same time.

My ability hums to life in my gut. "Tell me what you're talking about." I *push* my ability into the words and direct them at the old woman who seems to be more willing to talk.

The woman's shoulders stiffen and then drop. "I'll tell ye without compulsion, thank ye. There's a legend, a prophecy if ye must, of a moon-born girl with the mark of the Kinsman who will set fire to the hearts of all she comes across. Only by her hands will we unite as a kingdom. It was foretold by Irice the Voyant years ago before ye were born when the eldrin weren't so corrupt, nor the mages so powerful. No one thought we'd come so far away from what the Kinsman created us to be. Nobody believed it except the nomads. Yet even some of us still scoff." She sends Nobbert a pointed look.

Lucas flutters in my hands and stands. He lets out a chirp, stretching his wings as he tries to keep his balance. *"My lady? What happened? Are you all right?"*

"I'm all right. Are you? One of these vermin hit you with a stone." I glance up at everyone. They're all staring at me and Lucas. *"I had to tell them you are my Watcher."*

His dark head bobs around, looking at the crowd before us. *"My head hurts. Luckily it wasn't a square hit or I might not have survived."*

My heart pinches at the thought and anger reignites.

"What are ye doing?" Arrin points the stick at me now, a too-keen gaze on us.

I glare at her. "I'm speaking to my Watcher."

Gasps drown out the trickle of the stream.

"I told you! She's trouble," Nobbert snaps. "Not even voyants have the ability to speak to each other like that."

"I'm not a voyant. I came here to search for my grandmother, Madrigal, from the village beneath the mountain. If you'd kindly point me in the correct direction, I'll be on my way." I tug once again at the gauntlet's cuff as I bend down to get the scepter. The silver glove isn't tight on my hand, however, it refuses to come off. Lucas coos lightly as my grasp tightens in frustration, and I loosen my hold.

Wide-eyed silence greets me when I stand. Arrin clutches a hand to her chest. "Did you say Lady Madrigal was your grandmother?"

Foreboding pricks at my scalp. Is she surprised or angry? I obviously shouldn't have mentioned her, especially since Arrin gave her the title of Lady. "I'll be going now."

I turn to walk around the group, but several of the small people encircle me, squealing excitedly. Before I can react, I'm engulfed in a lung-crushing hug. Lucas chitters in protest and flutters out of my hand to awkwardly perch on my head. His claws sting as they scratch my scalp.

"Oh, golly goodness!" the red-head exclaims, tears glittering in her green eyes. "It's true! You're the moon-born girl. You've come to save us!"

I'm astonished at the complete change of attitude. The eldrin, Garrett, breaks free from the women's hold, throwing them off him.

"Get him before he disappears!" yells Nobbert.

Arrin holds up the silver necklace with a white stone. "He can't go anywhere. Get the shackles!"

The eldrin runs through the crowd, headed straight for me, determination creasing his brows. He knocks off the women as they reach for him, his fine-looking clothes slick with mud and damp with water.

Lucas's weight lifts off my head as he darts away and I raise the scepter, holding it with my gloved hand. My hands tickle with sparks of blue. It's all I can manage to summon. The ball on the scepter glows purple.

Garrett's reaching for the wooden pole when a blinding, bluish-purple light flashes, knocking him back. He flies through the air, blonde hair and limbs splayed out from his body. He lands with an 'oof' on the ground not far from where he'd been held moments before.

A halo of blue light surrounds me. The stone necklace throbs against my chest with a rhythm separate from my heartbeat. I grasp it with my ungloved hand. It's warm to the touch, a magical essence pulsing from it. What could it mean?

Arrin grins as if she has a delicious secret.

Nobbert frowns at me, but the heat has left his bulging eyes. He jabs out his arm toward the unmoving eldrin. "Get him shackled! Maybe we can trade him for Colly."

Lucas rests on my arm as the group shackles the dazed eldrin. "Will those hold him?" I ask. If I can get them off, Garrett most certainly should be able to.

Nobbert grunts. "They're made of kinstone." He pulls out a thin strand of rope and ties it to one of the loops in the middle of the cuffs, jerking to make sure the knot is tight. "They should hold anyone since they counteract magic. Anyone except you. You're magical, yet you got out of two of our best sets. What are you?"

"I'm just a girl." I hedge. I'm unsure if I should trust him. Obviously, with everything he's seen me do, he feels the same.

"Now that's a lie if I ever did hear one." His ruddy, hairy face reddens.

Arrin steps in front of Nobbert and stands nose to nose with him. "Calm down, will ye? Ye're the reason the girl doesn't trust us, ya big oaf." She turns to me and holds out a stubby hand, well-worn as if she's used to working, though her skin is still wrinkled from the water. "I believe things have gotten off on the wrong foot. My name is Arrin."

"I'm Tambrynn." I stare at her hand, unsure what to do with it. Take it and curtsey? Give her mine so she can smack it like some of my former employers?

Lucas shifts on my arm. *"She wants you to shake her hand. Just place your right one in hers, and she'll do the rest."*

Belatedly, I do so. Arrin's grasp is tight as she shakes it vigorously. I tug to take my hand back, but like the glove, she doesn't let go. As suddenly as the shaking started, it ends, as she turns my palm over to look at it.

I yank it back to my chest, positive she's going to slap it. She doesn't, but she grins at my quick movement.

"Ye're not a trusting timper-bellied twit. Ye've known work." She nods. "That's good."

"For what?" I ask as I roll my shoulder, unsure what a timper-bellied twit is. My arm's still sore from all of the rowing, and the woman's jerking shake reawakens the ache. It throbs, the necklace pulses, and my heart beats, all separately, threatening to undo my sanity.

"Ye're the granddaughter of Lady Madrigal, High Cleric and Minister of Grace, correct? Her daughter being Lady Cadence, renown Cleric and Healer?" she asks.

"I know not of the titles. Cadence was my mother, yes, and Madrigal, I'm told, is my grandmother. Can you tell me how to find her? It's of grave importance." Once I mention my mother, my thoughts turn to my father, and I can't keep them from him. Though we'd escaped him after the dragon's attack, I'm confident I haven't seen the last of him.

Arrin's face puckers, her wrinkles deepening. She drops her arm to her side, the stick slack in her hand. "Cadence *was* ye're mother? As in—?"

"She died ten years ago." Emotion clogs my voice. I swipe

my hand across my nose without thinking. It's my gloved hand and the fabric, though flexible, is scratchy, quite like barbs inset into the fabric. I hold my other hand against my stinging nose and upper lip.

Lucas warbles a sad, lonely note.

"I see." Arrin stands a bit taller and lifts her face to mine. "Ye're grandmother, Lady Madrigal, is gone as well, dead five years now in the spring. She died defending the Holy Fortress against the evil mage Thoron. Kinsman bless her soul." She bows her head.

Heat leaches out of my body, leaving me chilled. Even the necklace cools at my neck. Lucas teeters on my arm and I fumble with the scepter to hold him closer. I can't feel him through the gauntlet encasing my hand, but I hope my embrace is comforting. Unlike Lucas, I hadn't known Madrigal. And since discovering my father, I'd lain all my hope on finding her. How would I learn more about my abilities? Who could help me, us, now? Unwanted tears prick my eyes. "I—don't know what to say."

The sun is getting low now, blinding me with its blaze of final light streaking across the land. Arrin stops beside me, and I turn toward her and away from the bright light. "Ye saved us from the illusion, the least we can do is feed ye."

"What about Colly?" I ask. "Don't we need to find her?"

"We know where she is." The others' mumbling groans accompany Nobbert's reply. Head down, he gathers the rope he tied to the eldrin's cuffs and yanks it. The eldrin stumbles to follow where he's led.

Arrin grasps my arm by the elbow. Once again, her hold is firm. "It's never good luck to set out on an empty stomach. Besides, too many things come out in the dark. Best to start after first light. Come on, then." She releases my arm and totters after the others at a good pace.

My mind flits to the froggen and I shudder. A glance around the darkening meadow assures me there are no better offers at the moment. I hurry after her, gently holding Lucas and using the scepter as a walking stick. "Where are we going?"

"Through the mines to our hidden city." She glances back at me. "Ye might have to duck a bit."

29

"**D**o you know where we're headed?" I ask Lucas as I follow behind Arrin and her group. The pasture around us thins as the ground changes to a rocky landscape. Thicker, heartier weed clusters replace the lush grass and flowers. Mountains creep their way into view as we weave along a trail down a hill beyond the pastureland.

"*As a child, I'd heard about the giant blackwood timberlands where stories told of them living high in the trees. Without magical wards, they can't defend themselves from the rogue beasts that roam the woods at night. I've heard of them living in mines but never knew where they might be.*" Lucas flutters around the group, avoiding Nobbert and Garrett, and comes back to rest on my shoulder. I'm relieved that he seems to be fleet-winged despite having been knocked unconscious earlier.

There are trees around the base of the mountains. Tall, slender ones with smooth bark. I can't imagine them supporting homes or villages of nomads. Bird's nests, surely. But not houses of any substance. Wind whistles through the treetops, bowing them to and fro, solidifying my opinion.

"How far are the mines?" I ask Arrin. She strides a few steps ahead of me and off to my right. Her tottering gait is aided by her handy staff. I keep to her left and out of easy reach of it. I also use the scepter for balance as I pick my way around the rocks and the patches of sharp grass blades that snag on my woolen stockings.

She chuckles. "Not far. They're hidden for our safety and protection. We don't bring anyone in for the same reason." She turns her grayed head to me and winks. "Something tells me ye're not the threat that doofus Nobbert thinks."

I step on an errant stone and stumble as it twists my ankle. "I was only protecting myself. They attacked me first."

"Yes, yes. Ye don't have to keep defending ye'self. Though he won't say it, his actions prove he thinks ye're the moon-born girl just as I do."

I think back on all of the wives' tales and superstitions I'd been subject to on Tenebris. All of the outrageous ideas of me being cursed and evil. This was just another in a long line of misled ideas, even if it was a kinder misconception. "What if I'm not who you think I am? What if I'm just a girl—"

Arrin cackles. "Just a girl! With silver-spun hair and stars in your eyes? Not likely. Ye're magic is blue like the light of the moon. And ye have magic, ye don't wield magic." One of her gnarled hands circles the air in front of her for emphasis. "All them eldrin ever do is wield magical items or siphon natural energy into magic by other means like those white stones. They have no innate magic as ye do. There hasn't been a pure magic user, even an eldrin one, in a dragon's age. That's probably why good eldrin Nyle is wary of ye." Sarcasm laces her last words.

I'm taken aback. "But what about the froggen? Aren't they magical?"

She stops, startling me, and spins to face me, her long, wild hair whipping around her head. "Froggens were created by abhorrent magic. Wielded magic that twisted and perverted what they were into something they shouldn't be. No matter how romantic the stories about them be, they aren't natural. They aren't magic-born. Not like ye. They're deviant, which is why they don't procreate like other beings. They siphon energy to create more of their own with the intent purpose of ruling this kingdom." Arrin grabs my arm and gives it a hard shake. "Don't trust them."

I wince, unsure what to say. She drops my arm and totters on ahead of me. The wind, which had mostly stirred the treetops, swirls around us. Above the noise of the gusts of air is a far-off, high-pitched sound. I stop to listen more carefully. "Did you hear that?" I ask no one in particular.

The red-headed girl spins around, her eyes wide with panic. "I did. Run! Get to the mines. It's those abominations!"

"They must've sensed your magic." Lucas darts off my shoulder and circles behind us in a wide arc.

I clasp the scepter tighter, panic clenching my gut. My body complains as I pick up my pace. Though sore, I can still outrun the smaller nomads. Nobbert is now wrestling with the rope as Garrett tries to pull away. Two of the other men grab him, and together the three of them scuffle forward with the unwilling eldrin.

"It's not far now. Keep up!" Arrin is sturdier than she appears as she uses the staff to hurry toward the mountains. The rocks and stones don't hinder her as they do me. She even passes a few of the others who keep glancing behind them.

"Don't look! Keep moving!" I grab one woman by the shoulder and direct her forward. She's the smallest one and quite round and stout for a small woman. Tears streak down her face as she tries to keep up, but her legs are too short, her significant body too low to the ground to move swiftly. I hoist her awkwardly with my free arm, balancing her with the scepter tucked under my other armpit. She flounders in my grip. It's like trying to lug a squirming pig across a farmyard, and I'm bent over, hurrying as fast as I can to follow after Arrin.

The mountains loom ahead of us now, the shadows from the trees swallowing us up in cool darkness. More rocks and scrubby grasses dot the area, and I send a stone hurtling with my foot. It flies out of sight among the scrub which covers the ground now instead of the barbed, sharp grasses. Chills spread across my skin as I fight to keep hold of the nomad woman.

"My name's Witta, by the way," the nomad introduces herself with a jerky voice thanks to my running. "Thank you for saving me."

My arms burn from carrying her. I'm not sure how much longer I can keep it up. "How ... much ... farther ... is ... it?" It's getting hard to breathe. My back spasms and I fall to my knees, Witta landing on her bottom and sliding slightly in front of me.

We'd strode ahead of a few of the other nomads. Now as they pass us, though they turn to glance our way, no one stops to help. They're all terrified and consumed with their own survival. I grasp the scepter and drag Witta up to her feet. "Go. Run. I can defend myself." I'm panting so hard I wheeze. A concerned frown creases her brow, but thankfully she listens and hurries on without me.

"My lady. Are you all right?" Lucas returns to my side.

I'm bent, trying to catch my breath. I'm unsure if the air is heavier or if I'm not as capable as I once was. "Fine. Make sure they get inside wherever they're going."

"But, Tambrynn—"

"Go!" I sense them, an evil that nicks at my bones, before I twist to see them—their bent bodies with broken strides, moving faster than should be possible. Though it's dark, a murkier gloom sheathes them. I shiver. There are six of them, their maws open with saliva flying. Disgust and fear pinch the inside of my stomach.

I glance around, searching for my father. Like the pungent odorous sting of salted brine, his malevolence taints the wind. My ability buzzes to life in my gut, and the stone pulses at my neck. He must be near. Warmth swells from my center outward. I stand to face the beasts, the scepter held tight in my gloved hand. My aches subside as blue light crackles along my skin.

As the beasts lurch closer, I find my father is there at the back, the gray streak of hair on the left giving him away. His movements aren't as smooth or confident as they had been before. I squint to try to make out what's wrong and discern that though he remains youthful-looking, his face is puckered along one cheek and down his neck. Like he'd been burned. By a dragon, no doubt.

"My lady, the nomads have made it to the mine entrance. If you change now, you might make it before they reach you."

I imagine the small nomad people as Thoron's undead creatures. I can't allow that to happen. *"Won't he follow us?"*

Lucas hovers by me, nervousness emanating from him. *"The mine is laced with kinstone. Like the shackles, it repels magic. I don't think he or his beasts can enter without their magic being eliminated."*

Before I can register my deep-set fear of their howls, my body lightens, my heartbeat quickens, and I'm in the air. Lucas hoots, and we're off flying toward the mountains. Wind washes around me like a caress. It's exhilarating to have changed to a bird again, and it was easier this time than it ever has been. A melodic song bursts from my beak and is answered by snarls.

I tilt my body, following the stream of wind just as a red ball of Thoron's magic grazes one of my wings. Heat and then pain register from the spot along my back beside my arm. Singed, iridescent feathers swirl out of my sight. *"They're getting closer. Where's the doorway?"*

"Just up ahead. Stay close." Lucas's dark feathers disappear as we fly deeper into the shadow of the mountain.

A gust of wind blows me to the side and another ball of fiery heat shoots between Lucas and me. He darts down and to the right to avoid it.

I wobble before regaining my balance. *"They're too close."*

"Keep going, my lady. It's right here." He flits toward a sparse section of bushes near the base of the mountain. The opening must be there. His tailfeathers disappear and I bob my head to get a better view of the spot he flew through. With a giant shove of my wings, I aim for that bare area. I'm almost there when something knocks me sideways. I'm falling.

Heat and pain slice through my body. I clench my jaw, unable to move as flames of agony surge through every muscle to my bones. Mouth open in a silent cry, I hit the rocky ground. Luckily, the shock of the landing enables me to breathe again. Unluckily, I'm changed back to my girl form. Whatever magic Thoron had just thrown at me proves he is still strong, no matter what he looks like.

"Tambrynn!" Lucas shrieks.

I sit up and caress a lump on my head from a particularly sharp rock. It stings, but there's no blood. Rustling sounds behind me, someone grabs me at my armpits. I grasp hold of the scepter as I'm dragged backward through the bramble bushes. I cover my face against the onslaught of vicious scratching, my hair catching and snarling in the offending shrub. More rocks dig into my backside as I'm dropped abruptly.

"Get the scepter. Don't let the mage get hold of it!" One of the nomad men calls out.

Someone knocks me sideways. My hair is a snarled mess with sticks and debris. I brush it away from my face to see what's happening.

Witta grabs hold of the scepter and a blinding light bursts from the rod, flinging her like a rag doll into the mountain wall. Something cracks, and I fear it's her head.

"No!" I reach out and *call* the scepter to me. Witta falls to the ground, a crumpled form among the rubble.

30

My head throbs. I clench the scepter under my arm and scramble over to Witta to grab her around her middle and half-drag-half-carry her to the fissure. My necklace cord is caught between us and snaps from the strain. It tickles my neck as it slides away. Immediately the warmth of the stone is gone. I can't stop to find it. I'll have to look for it later. Finally reaching the others, the rest of the nomads stand in shocked silence at the mouth of the mountain opening.

Nobbert fists the rope attached to Garrett as the hostage resists, probably hoping to catch his nomad captor off guard. He's too tall for the opening, as am I, and I don't relish the thought of going inside bent over.

Arrin is the first to speak. "Bring her this way. Careful, now."

"Where are you, Lucas?" I ask in my mind. I haven't seen him since Thoron's magic hit me. My father and the beasts must be nearby now.

My mind immediately fills with a garbling noise. And pain. So much pain.

"Lucas!" I jerk my head around so hard my neck cramps. I squeal. The air grows thick with the stench of the beasts. They're close. Too close.

My ability spins in my gut like angry bees, and my hands glow a brighter blue.

Before I can manage to place Witta down safely, one of the beasts breaks through the bushes, trampling them. I drop the poor girl to the hard ground. I try to nudge her sideways, but the beast is coming straight for me. I stand and hold the scepter up to protect us.

The beast stops mid-stride and contorts, its snout receding into a human nose and mouth. It stumbles back into the bushes and the snout returns. It shakes its head.

I have no time to process what is happening before two more beasts bust through the bushes, the stiff branches scratching at their fetid flesh. They knock the first beast down in their haste to reach me.

The first lands not far from me, but he writhes on the ground, a beast one moment and a man the next. The other two also stop mid-stride as they step onto the flinty ground at the base of the dark mountain. They jerk and sputter, their hideous forms distorted in differing stages of man and beast.

"The kinstone's stopping them," Nobbert shouts from behind me. "If you're who you say you are, do something to get rid of them filthy monsters."

I swing the scepter back and forth between the three monsters, unsure what to do. The fact that they change back and forth between a beast and their former selves would indicate whoever they once were is still in there. Could they be saved? Should they be saved?

I hesitate long enough that the two scamper back far enough away from the stone that they return to their awful, undead forms. The first one jerks back and forth until it, too, reaches some invisible boundary and it settles back into its grotesque shape.

"What're you waiting for? The mage will be here any minute!" Nobbert wakes me from my thoughts.

"*Lucas?*" I ask in my mind again. Silence answers me, and my heated body chills.

"Never mind the beasts. Get Witta to safety," Arrin calls out. A glance behind assures me she's speaking with the other nomads and not me. I continue to face the beasts who now stand a horse and carriage length away from us near the destroyed bushes. Thankfully, they don't seem to be inclined to come toward us again.

Witta is shuffled away, across the dirt and rock.

There's a tug on my arm. "Tambrynn, come on. Come inside the mountain. Ye'll be safe there."

I ignore Arrin. "Something's wrong with Lucas. I can't leave him out here unprotected. Just get my necklace for me, please."

"We don't have time for this nonsense." Nobbert barks out.

Arrin's grip on my arm tightens. "He can fly, can't he? He'll be fine."

Thoron steps through what's left of the bushes, a harsh smile on his blistered face. The three beasts shy away from him. Two bolder, salivating ones flank him. "Yes, he'll be fine." He holds a limp, black bird in his hands.

For a moment my head swims, but the sound of my father's hawking laughter makes the fuzz in my head clear. I stare into his haughty eyes, unsure what to do. This is the terror I remember from when his beasts murdered Mother ten years ago. I can't let it happen again. And no matter what, I will avenge her death.

I lock my knees which must be visibly shaking. I neither feel nor hear anything behind me. The nomads no doubt have fled into the mountain and away from danger. It's a welcomed relief as I can't protect them all, at least not while I'm focused on saving Lucas and destroying my father.

"Nothing to say, Daughter?" He flips the bird from one hand to the other. Charred skin and blisters cover his hand. If it hurts, he shows no sign of it.

My gut's on fire. I take a step forward, the scepter pointed at him.

"Uh, uh, uh." He takes Lucas's head in one hand and his body in another. The feathers on his neck stick out and my heart freezes. "Would you like to play a game?"

My blood runs wild and my hands flame with blue light. "I don't play games," I say through tight jaws. My eyes burn until they sting and it's all I can do not to blink away the sensation.

"No, that's right. Your childhood was taken from you at such an early age, isn't that right?" He holds Lucas up higher, his neck still stretched far too much. The taut feathers glow a bluish-purple in the moonlight. "I did apologize for that, didn't I?" He drops Lucas and whispers something.

The bird changes into Lucas' human form before it hits the ground. The maps we'd taken from Tenebris fall, scattering beneath the ruined bushes.

I reach out a hand to *call* him to me.

A red ball of magic flies from my father's hand, engulfing Lucas.

Lucas shrieks in a high-pitched tenor I've never heard him make before.

I can hear him both in my head and with my ears. It's like a chorus of dozens of Lucas's screaming in torment. Blue flames light up my body, and I swing the scepter in Thoron's direction. My blue energy mixes with the scepter's purple. It streaks at him, hitting him and knocking him back into the last two beasts.

I run toward Lucas, *calling* him to me.

Thoron flicks his wrist and flings a black ball of magic at Lucas. It splits, half of it coming toward me and the other half hitting Lucas, lifting him soundlessly into the air.

I throw my arm up to block the dark magic coming for me and it bounces off my protective blue sphere, flying to the side and behind me.

When the protective shield lessens, I hear the nomads screaming. I turn my head slightly just in time to catch the eldrin, Garrett, running straight at me. He tackles me to the ground, landing on top of me. The air is knocked out of my lungs and I groan. Though he's slight of frame, Garrett is heavy. Pain explodes in my left side. Still without air, I'm unable to make a sound.

"Don't let him get hold of that scepter," Nobbert screams.

Garrett grabs it, thumping my body back against the ground as he does so, allowing air once again to enter my lungs. Gasping, I wrestle Garrett for the scepter. Burning hot magic crackles around us, but my protective shield also protects Garrett as he continues to struggle to gain control of the scepter.

I'm tiring. Even my ability is fading. Fierce, hot pain breaks through my shield. Both Garrett and I scream as it washes over us, and then I'm jerking around on the ground. There's nothing but darkness and spots of light as the pain stabs again and again at my flesh until it is gone and I'm lying, panting on the ground.

I struggle to regain control of my errant limbs, which twitch but don't answer my inner pleas to grab Lucas and change into a bird and fly away. There's no awaiting buzz in my gut, no blue glow, nothing but a dim awareness of agony.

Garrett manages to rise but is grabbed by one of the beasts who offers him like a present before a grinning Thoron.

Another beast grabs the scepter from where it lies near my feet and takes it to his master. In the blink of an eye, the gauntlet is gone and on Thoron's hand.

I shriek in an effort to regain the scepter, but it's no use. I have nothing, no ability, no power to call it to me.

Thoron caresses the carved handle with the glove, a wicked glee lighting his blistered face.

I glare death at him, wishing I could send him up in flames like the dragon had, only this time I would finish the job.

Thoron glances down at me as if sensing my thoughts. "What a wonderful gift. Thank you, Daughter."

He places a hand on the struggling eldrin and mutters some nonsensical words. Whatever he's said is powerful enough to bend Garrett back, almost in half, his face twisted into a grimace. My father continues to speak strange chants over Garrett's stiff body, the beasts looking on, entranced.

Blood tingles in my hands and feet as whatever spell Thoron hit me with finally wears off. I reach out and touch the boy beside me. "Lucas?"

His alabaster skin is paler than I remember, and he's cold. So cold. His dark hair is mussed and sticks out like feathers from his head and across his forehead. I wish he'd open his eyes, but he doesn't move or answer me.

The necklace lays at my side and I scrabble with numb fingers to get it among the rock on the ground. It warms and a slight humming starts from my arm and skips across my splayed body to where I touch Lucas. Prickling replaces numbness, and the thump of my blood rushing through my veins returns. The pressure and pain from Thoron's magic ease until they're gone. With a thought, I change Lucas back to his bird form and gather him close to me.

Thoron still chants over Garrett, oblivious to my actions. White haze gushes out of Garrett's body and into Thoron's. At the same time, dark foggy energy pours back into Garrett, and his face and body twist in alarming ways.

I take advantage of the distraction and stumble to my feet, running toward the fissure. There, Nobbert and Arrin both peek around the rock to watch Thoron, horror clear on their faces.

"Watch out!" Arrin cries.

I duck and swerve to the left, away from the fissure's opening. Rock explodes at almost the same spot I was, right where Nobbert and Arrin stood. I can't stop, though. Conceding that I cannot overpower my father, I have to save Lucas.

Rocks rain down, blocking the entrance to the mountain. I've nowhere to go.

Howls erupt behind me. Garrett's transformation must be complete. Blood races through my veins as I change. I'm bigger than usual and I clasp Lucas's limp form in my claws. I don't stop to question the change. I don't have time. Thoron's magic snaps at me in the air, tugging at my tail feathers.

I fly into the dark night.

31

I can see clearly despite the darkness. I don't fly far. Large trees line the side of the mountain above the nomad's crevice opening. I pray silently to the Kinsman that Lucas was right—the beasts can't follow our scent in the air. Besides, it would be hard for them to scale the treacherous incline of the mountain to get to us.

Wind rustles through the tall tree I land in, redolent with sap and pine. I float into the branches and settle Lucas into a safe spot against the trunk, thankful the branches are thick but spaced far enough apart for my larger form to fit.

Shivers overtake me and I ruffle my feathers. *"Lucas?"* He still hasn't moved, though I can feel his heartbeat with my talons. I nuzzle him with my beak. *"Can you hear me? Lucas?"*

There's no answer. So, I wait. The biting in my bones remains for what seems like hours, though the moon's arc doesn't match. I'm anxious and horrified by what my father did with Garrett. My mind can't set on one thought before another one takes its place. Weary, I tuck my beak beneath my wing and guard Lucas.

A blast wakens me. Birds cry out and flutter away. The tree shakes but remains.

Lucas sleeps, undeterred by the noise, against the tree where I'd laid him. I totter to the end of the limb to see what the explosion was. Dust clouds rise from the base of the mountainside, the same side as the crevice. My sharp hearing distinguishes nomads yelling, but they're too far away to make out what's happening.

I waver between flying off with Lucas and leaving the nomads behind or going to investigate. My conscience pricks, and I know what I have to do.

I grasp Lucas carefully in one of my talons. Hopping, I make my way to a wider area and spread my wings. The chilled morning air flutters through my feathers as I circle down. Lucas stirs and chirrups.

"Lucas?"

His heart rate increases, but besides his panicked squeaking squawks, I hear nothing in my mind.

More shouts and another explosion rocks the area. Gray dust plumes into the air as I swing wide around the base of the mountain. Rocks and rubble clutter the ground around what was a crevice, now a massive hole blown out from the mountainside.

Several nomads scuttle about digging out the rocks and clearing the debris. I see nor sense any other threats close by. I land on the outside of the field of rubble, setting Lucas down gently. With a thought, I change back.

Lucas flutters about, his chatter drowned out by the shouts and noises of the nomads clearing a path into the mountain. Nobbert's clothes are caked with dust and sweat. He spots us and storms over.

"And where'd you get off to last night?" Vessels bulge along his forehead.

Arrin strikes a boulder three times with her walking stick, her face pinched. "Leave her alone, ye big lummox." She reaches Nobbert and yanks his shoulder back. "Everyone was scared last night. Do ye think she was any different? There wasn't anything else to do besides run."

"Run and leave us stranded in the mountain." Nobbert was nose to nose with Arrin now, his vein pulsing rapidly.

Arrin's arm moves in a wide arc. "Ye weren't stranded, ye big oaf. Ye just didn't like having to go all the way through the mountain and blasting ye're doorway wide open."

"It's an open invitation to anyone who wants to come and steal our kinstone, it is. Come on over everyone, it's here for the taking." He spins and turns back toward the mountain, grumbling under his breath.

"Don't mind him. His knees were knocking last night same as yers, believe me." She shoots one last nasty look at Nobbert's backside before turning back to me. "Now, how are ye this morning?"

Lucas has ended his chattering and started to pick at the few grass blades growing out of the stony ground. I frown. "I'm fine, but I'm worried about Lucas."

Arrin bends over, one hand on her stick to steady her, and studies Lucas who continues to peck at the ground. "Did he just eat a bug? Does he normally do that kind of thing?"

"Bugs? Not that I'm aware of." I pick him up, but he protests by nipping at my fingers. "Ow." I drop him back down. "I don't know what to do. I can't communicate with him, and he doesn't seem to remember me."

"Thoron threw a lot of magic at ye both last evening. It's sure to leave anyone a bit befuddled." She leans on her stick, her gaze locked on me.

A weight settles on my chest. "It's all a mess. Thoron has the scepter now, Colly's still missing, and Lucas is not acting right. I don't know what to do." Tears sting the backs of my eyes. I refuse to cry, but my traitorous body doesn't listen.

Arrin tsks. "Ye can't go back and redo a thing, so it does no good to sit in a pool of pity. Better ye be to get on with doing something than to stew about it all." She keeps Lucas close by guiding him with the end of her staff when it seems as if he's ready to wander off.

I sniff, frustrated. "Yes, but what can I do?"

Arrin groans. "What can't ye do?" She yanks my arm and turns me toward the mountain. "We nomads have no magic. We can't defend ourselves against any magic kind. Yet, we found a way to blast open this mountain to find refuge." She grabs a chunk of rock at her bare feet. "And then we found the metal in this mountain absorbs magic. We didn't whine when it got hard and stop trying. We did something about it."

She swoops down and picks Lucas up. "Ye have more magic in yer pinky finger than those eldrin do combined. I can tell ye're smart. Think."

Lucas clucks and fights Arrin's hold. She hands him to me. "Those who are given special gifts from the Kinsman have a great responsibility to use them faithfully. That doesn't mean ye won't fail. It just means ye'll have to work hard to make things right." She turns and strides away from me, her stick thunking against the rocky ground.

"Yes, but where do I start?" My shoulders slump. Lucas stops wiggling in my arms, his dark eyes peering up at me as if suddenly recognizing me.

"How about changing into a plow horse so we can use you to move these rocks easier?" One of the nomad men calls out, laughing. The others chuckle in response.

I ignore them and grab an armful of stones. At least I knew how to work hard.

———

By midday, two paths have been formed. One runs around the side of the mountain, just wide enough for the nomads to travel single file, leading to their hidden second entrance. The other winds through the rubble in veins leading from the bushes to the now-cratered crevice opening.

Arrin hands me a thick chunk of bread. "I hope you like dewberry jam. It's all we have."

Pink jam glistens on top of the crusty bread. My stomach twists in hunger. "Thank you."

She sits next to me. "This one's for yer bird." She tears off a piece and throws it at Lucas, who gobbles it up.

The jam has a tart sweetness that makes my mouth water as I eat. It reminds me of the boysenberries from Tenebris, though they were a darker red color. I'd only had them a few times, mostly when Mother had still been alive. I savor the flavor as long as I can. "It's very good."

"Ye stayed. Ye could've left." She lobs a piece that hits Lucas right between his eyes. He shakes his head then pecks at it.

I shrug. "It's my fault Thoron's magic hit your crevice opening. It's only right I stay to help clean up."

"Sure, true." She nods. "We've got it well in hand now. All we need is to plaster the stones back in place to enclose the opening. What're yer plans?"

"She needs to find another place to stay." Nobbert swings his canteen at me, spilling it. By the scent and looks of the liquid, it's some sort of ale. "It's too dangerous to have her around. I'm too old to rebuild a mountain every day."

Arrin huffs. "Where's she supposed to go?"

He punches the cap back on the canteen. "I don't care if she sets up camp in the Harrowstone Valley or if she returns to the eldrin Sanctuary of Elysium. She needs to go and take that chirpy nuisance with her."

I watch Lucas running about, pecking at the pieces of bread Arrin tosses him. "His name is Lucas, not chirpy nuisance, thank you. And I'd gladly go if I knew how to get there."

"I've got just the thing for you." Nobbert's voice lilts.

I glance up at him, suspicious.

He pulls out a heap of crumpled parchment from his back pocket. He sets them down on the ground and points to them. "The maps your birdboy dropped last night. I found them under the bushes when I was cleaning up."

My heart pinches at the memory of Lucas and me getting the maps and books from the cavern after the ball. Oh, how handsome he'd been that night. Lucas pecks at one of the papers. Some of the words I understand, others I don't know.

I shoo Lucas away before he tears them. He's determined to get to them, though, and I have to grab him to keep him from the maps. "I can't read everything. And I don't know what direction is what. If you could show me?"

Red colors Nobbert's face. "How should I know?" He stomps away.

Arrin rolls them up and hands them to me. "Nobbert can't read or write. I was always lame, ye see. I had time to sit and learn. Nobbert didn't have the same opportunity. Boys farmed, fished, or mined."

She stands up and points toward the mountains. "That is north toward the eldrin holy lands of the sanctuary." She turns. "Past the pastures where ye found us are the Durham Timberlands and beyond that is the Great River. If ye head west, ye'll run into the desert lands and the Valley of Harrowstone. They're dangerous for any folk. East is the Meridian Peaks and the sea of Marmara. Ye'll find the good

Councilmaster has taken over the towns in the Shrouded Mountains between the sanctuary and the peaks."

I clutch both a squirming Lucas and the maps. I consider what Lucas would do. "If I go to the eldrin lands, what will I find?"

"A mountain fortress, empty save a few of the older eldrin folk. After Madrigal and the other leaders were killed in the battle against Thoron, the younger clerics split, leaving the elders to fend for themselves. What Thoron didn't plunder, the young eldrin took for themselves. Then they waged war against each other. Each time one would come into power, they'd put new rules and regulations in place until it seemed just breathing was illegal." She tsks. "That's how so many of our clan have been taken, just like Colly. If they can't threaten ye into submission, they take the young'uns and use them as laborers in their fields and cities."

Lucas stills in my arms, his heart beating fast against my skin. Whether he realized it or not, he'd followed close by me while I helped clear out the rubble. It is a good sign. At least, I pray it is. Now, after gobbling up the bread, he tucks his beak beneath his wing and rests.

I contemplate the mountains in the north where Arrin pointed. "Are there any dragon lands that you know of?"

"Dragons?" She sounds surprised. "There haven't been dragons for ages. 'Course, there hasn't been anyone who could change into a firebird in as many lifetimes. If there were dragons, ye'd find their history in the Sanctuary. Is that where ye're planning to go?"

Tension creeps into my shoulders, weighing me down. I need Lucas's guidance, but so far, I've been unable to hear him or talk with him. I hadn't recognized how much I was attuned to his presence in my mind, my heart, until it was gone. I worry the bond between us is broken and may never be healed.

I take a deep, shaky breath. "I need to start somewhere."

Lucas coos in his sleep. *"Don't give up, my lady."*

The words are so clear in my mind they bring tears to my eyes. He's still there, not lost as I'd feared. I shudder and bend to kiss his soft feathered back. *"I won't."*

Arrin eyes us. "Well, ye'll need some supplies then."

32

Arrin returns with a bundle of clothing and a bag full of supplies. She thrusts out the armful. "Our scouts found these in the mountain ruins after the eldrin left the sanctuary. I wasn't sure why I kept them until now. They're women's clothes, the choicest fabrics on Anavrin. No use to us. I'm thinking they should fit just fine."

I set a sleeping Lucas down carefully and take the items from her. It's a shirt with a matching skirt, soft to the touch, with underthings and knee-high stockings. Along with those are a pair of hard-soled slippers made from pliable leather. Curiously, the clothes are all the same shade of the stone in my necklace, blue with a green iridescence that glitters in the sunlight.

I clutch them to my chest. "Thank you."

"Ye can change behind those trees. It'll be private now that the men are hunting." Arrin moves as if to walk away. "Fly over the green lake with its castle, but don't go near it. The fish and water creatures that live there are an abomination." She spits out the last sentence.

I wonder how much she knows about the froggen, Siltworth in particular. I had no intention of running into him anytime soon. I nod in understanding.

She continues, pointing at a far spot on the mountain range. "Then keep going north to the highest mountain. There, in a deep valley, ye'll find the sanctuary city of Elysium built into the mountainside. May the Kinsman give ye the answers ye seek there." With a nod, she hobbles away.

Lucas remains asleep as I carry him, the maps, along with everything Arrin had just given me to the shelter of the trees.

It looks like a laundry area with lines running between the trees and empty tubs with soap and scrubbers. I place Lucas on a folded cloth and change, admiring the close weave and slick texture of the outfit. The blue color changes as I move, and the fabric fits my slimmer body. I'm surprised that the skirt is actually wide-legged britches. The shoes stretch and cover over my feet like a glove.

My heart pricks, remembering that my father has the scepter with the glove. Nothing good will come from that, I'm sure. My old woolen clothes are in appalling shape. No doubt they'll be used for scraps or burned. I leave them by one of the washtubs.

Lucas's dark eyes watch me now. I run my hand over his sleek feathers. "Can you fly after me, or should I carry you in my talon?"

"Scree-coo."

Shaken, I stare at him, my heart palpitating? "Lucas?"

"Chirrup, hoot."

I swing him up to my face. He snuggles close, and I pull away to make sure I'm not just imagining it.

Lucas pecks gently at a single tear flowing down my cheek. "You're still there. I just need to bring you back. Somehow." I needed to find Audhild or the beggar who had sent her. They might be the only ones who would know how to help us. My heart aching, I hug Lucas to my chest and grab the bag and tuck the maps inside it beside some berries, nuts, bread, and a full flagon of water.

"Can you follow me?" I ask Lucas as I set him down on the ground.

"Scree."

I smile, taking that as a yes and praying I'm right. "Stay close." I change in an instant and take flight, glancing behind to be sure Lucas is behind me. He is, and I let out a melodic chirp of thankfulness.

Outside of the enclosed wash area, the sun is bright and the air full of the scent of pine trees. The wind caresses my body as we fly over the treetops. The day is alight with the essence of a storm not too far away, though I see no dark clouds.

Our backs are to the sun. Lucas wobbles every once in a while, and I try my best to keep his slower pace, though my wings itch to stretch out in long strides.

"Lucas?" I test out our mind communications.

"Scree."

I find a path closer to a tree line so we're not out in the open. *"Can you hear me?"*

"Scree-scree."

So, hopefully, our connection was broken but not completely gone? *"I don't know for sure what I'm doing. I wish I could talk with you."*

"Scree."

I inwardly sigh.

We travel until the sun is high in the sky and my throat becomes parched. I've seen no green lake so far, but below us is a small brook. The babble of water directs my path down to a stream cut through the forest. It's wide enough we cannot jump over it, yet shallow enough to be crossed. The blurbing of rushing water comes from further up the stream. I circle the area to make sure it's safe to land. I see nothing of concern and drop to the bank, changing back to my girl form the instant my feet hit the ground.

Lucas continues to circle.

"C'mon down. I'll share what Arrin packed us." I take the bag off my back and untie the opening.

The thin material I wear rustles with a slight breeze, but the sun has warmed the air to a comfortable temperature. I sit on a raised bank beside the stream and eat a handful of nuts and an apple using a small knife to cut the fruit. When Lucas finally settles, I feed him small pieces of the apple, crumbles of cheese, and some dry bread. He settles into my side and dips his beak beneath his wing.

Sitting back, I glance up at the clouds between the treetops. A few birds call out in the distance. There's nothing out of the ordinary, yet I clasp the knife in one hand as I cross my arms and settle in for a small doze. I close my eyes to enjoy the peaceful moment without the chattering of the nomads or the howls of my father's beasts.

The babbling burble of the water gets louder. I glance around and find nothing of concern. However, I don't trust it. I've had enough surprises.

My suspicions are confirmed when my necklace warms against my chest and my gut hums. Something is nearby, but I see nothing in the trees. A glance up reveals nothing in the sky. What can it be? I twist to my knees to stand, disturbing Lucas from his sleep. I grip my knife so hard it hurts.

A rustle from behind me has me spinning around, my back

to the stream. Cold water trickles around me, and I glance down.

I'm grabbed around my stomach and dragged into the stream. Water engulfs my open mouth as I try to scream. Lucas screeches above the flush of the liquid in my ears, and I'm gone before I can do anything.

Bubbling, icy water surrounds me, piercing my body like sharp blades. I dig at whatever is around my stomach, chopping with the knife, to no avail. It holds tight no matter how hard I cut at it. I kick, but there's nothing but water to kick against. There's no muddy land or grassy bank to grab hold of.

I try *calling* for tree branches to reach down, but I'm traveling too fast for it to happen. It's not long before my lungs protest and spasm, wanting to breathe, but my trail through the stream continues. My body numbs, easing the biting pain of the cold. My strength is quickly depleted. I stop fighting to conserve my energy and shove my hands into the pockets of the strange pants trying to find some warmth for my frozen fingers.

I can see a blurry view of the clouds and blue sky. The stream narrows and I reach out to grab the sides. My hand makes contact—I pull my head above the water. I gasp and drag in a breath before whatever is pulling me tugs me back down. I reach for the knife but struggle to find the slit of the pocket opening.

And then we hit a larger body of water, the swift movement slows me for a brief second. I wave my arms and buck my legs, but I'm sucked into a water funnel and whirled around and around, my head spinning until I'm dizzy. The roaring blast tears at my body. Pressure pushes on my ears and eyes, and my lungs spasm again. The more I'm sucked down, the darker it gets and the faster I spin in circles until I'm thrown out of the swirling storm, easing the pressure that's building behind my eyes and in my ears.

I fight the instinct to inhale. The cold settles in my bones, replacing the numbness with a deep ache. My twitchy body refuses to obey me.

A shadow passes over me, grasping my collar, and I'm jerked upwards. Fish dart away from me and light reflects off the depths as I travel upward, and then I've broken through the surface and dragged to a bricked platform. I choke and spit, trying to suck enough air into my lungs to make up for the time I was underwater. I'm exhausted and heaving.

Vaguely I hear Lucas twittering in the distance. It takes several minutes before the darkness in my vision is gone and I am able to see clearly once again. I'm no longer in the forest. Frog-like people stand on a paved-brick shore lining the brackish green water. Rising out of the middle of the large pool is a grand castle, with a wooden drawbridge dropping to the foamy edge leading up to a double-door entry. Turrets border the castle's side with narrow windows like the ones in the abandoned fortress Lucas and I found near the Zoe Tree.

It's the exact place Arrin warned me to avoid.

Siltworth, the froggen, stands over me and bows. A jeweled crown of braided seaweed adorns his glistening head, and a large necklace with an ornate pearl pendant hangs from his thick neck. I recall momentarily Lucas's story about the first froggen and his gift to the noblewoman of a pearl necklace. Does his necklace indicate the story is more truth than fable?

"Welcome, silver mage with the star eyes, to my clan's fortress."

Dozens of froggen line the brick bank. They're all sizes and shapes, though none of them have necks, their heads bulge directly out of their rounded bodies. Some wear smaller crowns or jewelry, mostly having blue or green stones, not pearls. A few hold weapons, such as pitchforks with hooked tines. None of them seem very welcoming.

My necklace warms beneath my new top, and I drag myself up to sit on my knees, thankful my clothing isn't a dress. Curiously, it isn't soaked. The fabric, though wet, sheds water like a duck's back. I dig a vine of some sort that's poking my arm out of the sleeve and toss it aside. "What am I doing here?"

"*Scree!*"

Lucas's call echoes in my mind, bolstering me. It's not words, but it's better than the detachment he'd had earlier. I work to show no sign of having heard him, unsure what the froggen wants with me. However, I reach out with the fleck of ability left inside me to assure him I'm fine.

Siltworth's bulging, yellow eyes glisten. "My apologies about your friend. He wasn't very welcoming before, and we wish to speak with you alone. Since Thoron came into the possession of a holy relic that heightens his strength, our situation has turned dire."

I school my face, but my chilled cheeks flush enough to give away my guilt. Out of the corner of my eye, I see a dark shape flying by, but when I look straight on, I see nothing but a wavering sky. An illusion. One Lucas must not be able to get through. "What has that to do with me?"

"I believe you know the answer." He reaches a webbed hand out to help me stand. I then saw what I had thought was his molted skin is actually a seaweed cloak he wears. It's dragging on the sandy ground behind him as if he were a king.

Maybe he is.

I ignore his hand. "Still, what has that to do with me?"

He drops his arm and turns to walk over to a stone bench. Flinging the seaweed cloak wide, he sits, crossing his long, thin legs at the knee. He kicks his webbed foot with its round, padded toes back and forth in a nervous kind of tic. "It is your job to take the dark mage down. It has been foretold. We request you join us in our quest to eradicate him from this kingdom."

My ability bursts to life in my gut. It buzzes almost as wild as the whirlpool. I keep my hands clutched in my lap so I don't squeeze his bulbous body enough to burst his insides. "So, you drag me up a mountain-long, freezing-cold stream, almost drowning me in the process, and you call that a request? I thought manners and decorum meant something to your kind."

His leg rocks back and forth in a calm manner. Too calm, if the darting of his strange eyes were any indicator. "I tried that the first time around. You refused to accept my offer."

I fling my arms out in frustration. When my hand lands back against my thigh, it hits something hard in my pants pocket. I still had the knife! I hide my triumph. "I had just made it to Anavrin. I was completely overwhelmed. How was I supposed to make any kind of a decision like you were asking? I didn't even know you existed until you popped out of the water."

Several of the froggen surrounding us point their strange-looking pitchforks my direction.

"Scree!" Lucas's voice is faint, but I know it's him.

"It is not my job to prepare you," Siltworth croaks.

"It's not my job to save *you*." My ability hums so strongly in my gut that it burns now. I slip my hand inside my pocket, grabbing for the knife's handle. "I tire of this conversation."

"That's unfortunate." Siltworth lifts his lean arm, and two other froggens drag a gagged and fighting Arrin from behind a brick wall.

Her eyes are glittering with anger, her hair ratty with seaweed sticking out. I can't make out any of the flowers on her torn, muddied dress. One of her feet is bloody, and her walking stick is missing.

I stand, my hands crackling with blue energy. I fist the one they can see at my side and clasp the knife tighter with my other, hidden hand. "What'd you do to her?"

A third froggen produces Arrin's stick from behind his back. He punches it into her stomach. She groans and coughs, bending over to catch her breath. Tears streak down her dirty face. But it's not only pain I see on her face. She's as furious as I am.

Blood pumps through my veins as hot as any fire. I spin and confront Siltworth, who sits calmly on the bench, his leg slowly swinging back and forth. "Let her go!"

"No. Not until Thoron is destroyed, his life force blotted out of existence. And I am made ruler over the eldrin and hold the Eye of Fate scepter." He uncrosses his legs and crosses them the opposite way, his other leg now swinging back and forth. His webbed hands grip the handles on the bench.

I think of Adelia, Cook's favorite snoop at the Broodmoor Estate, how she'd eavesdrop on everyone. She always knew what was going on and worked it in her favor. "How do you know so much? How are you spying on everyone?"

"*Water.*" Lucas's voice whispers in my mind. I surreptitiously glance at the pool surrounding the castle, bubbling at the edges of the bricked banks of the stream. It froths and babbles like it's rushing over rocks, but there's no current here.

"We are talented in observance. Do we have a deal? Or do we bury Arrin in our Sunken Forest graveyard?" His bulging eyes hold mine in a steady gaze.

I recall that stretch of water and the branch that wasn't a branch and shiver. The froggens holding Arrin shift their feet. Her tears are gone, and her shoulders are hunched. In defeat?

Anger sets my insides aflame. I won't let anyone else, especially Arrin, wind up in their gruesome excuse for a graveyard.

"I think not." I raise my hands, flinging the knife at Siltworth and *pushing* it toward my target.

33

The knife's blade finds its target: the pearl pendant around Siltworth's massive neck. It cracks the jewel in half, and an eerie light glows around both parts. I *call* the pieces to me, sure they mean something to the fishkin leader.

Siltworth lets out a loud croaking scream of surprise and fury. "Get her!" His sticky tongue darts in and out of his mouth as he gropes the chain and empty pendant.

Magic crackles around my hands and throbs inside me. I quickly put the two pearl pieces in my pocket.

Two froggen near the bench toddle toward me. They're fast. But I'm quicker.

I reach out and *grab* them, lifting them into the air. My eyes heat up and I'm invigorated.

I smash the two bulbous heads together, but four more armed froggen are jumping into action as their unconscious forms fall to the ground. I whip out my hands and strip them of the wicked-looking pitchforks they hold.

Six more come, then another group, and then another, until I have more than a dozen crazed greenish-yellow lumps coming toward me. The two holding a furious and fighting Arrin drag her behind the walled stone gate.

There are too many coming toward me. I can't stop them all in time. Siltworth has grown in size, puffing out in a decidedly sickly yellow color. It's more disturbing than his green skin, and I find I have only one choice. I pray it will work.

With a thought I am airborne. I fly in a circle to find Arrin. She struggles with her captors and regains her stick, swinging it valiantly in a wide arc. It strikes the first captor on its nubby head. They drop, lying prone and unmoving on the ground. She lands a second swing, incapacitating the second one. Without a look back, Arrin limps away from the castle.

The froggen throw rocks and the pitchforks in the air aiming for me. I dart around them, but one almost hits my wing. A silver feather spirals down to the ground. I need to get out of here.

Siltworth thrashes on the ground, his hands at his throat, his protruding eyes bulging more as he struggles to breathe. His yellowish body puffs out then shrivels. I look away from the alarming sight, praying he is no longer a threat to me or anyone.

There are too many items to dodge, however. There's not enough space to keep flying within the magical sphere without becoming too exhausted to elude the weapons forever.

I dart to where I spy Lucas out of the corner of my bird eye. *"Open! Let me pass!"* I *order* the bubble of illusion that surrounds the froggen's castle fortress. My head hits it and I bounce back, like it's a flexible wall.

A rock grazes my claws. I concentrate harder, willing it more than requesting it, and something pops. The thrum in my gut flickers and then is gone, leaving me chilled. The illusion, however, winks as it dissipates and disappears. I'm through instantly and join a fluttering Lucas.

"Chirp-caw!" Lucas flies a circle around me, calling out happily.

"Yes, good to see you again as well. Let's get out of here."

The last thing I see is Arrin in the thick grass. She waves me on, pointing toward some distant mountains. I chirp out my thanks and a sad goodbye and turn in that direction. Maybe Nobbert was right. I'm nothing more than trouble for the non-magical nomads.

———

The sun has already left its high point in the sky. I have no clue how far the froggen took me out of the way from my path to the eldrin's sanctuary. And I lost the bag with the maps when I was grabbed and dragged through the stream. I continue to fly toward the sun now and pray it will take me where I need to go.

We travel for hours until the sky becomes tinged bright orange and red with a sunset. I've almost lost hope of finding Elysium when the trees part, revealing carvings above tall stone buildings. The stone is pocked, and some have blackened stains. Signs of a magical fight? There's rubble at the base of the mountain village and foliage grows out of the cracks and through some of the windows.

Birds flutter in and out of the structures, unaware they nest on holy ground. *"It looks different than I imagined it would."*

"Scree!"

"I'm not sure what I expected. Just not like this, I guess." I answer though I'm unsure what Lucas said. I make an arcing circle downward until I reach the peaked tips of the roofs. The buildings resemble turrets that start at the top of the mountain and are built downward with its slope. Each building is separate, the gray stones carved smooth. There are a few

remnants of broken windows, their dark depths like watchful eyes.

I swing through a narrow channel where a road is carved out of the stone sides and pitched to follow the curve of the mountain. The wind howling through the shadowed area bites at my wings. The backside is bare, uncarved stone. It's a city unto itself, lining both sides of the mountains and dipping into a deep valley between.

I circle back, making sure to catch any movement. I'm still on edge from being taken from the pasture to the froggen's castle, and I no longer trust my instincts.

Closer, I see the stone glitters. Not with gems, but with flecks of something that catches the light, making it brilliant despite the dimness. It would've been grand once, but the whistle of the wind through the empty ruins makes my neck feathers prickle. Lucas, I notice, is flying closer to me.

I see no movement, no signs of anyone there, but I don't entirely trust it. Lucas follows my lead, dropping more behind as I fly. He must be exhausted. Even I am drained after breaking the illusion. My wings strain to push past the changing wind currents.

However, I don't wish to settle in for the evening here. There are too many shadows. It's too oppressive for comfort.

"*Follow me,*" I call to Lucas.

"Scree." It's faint, slightly panting.

Against my better judgment, I circle down, trying to find the best place to land. It's all slopes and rock-strewn walkways. Insects sing in choruses, filling the empty space with sound. At the bottom, there's one grassy spot by a smaller building in the front, and I head there. It's better than the dark recesses of the buildings by far, so I circle the area, and finding no threats, land on the grass and change back.

Lucas totters on the breeze, landing harder in my hands

than usual. I catch him before he falls. He's panting and leans against me.

I shiver. The outfit, which had easily shed the water from the stream, is now a bit light for the cool evening air. So, I stand and enter the first building. Its carved wooden door is split in half down the center and hanging on by the hinges. Inside, the table is overturned, and heavy wooden furniture is broken into kindling. Books and parchments are strewn about and soiled. Shards of dishes and glasses make the floor too dangerous to walk on.

Farther back, a light flickers. I stop, my heart pounding so loud I fear it can be heard. Is someone here?

"Who goes there?" a man's voice breaks the silence.

I freeze midstep.

"You're not eldrin. I can hear you breathing. We've nothing left to take." The light moves, and with it, an older, gray-haired man appears. He's handsome with an unlined face despite his gray hair. His voice wavers just enough to know he's not as confident as he seems.

I consider fighting, but Lucas quakes in my hands and I know there's no way he can fly any more tonight. I'll either have to hide or carry him to safety. My hands glow light blue and my necklace warms, but I don't wish for another confrontation this eve.

The man starts yelling, calling other names.

My feet hit the grassy land just on the other side of the doorway when three others come out of buildings close by to see what's going on. I try to avoid them, but more join, and I'm surrounded.

I grab a jagged rock from a pile near the base of the mountain. I don't want to hurt anyone, but I will protect myself and Lucas if need be. "Look, I'm sorry. I didn't mean to intrude. I was just trying to find a place to shelter, that's all. Let us go, and I won't bother you again."

"Who is it?"

"Why is she here?"

"She looks eldrin."

"Is it another thief?"

They call one after another, none of them bothering to speak directly to me.

"Who summoned me?" It's Nyle's voice. His words are clipped and his voice tight. He's facing away from me.

I'd back up, but there are as many behind me as in front. I wave the stone I grabbed above my head, knowing it's a useless threat against them all. Lucas remains still in my hands, his heart beating rapidly against my skin. I don't dare fly away. Or do I? I'd carried Lucas before. I just don't remember how or what happened after I changed. My hands light up, my anxiety latching into what's left of my ability. I can't hide them because of Lucas, so I don't try.

"I beckoned you," the old man from the house states. "We agreed that none of your clan would come back again. Tell her to drop whatever she has in her hands."

Nyle turns and sees me, his face hardening. "Stealing again, I see. This time you won't get away. You're surrounded." He waves his hand wide, a maniacal grin on his too-perfect face.

"I've nothing of yours." I step back, but the circle of people closes in on me. I see no weapons, but I don't trust what I don't know, like innocent-looking streams. And I'm much too tired to deal tactfully with anyone.

"If she's not one of yours, who is she?" a woman to my left demands.

"That's no eldrin. Look at her hands. She's a mage!" Someone yells from my right side.

Two men rush toward me, glowing ropes in their hands.

One lashes at my hand with the rock. The rope stings, and I drop the stone to cradle my hand to my chest.

My stomach spins in circles. Another situation where I'm too outnumbered to do anything but flee. I grind my teeth together in frustration.

"Don't let her get away," Nyle screams. He flicks his wrist and a ball of flashing light floats above his hand. It illuminates his face and the area around him. Frenzied energy surrounds him and the others in a grayish mishmash of light and dark swirling and colliding.

This can't be good. Lucas trembles against me. The energy that surrounded my hands is gone. I turn and flee, knocking two people down as I fling an elbow back and forth. My hand aches, but I pay no mind to that pain.

I get several paces before I realize the problem with my plan to flee—the mountain drops off, and I skid to a halt. It's too dark to see much of anything, and there's no moon in the sky for any kind of light. However, I do see the moving shadows of the people following me amid their glowing magic. They're not hurrying.

Nyle's harsh laugh grates at my nerves. "You've nowhere to go, mage." He throws the ball of light. It expands as it moves swiftly toward us. It pulses, and I can sense the intent behind the spell: death.

"*Hold on, Lucas.*" I clutch him tight and jump off the cliff's edge.

Lucas's panicked squawking cries follow us into the dark nothingness.

34

My heart sails to my throat and I instantly regret my choice. The wind rushes over me. As a bird, it's exhilarating. But at this moment, when I've no power left to change, it's too terrifying to even scream.

"Call on your fire, Tambrynn. It has awakened." It's Audhild's voice in my mind.

"I don't know how to do that," I answer, flailing the arm that isn't holding Lucas and pumping my legs as I had in the water earlier.

The cold air shifts and there's a shadow among the darkness. I can feel its heat. My skin prickles. A bright ball of fire sails out of the shadow, revealing Audhild's form before hitting me square in the face. This time I do scream. And drop Lucas.

Pure heat pours over my body, setting me aflame. But I'm not consumed. I'm lifted, my body shedding its weight as I'm changed. Once silver, my wings are scorching the air a fiery blue. I can see through the darkness to where the dragon slithers in the sky, wings spread as wide as the gorge between the mountains, and eyes blazing with orange light.

"*Lucas?*" A high-pitch shrieking-roar bursts from me. Birds call out in dismay and explode from the trees around us, flying away.

"*I have him, Tambrynn. He is safe. Follow me.*" There's a distinct female tone to the voice now. It's as if the fire has clarified my hearing or perception.

"*Where are you going? Where are you taking him?*" I demand, trying to converse only in my mind, but I'm unable to. My shrill song flows from my beak. It's not melodious anymore. It's fierce and loud. More creatures scramble and dart about. At this rate, the eldrin will surely find me.

"*To the beggar-thief's camp.*"

My heart skips a beat. Is my luck turning? Surely this beggar-thief will help me.

I follow the dragon's snaking path with a straight one of my own to keep up. We soar into a deep ravine between two mountains, the walls sometimes so close the dragon brushes the trees with its massive wings. It's several minutes before sparse trees turn thicker, shift back to jagged cliffsides, and then change to rock-strewn meadows. Finally, Audhild tucks her wings in and drops to land silently.

Beneath a large shelf of stone jutting from the bottom of the mountain, a fire is lit just at the edge, reflecting off the gray rock. A man bends over a sizzling pot perched on a grate over the flames, filling the air with savory fried scents, the smoke from the fire curling over the ceiling of the shelf's ledge.

I land less elegantly than Audhild, though I do change as my knees hit land. The warmth from my wings dissipates, and I shiver. I'm in a wide, lush meadow, much like the one I found the nomads in.

Audhild lifts her wings and, with a push from her legs, is

airborne. She hovers over me and drops something from her claws.

"Scree!"

I reach out and catch a fluttering Lucas and gather and him close. *"Thank you, Audhild."* Tendrils of my unruly hair snap at my face as the wind from Audhild's wings whips them around. I close my eyes, thankful he is safe in my arms.

"You now owe me a favor, young firebird." She disappears into the dark sky.

"Firebird? What does that mean?" I ask, though I know Lucas cannot answer me.

Lucas chatters, thrashing about, and I have to scramble to maintain hold of him.

"Come. Warm yourself by the fire." The man looks up. His face is long, overly so, almost stretched, and his ears are pointed on each end. Sleek clothes, resembling the outfits the eldrin wear, like I currently wear, grace his slim body. He stirs the food in the pot with a clawed hand. I shrink back at the sight of him. For a moment, I envision the beast who had stepped onto the nomad's flinty mountain and had vacillated between beast and man.

Who is this beggar thief? Is he friend or foe?

"Tambrynn?" His voice cracks, and he clears his throat. "It's good to finally meet you."

My hands grow cold. How does he know my name? "Who are you?"

He grins and chuckles, stretching his taut facial skin into wrinkles that frame his oversized mouth. Though it seems as if his teeth are too big for his mouth, he speaks clearly. "I'm the one who felt you call out during a storm not so long ago. You were desperate and lost and just wanted to find someone, something, that would bring you where you needed to be."

I'm at a loss for words. There's no way he can know about

the wreck in the haunted forest *on another kingdom,* nor my prayers. He does not look like what I pictured the Kinsman would. "I have no idea what you're talking about."

His grin spreads wider, which would've been terrifying had he been threatening me. "Ah, a cynic, good. You take after me." He holds his clawed hand out. The nails are dark and sharp. "Welcome home, Tambrynn. I'm Bennett, your grandfather."

I stumble back as if punched. "My grandfather is dead."

"Not so youngling. He is the beggar-thief. Show some respect. He bargained for your life. You owe him as well." Audhild's voice is clear in my mind though she is nowhere to be seen.

"How—?"

The man chuckles and looks to the sky. "I don't need your help, fire-dragon. She's right to be skeptical. I'm sure if she was told anything of me, it was not favorable." He glances back my way. "I did not die by Thoron's hand. I was his first attempt at changing someone to one of his beasts." He waves an arm up and down his body. "It didn't fully take."

"How did you survive?" I ask, surprised. I'd seen Garrett changed and knew the power, the darkness, that was involved.

"That's something I'll teach you if you decide to stay," he answers. He ladles some food onto a metal plate, adding a silver spoon. "Sit, eat. I'm sure you're tired after your journey from Tenebris. You are safe here in dragon territory. At least for now."

"Dragon territory?" Though I'd seen Audhild twice now, it's still bizarre to think such massive creatures exist. I relocate a sleeping Lucas to a different spot in my hold, and his feathers glow purplish in the firelight. The flight to the eldrin sanctuary and then the jump from the mountain must've been too much for him. I hold him closer, unsure how safe it is to be near this man who claims to be my grandfather. Someone Lucas said would have rejected me like so many others.

The man shifts and places the first plate on the ground, ladling more in another plate for himself. Still steaming, he digs in and takes a bite. He wipes his mouth after he swallows. "This is Brimstoke, the valley of the dragon. Though dragons first lived among the Harrowstone Mountains, a land on the other side of Anavrin, they've since moved here for safety. When the first scourge of mages appeared, dragons were hunted for their blood and bones. It took a generation," he lifts and points one clawed finger, "just one generation of mages to deplete their ranks." He takes another bite as if in deep thought.

I can't help the curiosity. "What happened then?" My legs ache. In fact, my whole body aches, so I sit down several feet from the fire. Close enough to feel it, but not close enough to be warmed by it.

"The eldrin were charged with keeping them safe. And they were. Until they weren't." He chews more of the stew, his large jaw moving, making him bare his massive teeth as he chews.

Regardless of the sight of the man eating, the scent of the stew makes my stomach pinch. And the fire beckons me with its heat. Careful of Lucas, I shuffle closer to the fire.

The man eyes me and nods at the food. "I ate from the same pot. It's not poison. And I'm not half bad at cooking."

I reach for the plate. The meat, pale vegetables, and mushrooms swim inside a seasoned, brown gravy. I set Lucas gently aside and taste the mixture. It's rich in flavor, the meat a bit burned, but not bad overall. Much better than the swill I'd had at many of my employers through the years. "Why weren't the dragons safe?"

He points his spoon at me. "The key in my cooking is the herbs I use." He then takes a deep breath, and his stretched face becomes shadowed. "Neither the dragons nor any of us are safe because power entices power, which enables corruption."

I finish half of the plateful before I realize it. My stomach bulges slightly from gulping it down so fast. "You speak in riddles. I don't understand your meaning."

The man sighs. The flames flicker in his dark eyes. Are they black? "There is much to say, and I fear not enough time to do so. And I'm unsure what you've been told. You know the eldrin are the holy keepers of the Kinsman's secrets?"

"Yes, Lucas told me." Stomach still longing for sustenance, I set the empty plate down, and the old man adds another ladleful to it. I stare at it, not wanting to admit I'm still hungry, nor wanting to owe this man any more than I already did. He'd saved me not once but twice. With a small "thank you," I accept the second helping.

He grunts. "You get that stubbornness from me, just so you know. Madrigal was grace personified. So was Cadence before —" he hesitates. "Before she left." He stares at the ground, his eyes glistening. "Since my Cadence didn't show up with you, I can only assume she didn't make it."

My hand shakes and I lower the plate, suddenly not hungry at all. "The beasts murdered her when I was eight years old. Somehow I survived."

My grandfather pours a cup of water from a canteen and takes a drink. "I've made so many mistakes." His voice is low and haunted. His shoulders slump.

Tears burn my eyes. "Everyone makes mistakes."

"Yes, so I'm told. Mine just have more consequences." His eyes are narrow and calculating as he gazes into the dark expanse of the night sky. Insects chirp and a gentle wind rustles leaves on the trees. The peace is deceiving.

Beside me, Lucas shudders in his sleep. He wakes and glances dully up at me. A band tightens around my heart.

"You're not the only one." I stroke his soft feathers, longing to hold his hand once more.

"The fire dragon told me that is your Watcher? He's part djinn, correct?" He ladles some more food onto his plate and continues to eat.

"Yes. His name is Lucas." The band across my chest breaks, and pain radiates in every direction. Unable to eat more, I shove the plate away and scoop Lucas up into my arms.

The old man grunts, which sounds suspiciously like a growl. "What happened?"

"A curse from Thoron in the passageway stuck Lucas in his bird form. Then, later, after I'd saved some nomads, Thoron found us. He used another spell which broke our bond."

"The fire dragon's been keeping secrets again," he mutters. "You've bonded with him, eh? You can mindspeak?" His dark eyes are sharp, but I sense something genuine in his voice. A warmth I hadn't encountered with my father.

"We did until the last spell Thoron threw at us." I squeeze my eyes shut at the memory. What if Lucas is lost in his bird form like before on Tenebris? I couldn't bear it.

A hand falls on my shoulder. Startled, I look over into the face of my grandfather. Though the elongated appearance had put me off before, it isn't unkind.

A hint of a smile curls his lips. "Well, there's no spell that I know of that can break a bond, except death. Something else must be happening, and maybe I can right some of my wrongs by helping you with that."

35

My heart races. Could he, my grandfather, save Lucas from Thoron's cursed spells?

"There's a reason why I wasn't fully transformed when Thoron attacked your mother and me that day. Cadence was a strong healer and protector, yes. But it was my amulet that saved me from being turned into one of those unholy beasts. A pearl of great price and power." He searches beneath his tunic and produces a silver chain with a pearl pendant attached to it.

It's identical to Siltworth's—only smaller.

I stand and dig in my pocket, startling Lucas, who chirps in objection. I pull out the two broken pieces of the froggen's pearl and hold them out to the old man. Though it's dark, I can still see that peculiar glow around them, faint but present.

Concern deepens the lines around his eyes and mouth. "Where'd you get those?"

I drop my hands, unsure. "From the froggen, Siltworth. He'd dragged me to his castle fortress and tried to make me form a pact with him to destroy my father." I rub the uneven chunks in my hands. They're smooth despite the edges where they broke. "He had captured one of the nomad women who'd helped me. He threatened to kill her and put her in his watery graveyard if I didn't agree."

He blows out a breath. "You must not have agreed?"

I clench my jaw, still furious at the froggen. "I didn't agree. I threw a knife the nomad had given me at him, and it broke his pendant."

Eyes wide, he whistles. "Then you broke his spell as well."

Trepidation creeps over my skin, making the hair rise uncomfortably. "I broke Siltworth's spell? What spell? He said he was an authentic magical creature."

My grandfather's chuckle holds no humor. "He may have hatched as a froggen, but nothing born of dark magic, or evil, is authentic. There's only one creator. His kind were contrived under the worst motivations: greed, lust, a need to control. The good news, however, is that because they are not as authentic as they claim, their magic link can be broken."

"And Thoron's magic? It can be broken?" Hope blooms in my heart, heating my cheeks.

"It can be, if one knows how to do it. It's your bond. You must perform the rite. It will take a small bit of blood from each of you, the pearl chunks, and holy fire."

I pick Lucas up. "Holy fire? How do we get holy fire?"

"You are a firebird, are you not? They are the Kinsman's sacred bird. As the dragons are his holy messengers, you are his divine protector." He takes a small knife from his pocket. "Nick your hand and somewhere that won't injure your Watcher. You need to smear the blood across the gem and then change to your firebird form. When your body is aflame, let it engulf the stones, and it will remove the curse and restore Lucas."

"It's that easy?" I ask, confused.

He shrugs. "You're blessed to have holy fire, so it's not that easy for anyone else. But, all magic is a mixture of motivations and the items to focus and make the energy do your bidding. Good or evil, it works the same."

"That isn't very comforting." I take his knife and make a small cut on one of my fingers, letting a drop of blood fall on the halves. "Lucas?" I glance at him.

"Scree!" He fluffs his feathers and nods his head.

I carefully slice a small spot on one of his claws and wipe the pearl pieces across it. I kiss his sleek head before setting him on the ground. In the flash of a thought, I become a firebird once more. Warmth awakens inside of me, growing and bursting forth from the center of my being to the tips of my wings, tail, and claws. Blue flames light up where I stand next to the bloodied jewel bits. I carefully step over and sit on them, calling the flames out to do my will: heal our bond and restore Lucas to his natural form and ability.

My flames turn white and flare into the sky around us. They engulf Lucas, brightening until I'm forced to close my eyes against the brilliant light.

Strength seeps from me as it feeds the pearls and then Lucas. In a flash, the white flames depart, and I'm knocked backward onto the ground.

"Tambrynn?" Lucas's voice is clear and the most beautiful thing I've heard for far too long.

I struggle to my feet, turning to see his handsome face. Lucas's grin is wide, his pale face crinkled enough to hide his narrow eyes. Those beautiful dark eyes. I throw myself into his arms, laughing and crying at the same time.

Lucas holds me tight. "Oh, Tambrynn. I didn't know if I would ever get to do this again." His hands tangle in my unruly hair. He pulls back and kisses my forehead, cheeks, and then softly, my lips.

My heart beats so hard I fear it might explode.

I lean back and smile, taking in the sight of him. I brush a lock of dark hair away from one of his eyes and glory in the feel of it in my fingers. "Thank the Kinsman! And my grandfather."

We both turn to find the old man grinning as well. He motions to the stew. "Hungry?" he grunts at Lucas.

"Starving, thank you." He pulls me with him to sit beside my grandfather. "Thank you for helping me. For helping Tambrynn."

"I've many things to set right. It's only fair I start with my granddaughter. Now, eat. I have many things to teach you, and I worry we don't have enough time to do it right."

EPILOGUE

Siltworth sits on a bench beside the babbling water he and his army dug upstream from his castle fortress. It's one of many streams they dredged across Anavrin since he began his rule ages ago. He's very proud of that accomplishment, especially since none of the other inhabitants of the kingdom knew their origin or meaning.

Sitting here usually relaxes him. But tonight, everything is too tight, like the pants he wore to hide his nakedness or the constricting skin that covered his bones. So many times, he'd sat here and listened in on the mumblings and gossip that drifted in on the bubbles from across the kingdom. So many secrets revealed, plans foiled, and interesting facts he'd used against others. Tonight, however, he couldn't make out what the voices were saying. All thanks to that stupid girl for breaking his great-grandmother's precious pearl!

He screams until hoarse, then rakes a hand across his bald head. It's a curious feeling now that his hand is no longer webbed nor ended in sticky pads. He glares at the shape and pale, fleshy color of his fingers. Disgust festers in his gut. It isn't the end. Far from it!

Nyle flashes into existence beside the bench. Displeasure shines from his blue eyes. He frowns, creasing his impeccably smooth face. "Who are you? I thought I was meeting with the frogking."

Siltworth clears his throat, still raw from his earlier wailing. "It is I, Siltworth. Though I have lost my froggen form, I am still their king."

"Are you?" Humor tickles the edges of Nyle's lips upward. "What happened to you?"

Siltworth darts his tongue out across his lips. He can't help it, it's a habit. But it's not nearly as satisfying without his long, sticky tongue. He grinds his nubby teeth. "Tambrynn happened." Even his voice isn't pleasant without the deep, croaking resonance it had before. "I have a bargain for you, *Councilmaster*. Neither of us wants the silver mage alive. I can help you. I know things the eldrin don't know. I can help you get rid of her."

Nyle scowls at him in disbelief. "What do I get in this bargain?"

Siltworth stands and places his hands behind him. His stout belly is gone, however, and it doesn't feel as intimidating behind his new scrawny body that is neither mage nor eldrin in stature, but something in between. "You get Bennett, the High Elder."

Though Nyle tries to hide his delight, Siltworth knows it is the self-proclaimed Councilmaster's dearest wish. The murmuring bubbles spilling his secrets had indicated as much. With the Council dismantled so effectively by Thoron's war, only a High Elder could proclaim a new leader. And they'd all been murdered. Or so everyone thought.

Nyle's brow twitches, a rare show of emotion from the eldrin leader. "Bennett is dead."

"He's not. He's been in hiding for years. It was by his hand, and that dragon pet of his, that Tambrynn slipped through Thoron's fingers when she arrived here. It's only a matter of time before his granddaughter finds him and he decrees she is the High Elder of the land. Neither of us desire this. Do we have a deal?"

Siltworth senses he'd hooked the ambitious eldrin. It was in the way the sleekly-dressed eldrin, slick as his own morals, leaned toward him.

Nyle had been ruthless when the froggens had gone up against him in the past. The fishkin had never won, which worked in Siltworth's favor now. The eldrin thought he had the edge over him, over his kind. All Siltworth truly wanted was to use Nyle and then steal back from the eldrin what should've been his all along. Anavrin was his kingdom to rule. And it would be soon.

A wide smile spreads across Nyle's face. "We have a deal."

SPLIT KINGDOMS OF THE KINSMEN

- Anavrin
- Tenebris
- Panacea
- Hevell
- Zoar
- Emporium
- Risan
- Benario Vale
- Pseminia
- Iolneo
- Far Starl
- Trithis.

CREATURE RACES IN THE KINGDOMS OF TENEBRIS AND ANAVRIN:

Nomads – non-magical people. Small and stout in stature, they are creative and industrial.

Eldrin – a noble, holy race charged by the Kinsman to guard and care for his holy writings and relics. They are an ethereal-looking people but pompous and condescending at heart.

Mages – dark magic users, can be any race. Evil resides in their hearts and souls.

Djinn – shape-shifters who can change into any living creature on demand, often mischievous and tricksters.

Voyants – telepathic beings able to communicate with other creatures in their minds and can sense other's emotions.

Sluaghs – (pronounced: Slew-aws) the undead creatures hexed by dark mages with a mortuus irrepo curse into becoming part-beast and part-person. Evil permeates their beings and they are controlled by the necromancing mage.

Froggen – a cursed race of fishkin. Genteel in manner but swindlers at heart, they are untrustworthy. Hexed into creation, they live in waterways and seas which permeate Anavrin and rule it as a watery kingdom. They desire ultimate rule over Anavrin.

Dragons – holy messengers of the Kinsman, they are magic incarnate and sought after by mages for their blood and bone which hold magical properties. Their gift of fire burns away that which is corrupt. They are a rare and endangered species.

Firebirds – AKA phoenixes, also rare and endangered. Born healers, they are the protectors of the righteous and guiders of the lost and downtrodden. Their gift of fire heals rather than destroys.

ABOUT THE AUTHOR

Winner of the 2016 ACFW Genesis Award and finalist in the 2018 Grace Award and the 2020 Great Expectations Contest, Dawn has been recognized for her published and non-published works. Her flash fiction stories have been published in *Havok* magazine under both her real name and pen name, Jo Wonderly. Her debut novel, *Knee-high Lies*, was published in 2017.

As a child, Dawn often had her head in the clouds creating scenes and stories for anything and everything she came across. She believed there was magic everywhere, a sentiment she has never outgrown. Nature inspires her, and her love for the underdog and the unlikely hero colors much of what she writes.

Dawn adores anything Steampunk, is often distracted by shiny, pretty things, and her obsession with purses and shoes borders on hoarding. Dawn lives in Iowa and helps her husband run their foodservice and catering business out of Omaha, Nebraska. When not reading, writing, or catering, Dawn loves babysitting her grandchildren, is parent to Snickers the Wonder Beagle, and can usually be caught daydreaming.

MORE SPECULATIVE FICTION FROM EXPANSE BOOKS

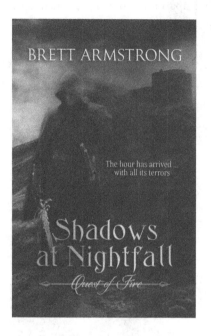

Shadows at Nightfall by Brett Armstrong

Quest of Fire - Book Three

The hour has arrived ... with all its terrors.

The shadows of Jason's past have caught him. Having stepped into the Quest of Fire, Jason is pursued by a league of assassins formed of pure darkness. To his horror he discovers these creatures also were contracted to eliminate Anargen and his friends as they sought to understand the Tower of Light's oracle. To unravel the mystery of who wants him dead and how he fits into the ages old quest, Jason must travel the lengths of the Lowlands. In the Ziljafu deserts a secret awaits him that will shake him to his core. He'll have to move fast and cling fiercely to hope, as Anargen's story twists down a bleak path to almost certain failure.

The creatures of darkness in the Lowlands have long waited for men to spurn the High King's laws. With few concerned for the light and everything falling apart around them, Jason and Anargen will face the shadows of night's falling as their world hangs in the balance.

Get your copy here: https://scrivenings.link/shadowsatnightfall

———

Beyond the Gates by Erin R. Howard

Gates of Deceit - Book One

Available May 17, 2022

If playing by the rules means it keeps you alive, then seventeen-year-old Renna James should know better. She is, after all, the one who broadcasts these rules to the Outpost. What lies beyond the gates had always lured her, but her venture outside wasn't supposed to leave her locked out. Now, Renna's one chance to survive the next seventy-two hours just ran into the forest she's forbidden to enter.

Get your copy here: https://scrivenings.link/beyondthegates

Quench your thirst for story.
www.ScriveningsPress.com

Stay up-to-date on your favorite books and authors with our free e-newsletters.

ScriveningsPress.com

CPSIA information can be obtained
at www.ICGtesting.com
Printed in the USA
LVHW080053050422
715224LV00011B/366